THE PERFECT MATCH

ADIBA JAIGIRDAR

ORION

First published in Great Britain in 2026 by Orion Fiction,
an imprint of The Orion Publishing Group Ltd.
Carmelite House, 50 Victoria Embankment
London EC4Y 0DZ

An Hachette UK Company

The authorised representative in the EEA is Hachette Ireland,
8 Castlecourt Centre, Dublin 15, D15 XTP3,
Ireland (email: info@hbgi.ie)

1 3 5 7 9 10 8 6 4 2

Copyright © Adiba Jaigirdar 2026

The moral right of Adiba Jaigirdar to be identified as
the author of this work has been asserted in accordance
with the Copyright, Designs and Patents Act of 1988.

All rights reserved. No part of this publication may be
reproduced, stored in a retrieval system, or transmitted
in any form or by any means, electronic, mechanical,
photocopying, recording, or otherwise, without the
prior permission of both the copyright owner and the
above publisher of this book.

All the characters in this book are fictitious, and any resemblance
to actual persons, living or dead, is purely coincidental.

A CIP catalogue record for this book is
available from the British Library.

ISBN (Mass Market Paperback) 9781 3987 2773 1
ISBN (Ebook) 9781 3987 2774 8
ISBN (Audio) 9781 3987 2775 5

Typeset by Input Data Services Ltd, Bridgwater, Somerset
Printed in Great Britain by Clays Ltd, Elcograf S.p.A.

www.orionbooks.co.uk

Praise for *The Perfect Match*

'Sweet and fun the whole way through!'
Nisha Sharma, author of *Dating Dr. Dil*

'LOVE, LOVE, LOVE! This was such a fantastic contribution to the sapphic sport romance genre and was one of the best women's football books I've read'
Joanna B, Reader Review

'Fans of Jaigirdar's debut sapphic adult romance will stamp and cheer like Dina and Maya's #1 fan'
Lillie Vale, *USA Today* bestselling author of *Wrapped with a Beau* and *The Shaadi Set-Up*

'I highly recommend checking out this wonderful book!!! I know this will be one of my favourite releases of the year!!'
Green G, Reader Review

'This sapphic sports romance should be on everyone's radar! I truly couldn't put it down'
Anam Iqbal, author of *The Exes*

'I really loved this one. Great complex characters, a messy and captivating plot, what's not to like?'
Manon D, Reader Review

'Adiba is the queen of friction and feelings!! I loved Maya and Dina and their inability to escape their pasts and each other. Pacy and pitch-perfect!'
**Lizzie Huxley-Jones,
author of *Make You Mine This Christmas***

Adiba Jaigirdar is the critically acclaimed and bestselling author of *The Henna Wars* and *Hani & Ishu's Guide to Fake Dating*. A Bangladeshi/Irish writer and teacher, she has an MA in Postcolonial Studies from the University of Kent, England and a BA in English and History from UCD, Ireland. All of her writing is aided by tea, and a healthy dose of Janelle Monáe and Hayley Kiyoko. When not writing, she is probably ranting about the ills of colonialism, playing video games or expanding her overflowing lipstick collection. She can be found on Twitter @adiba_j and on Instagram @dibs_j.

Also by Adiba Jaigirdar

Rani Choudhury Must Die
Four Eids and a Funeral
The Dos and Donuts of Love
A Million to One
Hani and Ishu's Guide to Fake Dating
The Henna Wars
Nadia Islam, on the Record

This book is dedicated to all the trailblazing women of colour who have paved the way, despite the uphill battles and the struggles to be seen and recognised.

Prologue

There's an electric energy around Snapdragon Stadium. The Vikings vs the Red Stars. The score still 1-1. This is still anybody's match. But I'll be damned if the Vikings lose now. Today.

It's the last minute of the game and the Red Stars have the ball. I try to keep up, but it's hard to drown out all the noise. My heart is beating too fast in my chest, and I can hear the rush of blood in my ears. Our team captain, Stacey, gives me a concerned look as she races past me to get back to defend. She's counting on me – the whole team is. The roar of the fans reminds me that they are too.

The referee blows the whistle, but the noise from the crowd doesn't stop. I slow down, take a deep breath. I can feel them looking at me. When I missed the goal earlier, they were booing me, and I can already imagine their comments online.

Maya Alam didn't seem like she was on top form today, did she?
The Vikings lost because Maya couldn't get her shit together.
Maya Alam let the team down. Again.

'Hey, you OK?' Stacey's hands are at my elbow, her bright blue eyes peering down at me.

'Yeah. I just can't believe we're still tied.' I sigh, trying to catch my breath.

She gives me a sympathetic smile. 'We can still pull it off. We've got extra time.' She gives me an encouraging pat on the back before she heads off to speak to the other girls on the team.

We've got fifteen minutes to turn things around.

I jog up to the field, taking my position for the final kick-off of the match. I close my eyes for just a moment, trying to tune everything else out. I have to be here, in this moment. In the match, thinking about the game. I can't be worrying about what comes next.

You're Maya bloody Alam. If anyone can do this, it's you.

The words are like a balm.

My eyes flicker open as the referee blows his whistle. I head straight for the ball, almost running into one of the players from the opposing team. I manage to get it before her, dribbling it in front of me, past the other players. Right towards the goal.

I'm laser-focused, sharp-eyed. I'm *not* going to miss this time. I race forward with the ball at my feet, dodging other Red Stars players around me. And then, the goalie is in front of me, shifting from one side to the other, hands outstretched, waiting for me to mess this up.

I drive my foot forward through the ball. It flies through the air and I watch with bated breath as it moves right past the goalie and bounces into the net.

The crowd around the stadium erupts into cheers, just as the final whistle sounds.

Game over – 2-1 to the Vikings.

Around me, the blue-uniformed Vikings – my teammates – are jumping and clapping, hugging each other happily, but I can barely muster a smile.

All the adrenaline that has carried me through the game is gone now and all I'm left with is this empty, deflated feeling.

Because this was my last win. My last match. It's the last time I'll ever be in a stadium like this, surrounded by my teammates and the cheering crowd.

When I go back to the changing rooms, I'll change out of my kit for the very last time and that will be it. I'll no longer be a Viking.

I'll just be Maya Alam. Retired footballer.

Not a winner, but a failure. And in light of all of that, I can't bring myself to celebrate the win, even though I was the one who scored the winning goal.

My teammates clap me on the back, tell me how great a job I did, but I just nod and plaster on a practised fake smile that slips away too easily.

All too soon, I'll be boarding the flight back to London.

Back to my old life.

And back to Dina Chowdhury, the girl who broke my heart.

Chapter 1

Dina

'Reading smutty fan fiction again?'

I nearly jump out of my chair at the sound of the door opening and quickly slam my laptop shut before anyone can get a look at what's on there.

Deen sets down the dish that he has come armed with. The spicy scent of chicken biryani makes my stomach gurgle with hunger. I hadn't even realised that it was way past time for lunch.

We're not really supposed to eat in the restaurant's office – it's reserved for business meetings. But nobody else comes in here except for me and Deen these days, so there's no one to bust us for breaking the rules. It's not like Baba's around, pretending to be annoyed at us running into the office during rush hour to play hide-and-seek, or doodling all over his envelopes full of overdue bills.

'I don't read fan fiction; I'm pretty sure that's you,' I accuse teasingly, though, in truth, we both know who reads the smutty fan fiction in our family. Putting my laptop back into my bag, I eagerly accept a plate of the steaming-hot biryani from Deen.

'It's an old Bengali recipe,' Deen says, as he sits down at the other end of the table with his own plate. 'Apparently, it was derived from the Mughal era, and they used to serve this in an old Dhaka restaurant back in the day.'

'Where do you even find out this crap?' I ask, while digging into the rice and chicken. Of course, it's the best biryani that I've ever had in my life. Somehow, Deen has the ability to make anything he touches taste like God's gift to humanity. I'm not envious of his gift, considering I would rather eat my own arm off than spend all my day in the kitchen, but I *am* a little envious of the fact that he's so damn talented at what he does.

'A little research goes a long way,' Deen says with a grin. 'So . . . what were you looking at then?' He nods to the laptop peeking out from my backpack under the desk.

I don't want to talk about it, but I know Deen won't let it go.

'Job applications,' I admit, reluctantly. 'It's grim out there, did you know that?' I don't admit that it's less about the prospect of jobs and more about how little I want to actually *do* any of those jobs. There are plenty of HR positions going, but the financial firm that I worked at before felt like it was sucking my soul dry. I'd applied to other HR positions, and a few had even invited me to interview, but they all had the same putrid smell of corporate greed behind their sheen of fancy office buildings. I didn't quit only to jump back into the corporate world again, no matter how well it paid. The depression was not worth it.

It's not like things are much better *now*. I've been doing a few waitressing jobs here and there to make ends meet, but that's not exactly the pinnacle of my dreams. It truly sucks to be trying to start over at twenty-eight, when I thought I'd have my life all figured out by now.

'You'll find something,' Deen says with uncharacteristic optimism as he shovels biryani into his mouth.

'This is good,' I say, nodding at the half-full bowl still on the desk between us. 'You should put this on the menu. We could have an old-Bengali cuisine theme. Go back to the world of the Mughals. I bet people will be intrigued by that, huh?'

'Yeah, I can imagine it.' Deen nods along, and I note the familiar glint in his eyes. 'We could redo the walls and ceilings with that Mughal flair, get some paintings from that era.' Deen quirks his head at me, as if he is thinking it through. 'Hm, it'll be mood lighting, romantic and sophisticated. But it'll still have that cosy, homey feel at the same time. So that people who come here can feel, you know . . . like this is their place. A home away from their own homes.'

He pauses, and I can almost see the restaurant the way that he's described it, instead of the one on the other side of the office door, with chipped paint and furniture that creaks every time someone uses it, which is rare these days.

'We could get some old-timey chairs and tables, some kerosene lamps,' I suggest, noticing how Deen comes to life when he talks about the restaurant. About his dream. 'You know Mustafa Uncle? Ma told me he has a new place at Whitechapel Market, selling second-hand furniture. We could go sometime.'

'Maybe someday,' Deen says with a sigh.

Just like that, we snap out of the dream and see it how it is. He has big dreams about the restaurant but has yet to bring up any of them with our mum. She's never been one for shiny new ideas. She likes the fact that the restaurant's menu hasn't changed in decades. She likes that she hasn't updated the decor; that the chairs squeak when you sit on them, and that the tables wobble whenever you set down a dish. She likes that all the customers are regulars and that we never get busy enough to need more than one person running the place.

Or, at least, she pretends that she likes all of those things, and she won't hear a single word about updating anything.

'Why put more money into a money pit?' is her tried-and-tested mantra.

By the time Deen and I finish with our lunch, it's time to prepare for the dinner rush. If you can call our slow trickle of customers a dinner rush.

Deen grabs the bowl of leftover biryani, while I gather our plates, and the two of us make it out of the office, through the deserted restaurant, and into the kitchen.

'Maybe you could serve the biryani as a chef's special,' I suggest while I scrub the dishes, and Deen gathers cauliflowers and carrots from the fridge.

'Maybe,' Deen mumbles, though we both know that he won't. Despite his teenage years of rebellion, which earned him quite the reputation, Deen has the utmost respect for our parents, especially when it comes to the restaurant. It might be dilapidated and a money pit *now*, but it's still what's kept us afloat for all of our lives. The restaurant and our parents' hard work are the clothes on our back, and the food on our plate.

Besides, it's Ma who taught Deen how to cook, when he got suspended from school for smoking weed in the bathrooms. She forced him to make dinner for the family for a whole month as punishment, birthing his lifelong love for cooking. So, if Ma doesn't want Deen to serve his food here and change up the menu, then he won't.

No matter how much he wants to.

I leave Deen to his cooking, since I would probably only help set the kitchen on fire, and start making my way back to the office, pondering whether I should even bother to go back to LinkedIn or if I should spend the rest of my day hiding in the office and binge watching whatever I can find on Netflix. But then the restaurant door opens, and in comes a horde of teenage girls, along with their buzz of talk and laughter. They're led in by a woman who looks strangely familiar.

'OK, guys, grab a table, and I'll go up to the—' The woman's voice is drowned out by the increasing sounds from the group of girls, who are now rushing to the empty tables by the corner, pushing them together until they make one long line.

I look back towards the kitchen door, expecting that Deen will come back out, ready to wrangle the kids, but when he doesn't, I march towards the woman in charge of the group with a frown.

'Sorry, they really shouldn't be rearranging the furniture like that,' I say, though I can't muster up enough energy to actually be frustrated. The girls have drawn up their chairs to the tables now, sitting elbow to elbow as they grab at the menus and shout over each other to be heard.

'Dina?' the woman asks.

When I turn to look at her – really look at her – I place her immediately.

'Jen?'

Jen smiles, and it almost feels like I'm suddenly transported back to school. Back to the football field, where Jen's encouraging smile led me to every victory that I ever had. It's been so many years since I saw her – too many years – but somehow, she looks almost exactly the same. Only her brown hair is a little shorter, and she looks a little older, like age and experience have settled into her youthful face.

'It's so good to see you,' Jen says, extending her arms out towards me. I wrap my arms around her too, almost out of instinct.

'You too. What . . . what are you doing here?' I ask. 'Those . . . aren't all your kids, are they?' I ask with a hesitant laugh, nodding at the group of girls that are still shouting to be heard by each other, despite the fact that the rest of the restaurant is completely deserted.

Jen chuckles. 'No. Not my kids. I'm coaching a football team for the local council, and we just had training.'

'Wow.' Now that I look at the girls a little closer, it's easy to see that they're wearing what could almost constitute football attire. They're not decked out in matching jerseys and football boots, but there's an array of loose T-shirts, shorts and brow-beaten trainers.

'Yeah, I'm sorry they're . . . a little excitable,' Jen says. 'I'll try to get them to calm down, and I can have them put the tables back if—'

'No, no. It's fine,' I say, shaking my head. It's not like any other customers are going to use those tables anyway. 'It's good to see that you're still coaching.'

'I like doing it.' Jen shrugs. 'I had to step away from the school to take care of family, but honestly, I had kind of missed coaching.'

I glance at the girls from her team again, and wonder what she missed about it. It couldn't have been dealing with teenage girls all day.

'Well, you were good at it. I bet the school misses you.' I still remember all the times she cheered me on from the touchline, and how she always fought for the school to fund the girls' football team when it was often only interested in the boys' team.

Jen rolls her eyes in good humour. 'Please. I don't think sports teachers are that hard to come by and I wasn't trained in coaching football teams. Besides, I was still learning the ropes back then.'

'It never felt like that to me,' I say. Jen had seemed like someone who had been coaching football her whole life. She knew how to get the best out of us by caring about us. Each and every one of us.

'You made it easy,' Jen says. 'You were already so good at football.'

A bloom of pride warms me. I can't remember the last time someone complimented me on doing something well. But my high comes crashing down as fast as it came when I remember *her*. It's like I can't even think about football without her face appearing in my memory.

'Well, I'm glad another team gets to experience your amazing coaching,' I say, trying to shake my memories off.

Jen's smile wavers a little. 'Thanks, Dina. Though, truthfully, this coaching job is a little different from when I was doing it at school. I mean, back then, it was part of my job, and I was younger and had so much energy. Now, I always have a million things on my plate. Sometimes, I feel like I can barely fit coaching into my schedule, so it falls to the wayside. Which is pretty unfair on the team.' She pauses, looking at me closely. 'I'm actually looking for an assistant coach to help me out. The council finally managed to find some funding for a part-time position, but I've had no luck with finding someone so far.'

The way she's looking at me makes me think for a second that she's considering *me* for the position.

'Well, a sedentary office job doesn't really qualify one for an assistant coach position.' I chuckle. 'I'm sure you'll find someone soon.'

'Yeah, I hope so,' Jen says. 'I shouldn't be talking your ear off about all of this anyway. How have things been with you?'

'Things have been . . . good, yeah,' I say, nodding, though the last thing I want to get into is details about my life. Being unemployed and having no future prospects is not the kind of thing you want to share with your former mentor. 'I should, um, get you some water and then take your orders. Why don't you take a seat and I'll be right back?'

I turn around and almost run right into Deen, who is already heading to the table with a jug of water and a stack of metal cups.

'Whoa, careful there,' he says, weaving around me. He greets Jen and the girls with a grin, serving them their water and taking their orders with his signature charm.

Jen flashes me a smile as Deen leaves the table, and it's clear that she wants to catch up some more, but catching up would require me having to share things about my life too. And I'm definitely not ready for that. So, I give her a small wave, before retreating back to the office and closing the door behind me.

'So . . . that was your old coach, right? What was her name again? Anne?' Deen asks later as we're closing up the restaurant.

'Jen,' I say, clearing up the area where the girls had been sitting. They made a total mess of things: the tablecloth is half off the table; rice and curry stains all over it. I pull it off the table and toss it aside. It will have to go in the wash, and even then, I'm not sure if those stains will come off.

'It's nice that she's still coaching,' Deen comments.

'Yeah, a rowdy bunch of teenagers,' I grumble. 'She said it's part of her work for the council.'

'And she said she was looking for an assistant coach . . .' Deen raises an eyebrow at me, and even though he doesn't say it outright, I know what he means.

'No. No way,' I say.

'Why not? You were her star football player, if I remember correctly,' Deen says.

'Yeah, an entire lifetime ago. And it's not like it led anywhere . . .' I almost think back to those days.

To *her*.

I shake my head, clearing my mind of those thoughts. 'That was my past, and in case you don't remember, I didn't exactly have success in football. So, why would I be a good coach? All I can teach those girls is failure.'

'That's dramatic,' Deen mumbles, before turning to me with a determined look in his eyes. 'You didn't fail, Dina. Plus, having someone who has life experience as a coach can be good. I mean, it's not like Jen was a mega-successful football star. Did that make her any less important to you as a mentor?'

When Deen puts it like that, it almost makes sense. But no, there is no way I am going to go back to football. Not after it chewed me up and spat me out.

'I'm not doing it. She would have tried to convince me to take the job if she wanted me, but she didn't, so obviously she doesn't think I'm good enough either.'

'Or . . . she remembers what happened and she didn't want to ask outright in case you were still sensitive about it,' Deen points out. 'Which, in case you were wondering, you are.'

'I'm not sensitive about it,' I say darkly, which probably isn't helping prove my point. Maybe I *am* a little sensitive about it, but I've earned the right to be.

'Look, Dina. Dreams die in our family. Ma's dreams of being an actress failed. Baba's dreams of this restaurant died with him. But you still have time to make something of your dreams,' Deen says. And I realise that he's being extremely serious about all of this from the way he holds my gaze. He really thinks that, somehow, *I'm* the member of our family who can go out there and achieve my dreams; end our cycle of settling for a life that we're ultimately unhappy with.

'What about you?' I ask.

'Me?' Deen asks, as if he has never even factored himself into this equation.

'What about your dreams of the restaurant? The new menu? The new decorations? Sprucing it up, bringing in new customers? Really doing the cooking thing?'

'That was just . . . talk.' Deen waves his hand dismissively.

'You talk to Ma about the menu, and . . . maybe I'll apply for the coach position.' I shrug, going back to clearing the tables. I expect that to be the end of the matter, because there is no way that Deen will actually brave that conversation with our mother.

'You know those two things are not the same,' Deen says after a moment. 'But . . . I'll consider talking to her.' I stop mid-cleaning and turn to Deen.

'Seriously?'

Deen shrugs, acting as if the idea of talking to Ma is not a big deal, and not something he's been avoiding for months and months now.

I stand up straight, looking Deen square in the eye. He seems sincere in his intentions. Maybe he *will* seriously think about it. Maybe he'll actually do it.

But knowing Deen, and knowing our family, I don't have much hope.

'OK. Then I'll think about applying to be a coach,' I say.

Deen's face breaks out into a grin. He knows this is the most he can hope for, and I know that it most likely won't amount to anything.

But at least the two of us are happy living in our denial.

Chapter 2

Maya

The dinner table is almost completely silent, save for the sound of chewing and the occasional scrape of cutlery. When I look up from staring down at my plate, I realise that Amma and Abba are exchanging meaningful glances between each other, like they're having a silent conversation.

Probably one that's about me.

I have to stop myself from physically recoiling. I miss the times when our dinner tables were filled with lively discussions and debates. When *I* was in on the meaningful glances, and not the object of them.

'So, Maya. How was your day today? You went out, right?' Amma asks when she notices me looking at her. The smile on her face is completely fake, and I can see the worry behind her eyes.

'It was fine,' I say. I wish I had something to offer, but I can't tell them that I spent the day scrolling through online hate about myself while lying in bed. Exactly as I have done every single day since I got home.

It doesn't help that in the first week of my return, journalists had hounded me, trying to get the scoop on why I had really retired. Some of them had even found out my parents' address, ambushing Amma and Abba with questions.

Things had since died down, but the news articles full of pure speculation hadn't stopped.

Worse, the Bangladeshi aunties and uncles had been calling my parents nonstop, trying to find out exactly what had happened with me and my career. I'm sure they're not loving having to field that line of questioning. Even though it's mostly just morbid curiosity that'll fade soon.

'Did you do some unpacking?' Abba asks, a little too casually.

'No, not yet.' My voice comes out sharper than I intend it to. It's been two whole weeks since I've come back home and I'm fast running out of underwear, but the idea of unpacking feels overwhelming. It feels like admitting defeat.

'We can help you unpack if you need us to,' Amma says gently. The kindness in her voice makes me feel more angry than soothed.

'I don't need help unpacking, Amma. I'm a grown woman who can unpack on her own,' I say. A grown woman who has no job and has moved back into her parents' house, I think to myself. A grown woman who is somehow right where she was as a teenager.

'OK. Just . . . offering.' Amma and Abba exchange another glance across the table, and that's about all I can take for one dinnertime conversation.

With a sigh, I stand, despite my half-full plate. I'm not even that hungry, if I'm being honest with myself. I have missed Amma's cooking over the past few years – obviously – but the taste of it now reminds me less of home and more of my failure.

'I think I've lost my appetite. I'm feeling a little sick,' I mumble, grabbing my plate and walking over to the compost bin to dump the rest of it out. I toss the plate itself in the sink before hurrying up the stairs. All the while, my parents say nothing, even though I know the idea of wasting food is probably killing them.

My old bedroom is not the sanctuary that it once used to be. My two suitcases from America are still standing by the door. The walls are plastered with old paraphernalia from when I was a teenager. Posters of the bands I used to listen to – Evanescence, Breaking Benjamin and Paramore – and merch of my favourite football team, Arsenal. There are the old football trophies lining the shelf above my desk: MAYA ALAM proudly displayed on all of them. And then there's the stack of farewell cards from my family and friends – half of whom have moved away or started families now. The cards say things like, *Good luck, Maya, you are going to kill it!* and *I always knew you were meant for amazing things!*

It hurts to look at them. It feels like I'm staring my failure in the face every day.

I pick up the cards one by one with trembling fingers – the bright, colourful flowers and balloons on each of them now seem mocking – and shove them into the bin in the corner by my old desk. It's bad enough that I have my parents' sympathy-filled gazes to stare at every day – I can't look at these cards too.

With that done, I toss myself onto the bed, staring up at the ceiling and taking a deep breath.

'This isn't the end of the world,' I say to myself, mostly because I need to hear it. Being back home with my very loving parents is definitely not a bad thing. Sure, I may be unemployed now and, yes, maybe all my dreams have been dashed at the ripe age of twenty-eight. But that doesn't make me a failure, even if I *have* technically failed. I may have had a budding career, but now, in the blink of an eye, it's all gone. And it's because of me – because I'm not strong enough to persevere through all the rumours, the criticisms, the blame, the jeers.

I turn to my side, glancing out the window. This is the view that I've had growing up my entire life. The back garden with the little shed; Amma's prize rose bush and the overgrown birch tree from Mrs Sardar's garden that my parents hate but would never complain about. I try not to dwell on all the times I kicked around my football out there, how Amma fussed about ruining her roses, how Mrs Sardar always tried to hold the ball hostage whenever I kicked it into her garden. They were simple times when I had such bright dreams for everything.

If only that Maya knew where she would end up.

My alarm goes off at its usual time the next morning, as it has done ever since I got back. I turn it off but make no move to get up. The idea of getting up, of starting my day – whatever that means now – fills me with dread.

This is what things have been like since I returned home two weeks ago. It's like I'm stuck in a weird limbo – halfway between still being that girl who woke up early in the morning for training and the one who can barely even muster up the energy to get out of bed these days.

I turn onto my side, blinking at the thin rays of light peeking through the curtain. I miss the routine of still being a Viking. I miss getting up at the crack of dawn, the cold shower and cup of strong coffee that woke me up. I miss the early-morning jog. The weekly scheduled workouts: weight training on Mondays and Wednesdays, team training on Tuesdays and Thursdays. I miss having things to do, people to see. I miss having a *goal,* things to look forward to.

I used to think that having everything scheduled to a tee was something I would struggle with, but I quickly learned that I actually thrived on it. Having everything set out, trying to figure out how to push myself to be better and better during every single training session. In the beginning, I could feel how my body was changing. I could feel myself becoming more competent, a better player. On the field, I was getting faster, better at tackling and at defending the ball.

I still remember my first match for the Vikings. My jangled nerves for the hours before. I could barely hold down any food. I didn't really know any of my teammates then and I wished I had somebody to talk to.

Or, rather, I wished that the person I wanted to speak to wanted to speak to me too.

But I had pushed through the nerves and even scored a goal. Afterwards, the girls from the team cheered at how well I had played, and we had gone out for drinks to celebrate. Not just the match that we had won, but my first match with them. I thought then that this was it. That was going to be my life going forward, and everything would be OK.

But it wasn't just about the game. My naive young self couldn't have even comprehended back then all of the other stuff. The things that I don't miss at all. Like the crowd jeering at me during every game, which I tried so hard to tune out. The journalists with their probing questions. The videos that captured me in my worst moments and spread like wildfire. The comments . . .

My phone buzzes, pulling me out of my thoughts. I tug it close to me, wondering if I have snoozed my alarm instead of turning it off. But what I actually see is a text from Isabel.

Isabel: Good morning

Isabel: I know you're seeing these texts and one of these days you're going to have to get up off your ass and start talking to me again!!!

I sigh, resting my forefinger on the notifications to swipe them away and forget about them until the next time Isabel texts. But it's been two whole weeks and Isabel hasn't let up.

I thought it would be easy to cut off all my ties to football. I'd had a brief farewell 'party' with most of the girls from my team, opposing teams, and more – if drinks at a cheap local bar could be referred to as a party. They hadn't asked many questions about my decision to retire, though they'd said they'd miss me over and over again. Afterwards, I'd swiftly exited all of our group chats and I thought that was that.

But Isabel has texted me every single day. I probably shouldn't be surprised, considering how close we've got over the past few years, but I also wasn't sure if I could bear to keep in touch with her. It reminded me too much of everything that I've lost out on. Which is exactly why I've been deleting all the message notifications from her. I've been leaving her on read. I figured after a couple of days, she'd tire of me ignoring her and write me off as a lost cause. But Isabel just hasn't been getting the message.

Which is why I hesitate with her text today. She's right – if she persists, one of these days I *will* have to start talking to her again. There's only so long that I can ignore her, and every time she texts to say *good morning*, and ask about how I'm doing, and how my parents are, and what it's like being back home, I feel this tightness in my chest.

Sitting up in bed, I rub sleep out of my eyes. Instead of

deleting the notification, my fingers go to the on-screen keyboard, typing an answer.

Maya: You are seriously persistent

Isabel's reply comes lightning fast, like she's been sitting by her phone, waiting for my reply.

Isabel: Hallelujah! She's alive!

Isabel: Please tell me you haven't been rotting away in bed and ignoring everyone for the past two weeks

It's eerie how well she knows me, but, in truth, Isabel was really the only person on the team who got me. It helped that she was Latina, which meant that often we were up against the same kind of problems. We talked about how the media seemed to have a grudge against us, and how even our 'fans' were quick to criticise us in a way that they never did the white players.

Maya: I've just needed time to myself. I still need some time to myself.

Isabel's reply comes more slowly this time. I can see her typing, stopping, typing, stopping. Like she's carefully choosing her words.

Isabel: Maya . . . I know it's been hard for you. And if you need to not talk to me for a while, I get that. But I'm here, whenever you need someone to talk to. You know that. Crossing the Atlantic Ocean doesn't mean you get rid of me. It's not going to be that easy.

I smile, and the movement almost feels unnatural. I can't remember the last time that I've smiled or laughed, or felt anything but an overwhelming sense of anguish. I miss Isabel, I miss my team. I miss my schedules and my training, and I miss football. But maybe being back home doesn't just have to be me going over my failures all day, every day.

Maybe it's time to start picking up the pieces again.

Chapter 3

Dina

I think about what Deen said while I cycle home from the restaurant, but I can't really wrap my head around the idea of being a coach. It's been so long since I've even touched a football. Whatever skill I thought I had has probably dissipated into thin air, and Jen likely knows that. She must have only mentioned the assistant coach position because she was making small talk and didn't know what else to talk about.

Yeah, that was definitely it.

I lock up my bike inside the foyer of the building before making my way up to my apartment. Outside the door, I can hear the mumble of *The Warm Up*, a sports talk show that Thea and I sometimes watch together. But when I step inside, my flatmates, Thea and Aisha, are in the sitting room watching what seems to be a very dry documentary about hairdressing – something that neither of them has ever expressed much interest in.

'Hey!' Thea says cheerfully over her shoulder.

'Hi . . .' I mumble, taking off my shoes and making my way towards the sitting room. 'What are you guys watching?'

'Oh, it's just background noise,' Aisha says, turning away from the TV and towards me, a bright smile pasted on her face. 'We were just, you know, having a catch-up.'

'Oh. Is there any good gossip that I've missed?'

'Um . . .' Aisha and Thea exchange a glance between them.

'My co-worker – the really annoying one who I'm convinced is the office lunch thief? She got engaged!' Thea offers.

'Oh . . .' I'm not really sure how to respond to that revelation considering Thea has only mentioned this co-worker a couple of times offhandedly.

'Uh, and they just opened this new restaurant like ten minutes away from where I work. We should go there for brunch sometime,' Aisha says enthusiastically.

'What's the place called?'

'Um . . .'

'What kind of food do they have?'

'I want to say . . . Mexican?' Aisha says.

'OK, what is going on?' I ask, frowning at Aisha and Thea. 'Neither of these things is gossip, and why did you change the channel when I walked in the door?'

'We didn't do that,' Thea says a little too fast, while Aisha shoots her a glare.

'I could hear the talk show from outside. Is there some big scandal running through the football community or something?'

Aisha and Thea exchange another look, before Aisha reluctantly picks up the remote by her side and flicks the channel back to *The Warm Up*. Erica Hadley and Karl Griffin are sitting across from each other on their comfy green couches as usual, but on the side is a blown-up picture of none other than *her*.

Maya Alam.

My mouth dries up just at the sight of her in her green

football shirt, her black hair tied back in a ponytail out of her eyes. Dark brown eyes looking straight at me as if they can see through me. Even though she's just an image on the TV, my heartbeat quickens. For a moment, it feels like she's right there in front of me, in my tiny living room.

It takes a minute for me to even register the conversation that Erica and Karl are having.

'I think it came as a shock to *everyone*, especially given how well she has been doing over the past few years. Nobody could have expected that she would go into early retirement,' Erica says.

'Right. I think just a few months ago, we were discussing that she might be one of the players we're seeing a lot of during the transfer market. She has – well, *had* – a lot of potential,' Karl says in agreement.

'There were a few incidents, though, and it's not like she has endeared anyone to her with her prickly attitude. Could that be part of the reason why she has decided to retire?'

'Was she forced into it, do you think?' Karl asks, leaning forwards towards Erica, like she has some great insight into Maya Alam's life.

'We heard that she's moved back,' Aisha says, looking at me tentatively. 'But it's probably temporary, and you'll probably never even see her. I mean—'

But I don't wait to hear any more of Thea's or Aisha's consolations. Instead, I turn around and head into my bedroom, slamming the door shut behind me.

I should have just left it alone, let them talk about co-worker engagements and brunch spots that they clearly know nothing about. The last thing I want to think about is Maya Alam. The last thing I want to do is run into her again. But if she's moved back here, I don't know how that *won't* happen. And with my life currently in shambles, seeing me at my worst will probably be like a victory lap for Maya.

A buzzing in my pocket pulls me out of my thoughts momentarily. I slip my phone out to find a message notification. From Jen.

Jen: Hey Dina! Hope this is still your number, it's been so long since I've texted you. Anyway, I just wanted to say how nice it was to see you today and sorry for the girls making such a mess of your family's restaurant! About the coach position . . . I know you probably have better things to do, but if it's ever something that takes your fancy, please let me know.

I think back to Deen, and to Maya's picture on the TV.

Then I text Jen back.

'They can be a bit of a handful,' Jen says the next day. We're sat across from each other in a small corner coffee shop by Victoria Park. I used to come here all the time with Maya, but I try not to think too much about that. 'You saw yourself at your restaurant the other day. But they're great kids all the same, and I think you're the perfect person to get through to them.'

I chew on my lips. When I texted Jen last night asking about the assistant coach position, I was fuelled by my resentment for Maya. But now, in the cold light of day, I am rethinking the whole thing. I haven't played football in almost a decade. And I've never coached before, or even been a team leader for anything, let alone of a group of teenage girls. I don't know what I was thinking in entertaining the idea of being a coach.

'I don't have any experience,' I say. 'I mean, I last played football . . . so long ago.' *And it didn't end well*, I think to myself but don't say aloud.

'Yeah, but it's kind of like riding a bike.' Jen shrugs. 'I know you haven't forgotten all the ins and outs of it. You were one of the best players on the team, Dina. The position is yours, if you want it. And I really hope that you'll take it.' Jen looks at me with so much pride in her eyes that I'm not sure how I can turn her down.

It was definitely a bad idea to meet up to discuss the coaching position. If we had had this conversation over the phone, I wouldn't have to deal with the weight of her crushing disappointment. There's a part of me that wants to say yes to her desperately – of course, there is. Since seeing Jen at the restaurant, I've been wondering what it would look like if I went back to football. But there's that other part of me, the one that's always whispering at the back of my head, that can't stop reminding me of what a disaster football had been in the end. How I had promised myself that I would never, ever go back to it.

'I don't know Jen,' I mumble, staring into the depths of my coffee, and trying to think of a way that I can let her down gently. I just need to explain to her that I'm not the Dina she remembers. That I'm not that girl who used to leap out of bed in the morning thinking about football practice. Who went to bed thinking about strategies and tactics. Who practised drills in the park by her house until dusk.

It's as I'm trying to come up with my reasons and excuses that the doors to the cafe open and a figure strolls in, looking around the shop. I'm hoping against all hope that it's not her because it can't be her. But I know that it *is*, because I'd recognise her anywhere. We spent the best part of our teenage years together, after all. Playing football together in Bethnal Green gardens, sharing the same earphones to listen to the latest Breaking Benjamin album, feeling like we had everything figured out when we had nothing figured out.

She doesn't seem to take notice of me and Jen. Instead, her eyes are glued to her phone, even as she marches forwards. I know that I should look away. Maybe duck my face and hide, but I can't stop staring at her.

Because she's Maya Alam, the bane of my existence. The reason for my heartbreak. The reason for all my heartbreak. The one person that I never want to think about, and never wanted to see again. But also somehow the one person that I can never seem to escape; definitely not in my thoughts and now, apparently, not even in reality.

For a moment, I'm sure that she'll go right past us. That we'll be like ships passing at night. And I prepare for just that, looking back towards Jen just as Maya approaches, closing my eyes and pretending that she's not there, that I can't already smell the familiar scent of her; it may be cloaked by her perfume – something citrusy – but there's the undertone of earthiness that's all Maya. It makes me a little light-headed.

But then Maya bumps right into me, almost sending me stumbling off my chair. Her phone falls to the ground with a loud clatter.

'Oh my God, I am so, *so* sorry,' Maya starts, even as she follows up her apology with a string of curses under her breath as she ducks for her phone on the ground. 'I wasn't looking where I was going and—'

It's only then that her eyes seem to land on me and there's a flicker of recognition in her dark brown eyes.

'Dina.' Her voice is barely a whisper as she says my name. It should fill me with rage, how casually she says it. Instead, it sends a jolt of electricity through me. Because nobody else says my name quite like *that*.

Thankfully, before I lose all my sense of self, Jen comes to my rescue.

'Maya!' she exclaims, a smile breaking out on her face.

I look down at my coffee, trying to get my heartbeat under control.

'Jen . . . hi.' Maya sounds strained, and when I glance up, I notice that Jen has leapt up from her chair to wrap Maya in a hug.

'I'd heard that you were back. How have you been?'

'Yeah, good,' Maya says. She glances at me, and I look away once more. At the walls of the cafe, at my coffee mug, at the blue-and-white tiled floor. Anywhere but at Maya. 'How are you? What have you been up to?'

'I'm doing good, I've been bouncing around between a few things,' Jen says. 'Now I'm actually running a youth football club for the council.' Jen turns to me, and I can sense her next line coming. The assistant coach position that we're discussing. With Maya here now, maybe I'm not Jen's only option anymore. Unlike me, Maya was a professional football player. And even if coaching a council team is probably beneath her after all the flash and pomp of her career, what if Jen offered it to her? The thought makes my stomach sink.

'Dina and I were actually just—' Jen begins, but I cut in before she can finish.

'Talking about the team. I'm the assistant coach. Just started.' I can't really avoid looking at Maya anymore. My eyes flicker up, meeting hers. I try to keep my expression unchanged, but the sight of her makes my stomach lurch and my mouth dry up. I can't figure out what emotion I'm even feeling – anger, guilt, or the resurfacing of old feelings that definitely should *not* be resurfacing? I'm not sure which one would be the worst.

It's been nine years since I saw Maya in the flesh, but that doesn't mean I haven't *seen* her. As much as I've tried to avoid any news about her since she left, I've stumbled across photos of her in newspapers and magazines, glanced at her interviews, and even caught glimpses of her matches. She always looks different in them. Kind of fake, filtered and airbrushed. Here, she looks more like the Maya that I used to know, the one that I have missed all these years. Her black hair has only grown longer over the years, and now it looks slightly dishevelled. She's wearing a simple T-shirt and jeans, like she's just thrown it together, but the clothes cling to her in just the right way.

'Oh, cool,' Maya says. Her eyes snap back to Jen.

Jen looks between the two of us and I don't know if she can read something in the air between us. I don't know how she would when I don't even know what it is. I want to be angry at Maya, want to hate her with every fibre of my being, but the sight of her has made me thaw a little. Made all our memories of the past come rushing back.

'I know you've just returned from your whirlwind football career. The football clubs here must be going crazy for you,' Jen says.

Maya smiles, but even I can tell that it feels a bit forced. There's something different about her – there's less of that haughty fierceness that she used to have when we were younger. It's been replaced by a strange kind of coldness.

I wonder if this is what Erica and Karl were talking about in *The Warm Up*.

'Yeah. Um . . .' Maya's eyes flicker down to her phone screen, the one that she seems to be holding in a death grip. 'I should actually get going, leave you guys to it,' Maya says. 'It was . . . nice to see you, Jen.' She glances at me again – only for a moment – before she's turning around and walking out the door.

Jen turns back to me, smile still in place. 'So, you're taking the job?' She raises an eyebrow as if asking what exactly that was all about. It's not like she doesn't have some idea about what things were like with me and Maya back in the day, but she doesn't know how it all ended. That we haven't spoken in almost a decade, even if I've thought about her more often than I want to admit.

'Yeah,' I say. 'I'm taking the job.'

Chapter 4

Maya

Outside the coffee shop, it takes me a minute to catch my breath. I close my eyes, and gulp in lungfuls of air. It's only the feel of plastic against my skin that reminds me that I'm still holding onto my phone tightly, like a lifeline.

It's ridiculous that someone I haven't seen in nearly a decade can have that kind of an effect on me – should be *allowed* to have that kind of an effect on me. I feel angry at myself, angry at Dina, angry at the fact that of all the coffee shops in the world, it's this one that I decided to stumble into.

I stand up straight, trying to shake the emotions out of me. Through the windowed door of the cafe, I can still make out Dina, though she's almost turned away from me. She and Jen are in an animated conversation. Unlike a few minutes ago, when she refused to speak to or even look at me, she looks happy as she speaks to Jen. She waves her arms around to punctuate her words, a smile lights up her brown eyes, and there's just a hint of pink dusting her sandy brown skin. Seeing her like this makes my stomach do familiar somersaults.

I turn away, forcing myself to stop studying her. I definitely can't be having those thoughts. I can't be doing this again. Especially not now.

I have been trying to get myself back on track ever since I started texting with Isabel again a few days ago. But it's easier said than done. Between finally unpacking my suitcase and trying to venture out to old haunts once more, I've also been glued to my phone, reading through any and all articles about me that pop up. I know it's a bad idea, but I also feel like I can't look away. Like, somehow, knowing about the things people are saying is better than not knowing, even if sometimes the comments feel like a knife to the heart.

When I'd walked into the coffee shop, I'd been reading through an article titled 'The REAL Reason for Maya Alam's Hasty Retirement'.

Now I close out of the article quickly. There's an irrational part of me that feels like Dina can still see me through the cafe doors, that she can somehow read the article on my phone and sense my insecurities emanating off me in waves.

Trying to put it all out of my mind, I start to make my way back home.

The next day, Dina's face stares at me from my computer screen. I spent enough time online stalking her after I left, but it's been several years since I've looked through her Facebook posts (not that she ever posted much). She promptly deleted our old photos together from her profile back then anyway.

Her Facebook account doesn't even exist anymore, and all I find is a sparsely used Instagram account, with a scattering of photos. There's one from a year ago of Dina and her brother, Deen, standing side by side, grinning at the camera. Then another from several months ago – a selfie where she's squeezed in the middle of two girls. The most recent picture she's posted is of a bouquet of flowers on a table, and it makes my heart squeeze together painfully, though it really, really shouldn't. She's clearly dating someone, and it shouldn't matter to me at all.

But for some reason, it does.

I close the lid of my laptop and take a deep breath, trying to erase Dina's face from my mind, hard as it is. I knew being back would be difficult, and I knew that it wouldn't be easy to steer clear of her. I just wasn't expecting everything to rush up at me at once; the good memories, and then all of the bad ones too.

The creak of the door opening sounds from downstairs, and I stand up, hurrying down the stairs. Amma is at the front door, her hands full of groceries. I step forward, taking the bags off her as she smiles and turns to lock the door behind her. Carrying the bags into the kitchen, I set them down. Amma follows me in.

'You don't have to help me. I'm used to doing these things on my own,' she says, shifting around the grocery bags. Her words send a little pang of regret through me. She and Abba shouldn't have to do all of these things on their own. If I had been around the last couple of years, I could have helped them out. But I have been all the way across the ocean, and my parents have had nobody here. Even since I've been back, I've just been moping around the house.

'I don't mind helping,' I say.

'I thought you were going to try to catch up with some old friends?' Amma asks.

That had been the plan, after all of Isabel's encouragement, but after running into Dina, I'm not so sure about anything anymore.

'They're all probably busy.' I shrug, while diving into

Amma's grocery bags to pull out eggs and a loaf of bread and putting them away. 'They've got jobs and families and lives.' I think about Dina for a moment, wondering exactly what kind of a life *she* has now.

'Hmm.' Amma frowns. She slowly starts putting vegetables into the fridge. 'So you didn't go out today at all?'

My stomach sinks at Amma's line of questioning, like I can sense that she can see I'm going backwards again. I should be getting over everything, moving past my football days and trying to forge a life for myself here. And something as simple as seeing my ex-girlfriend in a coffee shop we both used to frequent shouldn't be enough to send me spiralling.

'Not yet . . .'

'Maybe it's time to start looking for some kind of a job. It could be a good way to get you out of the house. Your abba and I could help you find something.' Amma offers me a hesitant smile. She's still walking on eggshells around me and I hate it. When I was younger, Amma, Abba and I could always speak honestly with each other; I never felt like I had to hide anything from them. They knew almost every detail of my life, from school, to my friends, and even Dina. Amma was the first person I told about Dina, the first person that I ever came out to as bisexual.

But now, it feels like our relationship has become distant. Like the long distance between us for the past nine years has persisted, even though I'm home now.

'I don't even know what I'd do. I mean, it's not like I have a university degree.' It wasn't something that bothered me when I was playing professionally. Other football players who had retired went on to coach professional teams, write books, take modelling contracts or sponsorship deals for sports drinks and gyms. But after the way I retired, I doubt any of these jobs will be coming my way any time soon. My options feel limited. Maybe even non-existent.

'We can talk to some uncles and aunties. They'll help find you something. You could . . . go to university, if you wanted. Your Malik uncle decided to do an undergrad in economics to help with the family business a few years ago, and he even got a mature-student scholarship to help pay the fees!' Amma sounds excited at the idea of it, but I only feel a pit in my stomach. Starting fresh in university is not my idea of fun. I can't even think of what I would want to study, and I haven't been able to bring myself to envision a future where I don't play football anymore.

'I'll figure something out,' I promise Amma. I know that I have to.

Chapter 5

Dina

Fifteen years ago

'Baba, come on! We're. Going. To. Be. Late!' I say, punctuating my words with subsequent knocks on the door. The clock in the hallway reads 7.45 a.m., which means that if we don't leave the house within the next ten minutes, we're definitely going to be late.

The door finally swings open, and Baba blinks at me tiredly. His eyes are bloodshot, his hair unkempt, though he's changed out of his pyjamas at least.

'I'm up, Dina.' He stifles a yawn and shuffles past me towards the stairs.

I hold in the scream that has been building up in me for the past half-hour. For my friends, the first day of secondary school meant getting excited about wearing their new school uniform for the first time, making sure that they had their hair brushed to perfection and eating a hearty breakfast. For me, it was desperately trying to wake up my dad in time, after all of his overworking at the restaurant.

I follow Baba down the stairs, but instead of heading to the front door, he makes his way to the kitchen and starts up the kettle.

'Baba, we really don't have time for—'

'It'll just be five minutes, Dina,' Baba mumbles between

a yawn. 'I definitely shouldn't be driving without having a cup of tea, at least. Don't worry, we won't be late.'

I check my watch, and I know that he is definitely wrong.

At least he has the foresight to make his tea directly in his tumbler before grabbing his car keys.

I follow him out of the front door and climb into our old beaten-up Toyota while Baba locks up the house. Whatever excitement I may have felt about the prospect of starting secondary school at some point has evaporated; replaced now by dread in my stomach.

Baba starts up the car and pulls out of the driveway. It's not long before we merge into the rush-hour traffic on the main road. I keep checking my watch, counting down the time until I'm officially late, and it doesn't take long, all things considered.

'It's going to be fine,' Baba says, noticing me check the time. 'All the teachers there already know Deen, so . . . it'll be fine.'

Deen has gone ahead to school with a group of his friends, so I haven't even thought about that. Instead of comforting me, it just makes my dread build up even more.

By the time we pull up to the school building, we're twenty whole minutes late. Baba has barely pulled to a stop when I throw open my door and climb out.

'Have a good day!' Baba shouts after me, though I barely register his words as I hurry through the front doors. My first class is supposed to be English with Ms Nichols in room 203, but I have no clue where that classroom might actually be. I duck into the East hallway, but all the classrooms seem to be 1-0-something, so I turn to make my way to the other hallway, when I nearly stumble into a teacher.

'You should be in class,' the teacher says, frowning down at me. 'What's your name?'

THE PERFECT MATCH

I shift from one foot to another. Surely, she will have to understand that it's my first day in this school and that I'm lost. 'Um, Dina Chowdhury. I'm looking for class 203 but—'

'Dina *Chowdhury*?' Her face turns sour as if there's something unpleasant about my name. 'Of course, you must be Deen's sister. Already skipping classes on the first day and not even dressed in the right uniform.' She looks me up and down, her lips curling with distaste. All the while, I'm wishing that the floor would open and swallow me up. That would be far better than standing here in this empty hallway being scrutinised by this teacher who I've never met before.

'I . . . My mum got the uniform from, um—' I don't even get the chance to explain that she found a discount shop with skirts and jumpers that were (according to her) *exactly* like the school uniform. It was easier to justify buying those than dropping a couple of hundred pounds on the official school uniform. Ma said I would just grow out of it within the next year anyway.

'I think detention should set you on the right track,' the teacher says with a nod, as if I haven't even attempted to speak. 'Though that didn't work on your brother, did it? Now, off to class you go.'

She doesn't even wait for me to respond before pushing past me in the hallway. For a moment, I can only just stand there, wondering how I've managed to get detention within the first five minutes of being in school. That seems like some kind of a world record.

I don't have time to wallow in the unfairness of it all, though, because I still have to find my classroom.

I'm wishing that life came with a redo button as I restart

my search for room 203. After a few more minutes of looking, I finally find the classroom. I can hear the buzz of conversation coming from inside – class is well underway, and I'll have to walk in and interrupt everything. Explaining why I'm late.

Pausing for a moment, I take a deep breath.

Then, I open the door and step inside.

'. . . And I think that he's really—' The girl speaking cuts herself off and stares at me, with the rest of the class.

But she doesn't just stare. Her expression has contorted into a glare directed at me. As if me interrupting the class is some kind of a personal affront against her.

'Are you supposed to be in this class? You know we started twenty minutes ago, right?' Ms Nichols, who is perched on her desk at the front of the classroom asks, frowning at me.

'Sorry I'm late,' I mumble, feeling my face flush.

At least the rest of the class seems to have lost their interest in me, even if the girl is still glaring daggers at me. Weaving through the desks, I find one at the very back of the classroom. I'm ready to disappear into the walls, if the walls would have me.

Ms Nichols nods to the girl and says, 'Thanks for that, Maya, let's move along.'

I watch as the girl – Maya – relaxes a little in her seat, her posture perfect and her fingers tapping the open notebook in front of her with her pen. She has the proper school uniform, down to the knee-length white socks with maroon stripes. Even the English textbook atop her desk is sparkling and new, while the one that I reluctantly fish out of my own backpack is tattered and filled with marginalia from a previous owner.

THE PERFECT MATCH

I open my textbook to the right page, reading over the poem that the class has been discussing, while Ms Nichols guides everyone towards the questions at the bottom of the page.

The class goes quiet as everyone picks up their pens and starts writing their answers. I skim over the questions and the poem again, jotting down notes first, before actually getting to the questions.

I'm still trying to finish my last sentence when Ms Nichols starts looking for the correct answer to the first question.

Maya's hand shoots up before anyone else's.

Could she be any more of a teacher's pet?

And on the first day of school, no less.

I roll my eyes. I've met girls like Maya before – prissy and perfect and with zero problems in their life, always dying to show off just how amazing they are to anybody who'll give them the time of day.

'I think there are a few different literary devices that are used in this poem,' Maya says in her haughty voice. Even though the question asked to give one example, Maya seems determined to use this chance to show off. Is this what every single English class is going to be like this year? 'In the first line, we can clearly see an example of alliteration, and in the second . . .'

My ears perk up, my shoulders rise, and I lean forward in my seat, before my hand rises as if of its own accord.

Ms Nichols is smiling politely at Maya even though we all know that she's totally wrong in her answer. 'Ah, thank you, Maya. That's not quite . . . In the first sentence, it wasn't . . .' Ms Nichols's eyes drift towards me and she nods. 'Yes?'

I have to stop myself from beaming as I answer. 'There

are a few literary devices, but the first line is actually an example of onomatopoeia. I mean, a *tap*,' I say, quoting from the poem and tapping my finger against the wooden desk in front of me. 'It's kind of obvious.'

Maya has twisted around to look at me, her cheeks decidedly pinker than they previously were. If I thought her glare was bad before, it's nothing compared to her expression now. If looks could kill, I would probably already be dead. I don't return her glare, though, just give her a sickly-sweet smile, which seems to make her even more angry.

'Yes, thank you for that, and for the demonstration too,' Ms Nichols says with a smile. 'I don't think I got your name.'

'Dina,' I say proudly, not wanting to hide away for the first time in this class. Maybe sharing a class with Maya won't be the worst thing in the world after all.

We get through the rest of the questions and just as Ms Nichols is assigning us homework for the day, there is a loud rapping on the door.

'Come in,' Ms Nichols says and the door swings open.

A woman in a blue tracksuit walks in, smiling hesitantly at Ms Nichols. 'Hey, Olivia. I just wanted to make a quick announcement about try-outs, if that's OK? I won't take up too much of your time,' she says.

'Of course, go ahead.' Ms Nichols turns back to the whiteboard to finish writing up the homework assignment.

The woman looks at us, her smile warm as she takes us in. 'Hi, everyone. I'm Jen, I'm the sports teacher here and I'll probably be seeing all of you for class pretty soon. There's going to be try-outs for the girl's football team next Thursday after school, and we're always looking for new talent. So, I encourage all of you to come and show off your skills. I know there are already a couple of you whose previous schools have talked you up. Maya Alam?' Jen turns to Maya, her smile widening.

Maya sits up straighter at the mention.

I groan inwardly – how is this girl already in with every single teacher at this school? She only has a twenty-minute head start on me.

'Your old teacher told me about how great you were. Please do come to the try-outs, yeah? And that goes for the rest of you too. Hope to see you all there.' With that, Jen turns back to Ms Nichols, mumbles another thank you and ducks out of the classroom.

Maya is grinning from ear to ear and the classroom bursts into a curious buzz. I can already see a few of the girls around Maya turning to her, no doubt asking about whether she will try out or not.

But I'm already tired of the Maya show. So if Maya is going to try out, then I definitely have to try out as well. And when I get in, I'll outshine her on the football field too.

Chapter 6

Dina

'And then she just handed me the invite, even though the wedding is only two weeks away. Can you believe that? Totally shameless.' Ma shakes her head, like last-minute wedding invites are some kind of crime against humanity.

'I thought you didn't even like Maryam aunty,' Deen says through a mouthful of rice. His words would be completely incomprehensible, but Ma and I are too used to him and can understand him even in the worst of circumstances. Still, Ma frowns at his ill-kept manners, though she doesn't make a comment on it for now.

'I just think your Maryam aunty has . . . a few faults.' Ma begins to clear the table of the dishes, as a way to veer away from the topic of how much she actually dislikes Maryam aunty. The whole conversation about her eldest son's wedding invite has definitely elicited a sour mood from our mother. At another point in time, she might use a wedding invite to try to cajole Deen and me about *our* romantic relationships, but Deen has been all hands on deck with the restaurant for the past three years with no room for romance, and I blew up my last serious relationship when I quit my job at the financial firm. She – Anu – was determined to believe that I was just having some sort of a quarter-life crisis, and refused to entertain it by supporting my decision to quit. So that was that.

It's a good thing Ma was never a big fan of Anu anyway.

Deen gives me an encouraging glance from across the table, but I know now is not the time to start the conversation about football with Ma. Instead, I stand up quickly and start gathering up the dishes even faster than Ma can.

'Deen and I can clean up,' I offer.

Deen shoots me a glare, but quickly pastes on a smile when Ma looks from me to him.

'I don't mind,' Ma says. 'I like it when you both eat here.' She says it as if Deen hasn't been living with her for the past five years and doesn't eat here every single day. Or that ever since I quit my job in the city, I haven't come here twice a week for her cooking – which remains incomparable to anything else.

'We've got it, Ma,' I say. 'You want some tea?'

Ma looks at me with a hint of suspicion, which makes me wonder if the offer of tea was a little bit too much. Deen and I have never been the kind of kids who pamper our parents. In fact, Deen has a long and storied track record of being the problem child who would require my parents to have meetings with the school principal every couple of months. It's kind of a wonder that he grew up to be the person he is today.

'I can make the tea,' Deen offers now, standing up too.

If Ma is suspicious, she doesn't say it. Instead, she smiles and wanders away from the dining room and towards her prized garden. It's become a bit of an obsession for her over the last few years, but as far as obsessions go, it's been pretty fruitful.

Last year, she planted tomatoes, which bloomed into

small, green-ish red cherry tomatoes that were a little too sour to put into a salad. But being Bengali, Ma had the perfect solution: she made the tomatoes into achar. It was perfectly suited with the sour taste, and she even made enough to give away to a few of the aunties around the neighbourhood. Her home-made achar from her home-grown tomatoes was definitely one of her great sources of pride last year, especially since, as her kids, we hadn't brought home any accomplishments. Ever since Deen got his diploma in business three years ago, he's been whiling away his time maintaining the restaurant. Meanwhile, I had only brought home disappointment through my hasty decision to quit my job.

Ma has never expressed disapproval about either of our choices, but I know it's hard for her when her friends boast about their kids' high-paying careers. They've gone on to become doctors, engineers and lawyers. And if not that, they've at least had the good sense to get married and start families. Comparatively, Deen and I are failures as children.

I watch as Ma starts tending to some of her plants, unsure of how to approach her, when Deen passes by, elbowing me painfully in the ribs and whispering, 'Coward,' into my ear. He starts up the kettle and it hisses loudly as it begins boiling.

I turn to him with a frown. 'You weren't jumping to talk to her either.'

'Yeah, well. Mine is, you know . . . less concrete,' Deen says, looking at the boiling kettle instead of at me.

'Which makes your discussion easier to have,' I point out.

'No, it doesn't,' Deen says. 'Yours is more important. I mean, aren't you supposed to start next week?'

'Yes . . .' The thought of that doesn't bring me joy.

I'm due to start coaching soon, and the idea of it makes panic slowly creep through me. But there's also an electric pulse of excitement when I imagine stepping onto a football pitch again. It's been so long since I've touched a football, or even gone near a pitch. I never thought that I would again.

Deen is right – even if he is saying all of this because he doesn't want to be first up to talk to Ma.

'Just because I'm talking to her first doesn't mean you're off the hook,' I tell him.

Deen rolls his eyes as he places the familiar Hollywood star of fame mug on the counter, tossing a teabag into it. Deen and I bought Ma the mug when we were kids, back when she still went to auditions. Back when she still talked about her dream of becoming an actress. I barely even remember those days now.

Taking a deep breath, I make my way towards Ma in the garden. She looks happy and peaceful, shovelling the dirt around her blueberry bushes.

'Ma . . .' I say.

'Hmm?' she answers, though she doesn't look up.

I crouch down by the blueberry bushes next to her, unsure of how to bring up the topic.

'You think you'll make blueberry achar this year?' I ask.

Ma's eyes light up at the suggestion. She takes hold of some of the flowers that have bloomed on the leaves of the plant and studies them closely. 'If I don't let them ripen, I probably could. Do you think that would taste good?'

I'm definitely the wrong person to ask that question, but I nod happily, trying to keep Ma in this favourable mood.

Then, with a deep breath, I dive in. 'Ma, do you remember . . . Jen?

'Your friend with the bad haircut from school?'

I frown, wondering which friend she's talking about. I'm not surprised that she doesn't remember Jen. It was Baba who dealt with all the football stuff. He was the one who bought me my first football kit, who used to kick the ball around with me in the back garden while Ma despaired over the state of her plants. He attended every single match I had and always cheered me on. He and Jen were basically on a first-name basis.

'Um, no. She was . . . well, she used to coach football back in secondary school. You met her a couple of times, at some of my games. Well, she came into the restaurant the other day.' I pause, waiting for Ma to react, but she doesn't. She doesn't give any indication that she's even heard what I've said, but she must have. I worry that if I pause, I'll never get up the courage to tell her again, so I just plough on. 'She still coaches football. Not at the school anymore, though. She helps run a youth football group for the council, which is obviously very commendable. It helps the kids out, I'm sure. Anyway, um . . . well, she told me she was looking for an assistant coach and you know I've been feeling lost ever since I quit my job. And this felt like a good opportunity. So, I thought I would help her out.'

I pause once more, looking for some kind of a change in Ma's demeanour. Something that tells me she's disappointed or happy, though the latter is unlikely. She doesn't say anything, though. Instead, she studies the blooms on her plants with careful scrutiny, cradling them with her hands, feeling them with her fingertips.

'She's asked me to start next week. I just . . . wanted

you to know.' I stand up, brushing some dirt off my jeans, and trying not to feel too discouraged by Ma's lack of a response. Deen was definitely right not to want to talk to Ma – she's always been this way, shutting down instead of engaging in uncomfortable conversations. For Ma, it was better to bury everything, especially your feelings. It's become worse since Baba passed away. Sometimes, I wonder if that's why she's so hell-bent on not changing anything in the restaurant. If it's her way of preserving Baba's memory.

'I don't know why you're going back to the very thing that broke your heart and spirit.' Ma's voice – sharp and clear – surprises me. I may have expected her to be disappointed in my decision to pursue football again, but I didn't expect her to be disappointed *for* me.

'It's not – it's going to be different this time,' I say, but I can't stop the quiver in my voice. I hate that I don't sound convincing, even to myself. 'It's not a football team or the chance at a scholarship or anything. It's just an assistant coach position, and I can quit any time I want. I won't get caught up in it.'

I *can't* get caught up in it, though I don't voice that out loud to Ma.

Ma looks up to meet my gaze finally, studying me wordlessly. She doesn't believe me, and I don't blame her. I'm not sure if I believe me either. Will it be that easy to go back to football? Will it be that easy if I left it again? It took so much from me once before, and now I'm walking back to it as if all of that history has been erased, when I know that it hasn't.

'You changed after everything, you know.' Ma stands up, taking off her yellow gardening gloves slowly. 'I always noticed it in you. It took you so long to move forward, and I just don't want that to happen again.'

'It won't happen again,' I insist. More for myself than for her.

If last time had left me broken and hollow, I'm not sure I have it in me to go through that heartbreak again.

Chapter 7

Maya

Despite Ma's insistence that I get out of the house and start looking for a job, I spend the week holed up at home. Venturing out before only led to running into Dina and I'm not sure if I'm prepared for that to happen again.

It's one of those days when I'm languishing in bed that my phone buzzes. I reach for it, thinking that it must be Isabel, but it isn't. It's a Google alert with my name that I set up years ago. I've spent a little too much time scouring the internet for the responses to my retirement announcement since I got back and it hasn't exactly helped things. But I also feel like I can't look away.

Now, I click on the alert, and the headline appears in my screen, bold and bright: 'Maya Alam's TORRID history'. My stomach drops, but I click through to the article, my eyes scanning it quickly. It's not the worst piece about me, though it basically has no facts to speak of. There's speculation about my time on the team, how I was on the sidelines after my first couple of games, the rumours about me being unpleasant to work with. I've seen it all before. But, of course, I can't help but go down to the comments, my heart beating fast as I do. I know that I should just close my phone and put it away. But it's like a drug, being in the media. Having people who you have never met think they know so much about you – engage in speculation about you.

> *@coyotea: Thank GOD she's gone!*
> *@sealixir: The Vikings are sooo better off without her.*
> *@yakar: She couldn't play football to save her life, no wonder she retired.*
> *@deliverykail: This is why India never makes the world cup – they all SUCK at football!*
> *@warthawk: Women's football is full of total hacks and too much drama – and all they want to do is complain!!!*

I close my eyes and take a deep breath, finally putting my phone away. But my heart is pumping fast and I feel like there's adrenaline coursing through my body.

I need to find a way to deal with it, so I go downstairs, pulling my trainers from the shoe rack.

'Maya?' Amma is standing at the kitchen door, a wooden spoon in her hands. 'Are you . . . OK?'

'I'm fine,' I lie quickly. 'I'm just . . . I'm going to go out for a run.'

'Oh.' Amma seems to be trying to hide her surprise, but I read it in her wide-eyed expression just the same. I've barely left the house since I got back. I definitely haven't just nipped out for a run. 'Well . . . OK. Will you come back for lunch? I'm making daal makhani.'

'Yes, yeah. I'll be back . . . soon.' I finish tying my shoe-laces and give Amma a reassuring smile. 'I'll see you later.'

I jog around the neighbourhood for a little bit, the cool air and the rush of blood through my body feeling like relief. Thoughts of that news article and the accompanying comments are still buzzing around somewhere in my brain, but they're dull now. Instead, I'm thinking about this place, being back home. My memories of the past start rushing back as I pass familiar places: Victoria Park, where I used to hang out with my friends after school, the hidden off-licence near it where we would buy cheap meal deals for lunch. And finally, somehow, I stumble outside my old secondary school.

I pause to catch my breath, looking up at the building. Despite all the years that have passed, Westbrook Secondary School hasn't changed even a tiny bit. There's the car park always filled to the brim, the big block of a building with no colour other than grey, black or white to be seen on it, the cold glass doors, the too-small windows that barely let enough light or air in. And, of course, the football pitch that used to feel massive back when we played on it but now makes me wonder how it even contained our teams during matches. It feels strange to see it again, to think about all of our practice sessions, our matches. It feels so long ago and yet so recent at the same time.

'Maya? Maya Alam?' A familiar face appears in front of me, a much-needed interruption to my reminiscing.

My mind scrambles for the name of my old principal before it suddenly comes to me, just at the right time.

'Ms Jacobs,' I say, trying to smile with as much enthusiasm as she's showing me right now.

'What are you doing here?' she asks, beaming at me. 'I thought you were still in America.'

My smile almost falters. I guess the news hasn't travelled here yet. Or Ms Jacobs is too busy running a school to keep up with football news.

'No, I'm—'

'You have to come in and see everyone. They'll be so

excited to know you're here!' Ms Jacobs interrupts me, putting out her half-lit cigarette. I'm thankful for the interruption, since I don't really know how to explain why I'm here in the first place. But I'm also not sure what she means by everyone wanting to see me.

When she ushers me inside the school, I have no choice but to follow her. I think about trying to make up some kind of an excuse to leave, but my mind is drawing a total blank.

I follow Ms Jacobs through the familiar school hallways as she talks about all of my various successes and how proud the school has been to have me as an alumnus. I can barely focus on the conversation because my chest tightens with each passing minute. If they were proud of me before, how will they feel now that I've failed?

My mind finally starts piecing together an excuse about promising to take my mum to her doctor's appointment, but just as I'm about to politely interrupt Ms Jacobs with my lie, she flings open the double doors to the main hall, filled with what looks like every student and faculty member in the school. The near-silence of the hall is disturbed by our entrance, so it's not a surprise that most of them turn towards us. I feel like I'm back on the football pitch all of a sudden, being ogled by thousands of people in the stadium. A small electric thrill goes through me.

'Ms Jacobs, there you are,' a teacher on stage that I don't recognise says. She waves Ms Jacobs up, giving me a confused once-over.

'They're just about to finish up our last assembly of the year, so this is perfect,' Ms Jacobs says to me softly.

'Oh, I should—'

But Ms Jacobs is not listening to me. She takes hold of

my hand and drags me up on stage with her – only letting go of me as she approaches the mic.

'I'm sure Ms McMahon has already covered everything,' Ms Jacobs says into the mic while I longingly look at the now-closed double doors of the hall. 'So, I really don't have much to say, except that I found a really exciting guest outside the school. I know that all of you have heard of her, and she's going to say a few words for us this morning. Aren't we lucky? Let's give a round of applause for our very own Maya Alam.' Ms Jacobs starts off the round of applause as she steps away from the mic and turns her smile to me.

I can only stand there for a moment, wondering if I've stepped into some kind of a nightmare. But I'm sure even my subconscious couldn't have dreamt up this situation – standing in front of a crowd of former teachers and current students, dressed in a shabby old tracksuit that's a little too snug, uncomfortably aware of the fact that every part of my body is damp with sweat.

'Maya.' Ms Jacobs gives me an encouraging nod, and so the only thing I can do is take a step forward towards the mic. My mouth is dry and my mind is blank, but I know the sooner I say something, the sooner I can get the hell out of here.

'Um, hi,' I say, inwardly cringing at the way my voice rings out across the hall a little too loudly. 'I wasn't really expecting to be here today, but . . . it's so wonderful to be back at my old school.' I take a breath, trying not to look at anyone, trying to imagine the crowd as a mass of unknown people. 'I was so lucky to get my start here. If I hadn't played on the Westbrook football team, I probably would have never even dreamt of pursuing football. I really owe a lot to this school; everyone here who encouraged me to go for my dreams. And if you're anything like me, you should make use of your time here, and go for your dreams too.'

I smile, before taking a step back from the mic, and everyone applauds once more. My entire body feels hot with embarrassment.

As Ms Jacobs dismisses the assembly and I finally step off the stage, one of my old teachers appears from out of the crowd.

'Maya!' Mrs Fitzgerald says. 'It's so good to see you again, and it's been so amazing to see all of your success. I always knew you had it in you.'

Her words make a lump form in my throat. Mrs Fitzgerald was my maths teacher for almost all of secondary school, and even though maths wasn't my best subject, she never gave up on me. I always remembered her fondly.

'Thanks, Mrs Fitzgerald,' I manage to get out. 'It's good to see you too.' She's not the only one who seems excited to speak to me either; there are students who look too young to even be in secondary school looking at me with everything from shy admiration to fangirlish glee.

'Did your team really win the national women's soccer league last year?' one of the young students asks me, looking up at me with curiosity in her eyes.

I still remember that match, that victory that seemed completely unachievable. We'd been sweating under the California heat, and the Dignity Sports Park was filled to the brim. I could hardly believe at the time that we had made it all the way to the finals. That, in itself, had felt like a dream. Our opponents, North Carolina Courage, had already won the league twice before. Meanwhile, this was the Vikings' first time making it to the finals. We were neck and neck for most of the game, but somehow, against all odds, we had pulled it off. We'd won. The thrill of it was like nothing I'd ever felt before. It was shock and excitement and an overwhelming sense of happiness, all mixed in together.

'Yeah, we did,' I say, my chest swelling with pride. There's a certain thrill when it comes to winning any match, but that one was special.

'So, why did you quit?' the student asks.

I deflate immediately, even as Mrs Fitzgerald turns to give her a small glare.

'Daisy, that's really none of your business. Now, off you go,' she says, shooing her away.

Daisy gives me one last look before turning around and joining a group of girls in another corner of the hall. More students are passing me curious glances, but my face burns with the shame of Daisy's question – especially now I know that they probably all have that question. And many more. Questions that I can't give answers to.

'I'm sorry about that,' Mrs Fitzgerald says. 'Just ignore her, and ignore . . . all the papers and everything. I can't even imagine how tough handling all of that must be, but you should know that we are incredibly proud of you.'

She gives me an encouraging smile. It doesn't change anything, but it makes me feel at least a little bit better.

'Come on, Maya, I'll show you the brand-new gym that we just opened this year!' Ms Jacobs says, tearing me away from the crowd and Mrs Fitzgerald.

I happily follow her out of the double doors of the main hall, not wanting to deal with the inquisitive students anymore.

'New gym?' I ask. I guess something here has changed in the last few years.

'Well, ever since you got snatched up and made it big, more and more of our students have been getting involved in sports. We got funding for this new gym and, of course, we mentioned you and your success in our application for that,' Ms Jacobs says proudly.

That brings a smile to my lips. No matter what happened, it seems I made some kind of an impact, even if it's in the form of a new gym and a few more young girls giving sports a go.

'Here we are,' Ms Jacobs says, thrusting the doors to the gym open and stepping inside. I follow her in, and I'm impressed. This new gym is definitely a huge improvement. It's a much bigger space than the old one. It's brand new and sparkling, and there's new equipment pushed to the sides – gymnastic mats, badminton rackets and shuttlecocks, nets. When I walk around, the floor squeaks loudly and it echoes across the massive space.

'Wow. This is nice,' I say. I walk around the gym slowly, taking the place in, before stopping at the trophy cabinet by the door that I'd missed when we first came in. It houses our old football trophy, still gleaming as bright and shiny as the day that we won it.

I remember that day – a little too fondly. I'm not sure if even the national women's soccer league win compared to this one. Beside the trophy is a framed photo of our entire team. My eyes immediately find me and Dina side by side, her arms wrapped around me. Both of us grinning into the camera like this was the best day of our lives. I wonder if it *was* the best day of my life. If everything else after that pales in comparison. There's a dull ache in my heart as I think about that day and this picture.

'You know, we're looking for a football coach for the summer,' Ms Jacobs says, interrupting my revisit of the past.

I look away from the picture of me and Dina and turn back to her with a question on my face.

'The current PE teacher isn't available, and if we can't find someone, we'll probably have to cancel the summer football programme, which the students have been really looking forward to. I'm sure you have a busy schedule, but if you had some time, maybe you would be interested in filling in?'

An offer of a job is definitely not something I was expecting today. Especially dressed in my tracksuit, with sweat clinging to every inch of me.

'I'm not really a coach,' I say.

'Sure, but you know the game better than anyone, and the students would be so happy to have you as the coach. They really look up to you. And I know you're more than capable.'

I'm not sure if I agree. Besides, if I'm not going to be playing football anymore, I'm not sure if I want anything to do with it. Being sidelined during matches was bad enough, filled with longing for wanting to be in the game, kicking the ball around. Agreeing to a coaching position feels like agreeing to being sidelined forever.

But then I glance back at the picture from my days on the football team. The happiest days of my life, me and Dina together. I know that we can never go back to that. I know that I shouldn't cling to the past. That I should try to move on. But if Dina can be a football coach with Jen, why can't I? I imagine running into her again, back in the cafe. This time, I wouldn't run out, feeling my heart beating like a hundred butterflies' wings under my ribcage. I could look her in the eye, tell her that I'm back for good, that I'm here to stay. That I'm coaching a football team, same as her.

'OK,' I say. 'I'll take the job.'

Chapter 8

Maya

Fifteen years ago

Dina has her glare fixed on me as I run towards her. The ball is at my feet; it almost feels automatic as I dribble it forward. My breath is fast and heavy, and I know I've already outrun the other players on my team. It's just Dina playing in goal, and me. She's the only thing standing between me and scoring the goal.

I pause for a second, just at the threshold of the penalty area, my eyes meeting Dina's. If she sees my challenge in them, it doesn't cause her to back down or even pause for a second. She stretches her arms on either side, ready to block the shot.

I run forward, shaping as if to go to the right. Dina moves towards the ball, and my foot pushes forward, shooting to the left. Dina realises her mistake at the last second, stumbling and leaping towards the ball. But I'm too fast, and she's too late. The ball brushes against the tips of her fingers and hits the net, before bounding to the ground with a satisfying thwap.

I turn to the rest of the team with a grin, as Jen blows the whistle.

'And that's time. Well done, Maya,' Jen says. 'That was a great goal.' She gives me an encouraging pat on the shoulder, and even though she doesn't say it, I already know that there's no way Jen will leave me out of the team now.

To my dismay, though, Jen gives Dina an encouraging look as she leaves the goalmouth and makes her way towards the centre of the pitch.

'You did a good job too, Dina. If you'd been just a second earlier, you would have caught the ball,' Jen says.

Dina doesn't seem very encouraged by Jen's compliment. She just shrugs, her expression surly as she glances at me. I simply glare back. It's not my fault that I'm a better football player than her, and besides, if Jen's compliment is anything to go by, Dina will probably make it onto the team as well. The thought doesn't make me happy.

Dina has seemed determined to hate me ever since that English class and I'm not exactly a big fan of her either. Being on the same football team wasn't on my bingo card, but I can make it work.

Dina, though? I'm not sure if *she* can make it work.

'All right, girls, really good game. Unfortunately, we don't have enough spots on the team for everyone, but that was a great effort from all of you,' Jen says with an encouraging smile. 'So, the team is as follows . . .'

Jen starts calling out the names one by one. As each girl is called, they visibly brighten, many of them turning to high-five each other. I have no doubt that I made the cut, but I still wait with bated breath, my heart beating faster and faster as Jen calls each name that's not mine.

'Dina Chowdhury!' Jen calls out, and Dina's forlorn expression changes to one of surprise. She looks towards Jen, like she can't believe she was actually chosen. I frown at the act – as if Dina doesn't know that she was one of the best players trying out today. She blocked nearly every shot when she was playing in goal, and she scored two goals when she was playing up front. Her team probably would have won if Jen hadn't made them switch goalies halfway through the match.

Jen is quickly nearing the end of her list, and I'm yet to be called. My previous confidence starts to fade a little too fast, replaced with a slow-building panic. Is it possible that I didn't play as well as I thought I did? Or maybe Jen just thought that my last-minute goal was a fluke? After all, that was the only goal I managed to score, even if I did succeed in winning possession back from the other team multiple times.

'Last but not least, Maya Alam.' Jen gives me a smile as she says my name, and relief washes over me.

Beside me, Gwen and Nadine give me excited high-fives. Nadine and I have been obsessed with football since primary school and when we found out the secondary school had a team, we were desperate to try out, but we've only just met Gwen at try-outs.

'All right, that's everyone. I'm sorry to anyone who didn't make the team. We still have the football unit in PE later in the year. And maybe you can try your luck next year, all right?'

With that, Jen motions us towards the changing rooms and we all shuffle forwards.

'I'm so glad that all of us made it,' Nadine says in a relieved voice. There are a couple of dejected girls who walk with us. I'm definitely glad that I'm not one of them.

'Me too,' Gwen says. 'For a moment there, I thought maybe Maya wouldn't . . .' She drifts off, giving me a nervous glance.

'I knew I would.' My voice is a lot more confident than

I feel. I *was* the last person called and I couldn't help but wonder if that meant I was Jen's last pick. 'I mean, I was the one who scored that final goal. Did you see me? How could I not make the team after that?'

'Yeah, but . . . Dina almost blocked you,' Gwen points out unhelpfully.

I frown, glad that once we get to the changing rooms, her bag and locker are on the other side, so we don't have to talk about Dina and her goalkeeping.

Gwen parts ways with us, while Nadine and I get our stuff from the benches.

I sit down, starting to peel off my boots, but Nadine is giving me a weird look.

'What?' I ask, wondering if maybe my socks are smelly after all that running around.

'Dina made the team too. You're going to have to get along with her,' she says.

Dina and I have only known each other for a week, but it feels like everybody already knows just how much we don't get along. It's not *my* fault that Dina seems determined to show me up at every opportunity.

'Yes, I know.' I sigh, looking over her shoulder to where Dina is standing, rooting around in her bag. She pulls out her worn uniform – the one that is the wrong shade for the actual school uniform and doesn't even have the school logo. I don't understand why the teachers haven't made her change out of it, and into the proper uniform. Only Dina would get away with something like that. 'I just don't get her,' I say, lowering my voice. 'She's such a phony, and she's so . . . ugh. I mean, did you see how she pretended to be shocked when Jen called her name out? Like, of course she knew she was on the team, Jen couldn't stop praising her goalkeeping.' Once I get started, I can't stop, even though I know she's only a few paces away from me. 'And did you see how she was late for class *again*? Is it that difficult to set an alarm? I just don't get it. I don't get her.'

It would be one thing if Dina didn't act like she was better than everyone while being decidedly *not* better than everyone. But she walks around school like it doesn't matter that she has the wrong uniform or the fact that she's already had detention despite it only being the first week. And then there's the showing off – the always trying to one-up me. It started that first day and has persisted into every single class we've shared together. She even tried to one-up my lunch the other day. It's like she's determined to prove she's better than me in every possible way.

Nadine shakes her head, like she doesn't get her either. 'I'm just saying, we're all going to be on the same team. We'll probably have to see a lot of each other. I mean, practice every week, and then matches too. Plus, it probably helps when people on the same team don't hate each other's guts.'

'I don't hate her guts,' I say. I'm not sure if I sound particularly convincing. There is something about Dina that just rubs me the wrong way. Maybe it's the fact that, despite her many clear flaws, she seems to have the disarming ability to charm anyone. Like how quickly Ms Nichols seemed to forget that Dina missed half of our first English class, and how Jen was practically singing her praises just now.

And now I'm going to be stuck on a football team with her.

Chapter 9
Dina

'Wow, you really look the part of a coach,' Jen says when she meets me at the park on Monday morning. I've dug out one of my old tracksuits – black with a green stripe down the sides. Deen has even bought me one of those whistles that coaches wear around their neck. I tried to decline it, thinking it made me look a little too dorky and overenthusiastic, but he insisted.

Now, I feel a blush creep up my face at Jen's appraisal.

'My brother gave this to me. He insisted.' I hold out the whistle for her to see.

'Well, you'll need it, so it was good thinking on his part. Come on, I think the girls should be here already.'

She leads me through the wrought-iron gates and along a weaving dirt path to an open space, but there's no sign of the group of girls that were in the restaurant last week.

Jen frowns, checking the time on her phone. 'They're not always good at being on time. Don't worry, they'll be here soon.' She says it to reassure me, but she seems more worried than I am.

'It's fine. I mean, it's the summer, I guess,' I say. They didn't actually look like the most enthusiastic football players the last time I saw them, but I decide to keep that thought to myself.

Finally, after a few more minutes, I spot a few girls shuffling over, looking tired and uninterested, though they do pass me cursory curious glances.

'Good morning,' Jen says, in her stern teacher voice. 'You're late.'

'Sorry,' one of the girls says – she has long blonde hair and is, for some reason, wearing a full face of make-up. Never a good idea when playing football.

'Jade, you can't come to practice wearing that much make-up. And tie up your hair, for God's sake.' Jen tosses her a hair tie, almost as if she expected this.

'Will do, coach,' Jade says with a sickly-sweet smile. She catches the hair tie but doesn't seem to be in haste to tie up her hair. Instead, she takes out her phone and starts taking some selfies.

'They're not usually . . . They're usually better,' Jen says, checking the time on her phone again. Which doesn't really make me believe that they're usually much better.

'It's fine,' I mumble, trying to swallow back the worry already building inside me. I'm not sure how Jen and I are supposed to coach this group of girls. It's not like I expected our old team to show up in the park today, but I hoped for at least some kind of excitement about football, or getting a new coach, or *something*.

Definitely not this.

Slowly, more groups of girls come strolling in, though I notice a lot of them are not dressed ready to play. There's one girl who's wearing flats instead of trainers, another wearing jeans instead of tracksuit bottoms or shorts, and a few more with their long hair loose.

Jen seems prepared for all of this: she has extra kit, hair ties and even a beaten-up pair of boots that are a little too small for the girl that needs them. She reprimands all of them as she hands these out, but her words seem to fall on deaf ears. I try to remember if we were like this when Jen was our coach, but I mostly remember the excitement of my first football practice.

'All right, girls, good morning. Thanks for finally making it in!' Jen says with faux cheeriness.

'Morning,' the girls mumble back, barely sparing her a second glance. Some of them still cast me curious looks.

'I have some exciting news. This is Dina, our new assistant coach!' Jen waves an arm towards me.

I smile as some of the girls' eyes flicker up towards me, but their piqued curiosity seems to quickly dissipate. I guess I'm not as exciting as they thought I might be.

'Cool,' one of the girls towards the front mumbles, her eyes glazing over as she goes back to her phone promptly. Definitely not very cool.

'I thought *you* were our coach,' another one of the girls says, looking between me and Jen with a confused expression. She's one of the only ones who has come dressed to play football.

'I am, Sophie, but Dina will be helping me out with coaching,' Jen explains.

'That's why she said *assistant* coach,' another girl beside Sophie says, rolling her eyes. Which earns her a glare from Sophie and a frown from Jen.

'Sara, come on. It was a fair question. Now, let's do some warm-ups, OK?' Jen ushers all of the girls on to run some laps.

After some initial groaning, they put away their phones and head onto the field, jogging the length of it back and forth. They don't look happy about it, and they're not what

I would call fast or energetic. But at least they're doing it.

'They just need a little time to get going,' Jen whispers to me.

'Yeah, sure. We always did too,' I say, though it's not really true.

I check the time on my phone. We're already halfway through practice and most of it has been taken up with their tardiness, getting them prepared to actually play and with warming up.

'We'll get them to do some drills. What do you say?' Jen asks.

'I'll get the cones set up,' I offer, excited to finally have something to do instead of just despairing over the state of the team.

I pick up the stack of cones that Jen brought and start arranging them at different angles around the place. Once I'm done, my eyes drift to the touchline, for some reason expecting Baba's familiar face to be there, telling me what a good job I'm doing. Of course, he isn't there. It's been five years since he passed away, but sometimes it still feels difficult to wrap my head around it.

Soon, the girls are running drills around the cones, dribbling the ball from one cone to the next. They're not bad, but it's clear that they don't have a lot of practice. The main problem I notice is that they're a little too easily distracted. They argue and they fight. They want to gossip and talk about celebrity scandals. And one thing is perfectly clear: they have absolutely no interest in the game.

By the time practice is over, I'm reconsidering everything. Ma's words in her garden over the weekend are flashing in my mind. Why did I ever think that coming back to football was a good idea, even in this minuscule capacity? My mother always knows best about everything. I might as well throw in the towel, and maybe I should even tell Deen that he should forget about his dreams of the restaurant. Clearly, dreams are better left to our imaginations, because the reality of my dreams of returning to football feels nothing like I wanted it to.

Jen turns to me, and it's almost like she can see the panic in my face. She gives me a much-needed encouraging smile. 'I'll walk you out of the park, come on.'

She gathers up the last of her belongings and the two of us walk side by side, silence washing over us. All the while, my mind is whirring with all the reasons why I should quit right here and now. Surely, there's a better use for my time than coaching a team of girls who know nothing about football.

'I know they can be a lot,' Jen says finally, hesitantly. It's almost like she can read my mind. 'But you saw that they were talented, right?'

'They don't like football. They didn't want to be there and they definitely didn't want to play,' I say.

'They're kids, Dina. You have to cut them some slack,' Jen says. 'And . . . OK, maybe their dreams aren't playing football but—'

'They don't even like it.'

'But they'll learn to like it with time and practice. It's still the start of summer; they're getting the hang of things.' Jen sounds way more confident than I feel.

'I don't know, Jen,' I say. 'I didn't . . . I mean, I wasn't sure what to expect but—'

'You know why I wanted you to be assistant coach?' Jen stops in her tracks, turning to look at me with utter sincerity in her expression.

'Because I was the only one who would do it?'

Jen smiles. 'I wanted you to do it because I think that if there's anyone who can get these girls to like football – maybe even love it – it's you. You can show them what you liked about it, and you can help them hone their talents. If nothing else, you can get them to enjoy it for this summer, and maybe even win a few matches.'

Jen's confidence in me is baffling, and totally misplaced. Especially when I've never coached in my life.

'I know you can do this, Dina. And you've got me. I've got you. We're going to get this team into shape together,' Jen continues.

That, at least, brings a smile to my lips. It's nice to have Jen around again. Her energy is a little infectious, and the fact that she's unwilling to give up is pretty commendable. It was one of the things I admired about her back when she was our coach. No matter how much we struggled, Jen never gave up on us. She always believed that we could do whatever we set our minds to.

And she could be right – maybe between the two of us we really can do it.

Chapter 10

Maya

The first day of my coaching job rolls around fast. Ms Jacobs is bouncing on her heels when I show up at the entrance of the park. She waves me over, while putting out her cigarette.

'It's so good to see you again, Maya,' she says brightly. 'Let's go meet the team, shall we?'

She leads me through the park, towards the field, where a group of girls are already waiting. They're dressed in purple-and-white football shirts and shorts with the Westbrook school logo emblazoned on them, kicking a ball around between them. They stop as soon as Ms Jacobs and I make our entrance, and their eyes seem to light up.

'Good afternoon, girls,' Ms Jacobs says.

'Good afternoon!' they repeat in unison. Their eyes drift towards me instead of Ms Jacobs.

'This is Maya Alam. I know some of you probably already know her,' Ms Jacobs says, waving an arm towards me. 'We're very lucky that she's agreed to coach the team over the summer. I hope you realise just how fortunate you are that she's found time in her busy schedule to do this for us.'

I almost wince at that. My 'busy schedule' includes avoiding my parents' sympathetic glances, scrolling the r/womenssoccer subreddit to see what people have been saying about me and lying around in bed feeling sorry for myself.

'I'm excited to be here,' I say, smiling at the students as enthusiastically as I can, even if my enthusiasm feels put on. In reality, I feel out of my depth, having these young girls look at me with their admiring gazes. There's nothing to admire about me, and I certainly don't feel that I'm cut out to be their full-time coach for the summer. I'm sure it won't be long before everyone figures it out.

'Well, I'll leave you to it,' Ms Jacobs says, nodding to the students. 'I expect you to be on your best behaviour, girls.'

My stomach sinks. I didn't think Ms Jacobs would just throw me in at the deep end like this.

'Give me a call if you need anything,' Ms Jacobs says to me in a low voice. 'But I know you've got this.'

I offer her a weak smile before turning back to the girls. They're watching me expectantly and suddenly I feel weird and out of place. I've been practising all of the different ways I could start off today – how I would be cool and collected as I officially introduced myself as their coach – but now, as I look at their smiling faces, my mouth becomes dry. 'Um, so . . . wow. Our first official practice session. I'm, uh, Maya. It's really nice to be here, and I'm excited to get to know all of you.'

The girls don't respond. They blink at me in anticipation and I feel like they must know that I'm an imposter. After this practice, they'll probably go and tell Ms Jacobs that she hired a phony to be their coach.

'Could you show us how you scored that penalty kick in your match against the San Diego Strikers?' one of the girls pipes up finally, the enthusiasm clear in her voice. 'None of us thought you'd score, but you did.'

A flood of relief washes over me. Here's something that I

know – that match and exactly how we won it. The Strikers scored their first goal within the first fifteen minutes, and try as we might, we just couldn't find an equaliser. And while our defence did its job by not letting them score again, their defence had been tough too. They managed to wrangle the ball from us at every turn, and we didn't even make it anywhere near their goal until the second half of the match. It was only when we went into added-on time that we actually managed to score. The joy I'd felt at that had been overwhelming.

And then the penalties. The pressure as the time ticked by. Watching the goalkeeper with a keen eye as I calculated how to strike the ball. Where to place it.

Our entire team had already seemed to accept defeat because the Strikers were practically undefeated at shoot-outs.

'Do your best,' the captain, Stacey Morrow, had told me right before I took the penalty. It was make or break. I could lead the team to victory with this penalty, or lead us to defeat.

And when I scored, the entire stadium erupted into raucous shouts and applause. For an entire minute, everything seemed to unfold in front of me as if in slow motion: my teammates as they rushed up to me, their faces split into the widest grins I'd ever seen. The other team's looks of bafflement. Our coach on the touchline jumping up and down with joy. In that moment, I remembered exactly what I loved about playing football; the absolute rush of adrenaline, the thrill of victory, the shared camaraderie in all of it.

'How about we all practise some penalties?' I ask now, feeling a little bit more capable of being able to do this after being reminded of that victory.

The girls nod happily, moving into position before I even

have to give them any instructions. They remind me of my first practice session on the school team, when Nadine, Gwen and I were bouncing on our feet to get started.

I watch from the touchline as they line up to take their penalties. One by one they go about trying their best to score. Only a few of them manage to get their shots past the goalie, but all of them give it their best – I can tell from each of their determined expressions, the way they seem to weigh up everything as they step up to the ball.

Once they've each had a chance, I step in to give them some instructions on how they can improve.

'You should always have an idea of where you want to kick the ball when you approach it,' I say, coming up to the ball myself. 'Make sure you drive forward, and follow through, and don't change your mind. If you get confused, or change your mind, your shot won't land.'

I kick the ball, and it flies through the air and soars into the net. The team bursts into cheers and applause, and it almost brings me back to my own team. To being on the pitch, playing a game with them. But when I turn back, of course, all I see are the young girls of this new team, with their beaming, enthusiastic faces.

Yet, it doesn't seem that different, in a way. Maybe I can make a real difference here. Maybe I can love it even more than playing football myself.

'OK,' I say. 'Let's try one more time.'

The girls line up to take their penalties as my phone buzzes in my pocket. When I slip it out, Isabel's name flashes on the screen.

'Hey, I'm kind of busy right now,' I say, as soon as I answer the phone. My eyes track the girls as they take their penalties.

'Oh, sorry, I'll be quick!' Isabel says. Her familiar voice feels soothing. She's been a tether for me these last few weeks. I don't think even she understands that she is the reason I've managed to pick myself up and actually start to do things with my life.

'OK, what's up?'

'Do you remember Nina Hall? She used to coach for the Red Royals?'

'Yeah, I remember her.' We played the Royals a couple of times during my time on the Vikings. Nina always got along with our own coach and her team always seemed to have a lot of respect for her.

'Well, she's looking for—'

One of the girls stumbles as she kicks the ball, falling flat on her face. I wince, and rush towards her, Isabel's words a mumble in my ear.

'Are you OK?' I ask.

The girl stands up, tossing her brown ponytail behind her and brushing herself off like it's no big deal. 'Fine. Sorry . . .' She looks at me hesitantly, like I'll reprimand her for the accident.

'Nothing to be sorry about. Let's go again, I'll help you. Give me a second.' I press the phone to my ear again.

'. . . And so I think you should do it. Will you?' Isabel asks.

'Sure, yeah. But I really have to go, Isabel, sorry.'

'Oh.' Isabel sounds surprised. 'OK, great. I'll text you the details.'

I have no idea what I've signed up for, but it's Isabel so it can't be that bad. Maybe Nina is over in the UK and wants to catch up over coffee sometime, and that wouldn't be so bad. It would be nice to see her again.

I hang up the phone and turn back to the girl. 'What's your name?'

'Laila.' She sounds nervous as she speaks. I offer her a bright smile.

'OK, Laila. Let's do this again.' I place the ball down in front of us and show her how to fix her stance, how to approach the ball and drive her foot through it correctly.

She frowns, but seems to take it all in. I can tell that there's something distracting her, though, like she's not completely here. It's her furrowed eyebrows, the fact that she keeps looking over her shoulder.

She tries the penalty kick one more time, but there isn't enough power in her shot and the ball only dribbles forward slightly, instead of flying goalwards. I can see the other girls get frustrated, rolling their eyes and sighing. Meanwhile, there's a pink flush across Laila's cheeks.

'Let's call it a day,' I call out to the girls. 'We'll pick this back up tomorrow.' I look to Laila. 'We'll try again tomorrow, all right?'

She nods, not quite looking me in the eyes, before joining the rest of the team in jogging off the field. I watch with a frown. There's definitely something going on with Laila.

I fall into some kind of a routine over the next few days. It almost feels like maybe I'm back on track with everything, like perhaps it's not the end of the world that all my dreams were shattered at the youthful age of twenty-eight. Because I wake up in the morning and I have something to do with my life – even if it's something as simple as inspiring a young and enthusiastic group of footballers to play their hearts out.

I manage to finally get everything unpacked and put away, shoving my old football shirt to the very back of my wardrobe, where it will never, ever see the light of day again. Unpacking, sorting through my belongings and going out with a purpose to my day at least seems to put a smile on my parents' faces. Our dinners become less punctuated with awkward silence and tension, where nobody deigns to speak a word for fear of upsetting me, and more like the way they used to be. We actually speak to each other about what we've been up to, now that I actually have been up to something more than sulking in my bedroom, feeling sorry for myself.

Laila still comes to every practice a little distracted. She's seemingly the weakest of all the players, but I'm not sure if I totally believe that she *is* weak. Her heart just doesn't seem to be in the game. Instead, every chance she gets she sneaks glances at her phone, but she doesn't even seem happy about that.

After practice one day, I ask her to stay behind, and as the rest of the team slink away, she comes up to me, a pink flush colouring her cheeks.

'Did I do something wrong?' she asks, her voice meek. She doesn't look at me, instead toeing the grass with her football boots.

'No, you did nothing wrong.' I feel a tug at my heart at the idea that I've made her think she has. 'I was just wondering . . . if everything was OK. Your heart doesn't really seem to be in football.'

Laila shrugs, not giving anything away. I know that I can't force her to tell me anything. Maybe her parents are forcing her to be on the team, and she really doesn't like the game. Even though I don't believe that's true.

I'm about to dismiss her when her phone buzzes loudly in her pocket. She freezes, her shoulders tensing. But it's not the nervousness of someone who's been caught with a phone she's not supposed to have. It's something else.

Laila finally looks at me, barely, out of the corner of her eye.

'Sorry . . . I know I shouldn't have it on during practice,' she says.

I frown. 'It's OK. Were you waiting for an important message?'

Laila shrugs again, but there's still a terseness in her demeanour.

'If something is wrong, you can tell me,' I say.

'I'm fine,' Laila insists. 'Can I go?'

'Yeah, of course.' I offer her a smile.

She shuffles off and I take a deep breath. There's definitely something wrong, but I'm not sure how I'm supposed to figure out what it is.

I clear up our corner of the park and begin to make my way back home slowly, all the while thinking about what I should do. I take out my phone, navigating over to Instagram. A bunch of the girls from the team have started following me, even though I'm barely active on it anymore.

A quick scroll through my follower page leads me to Laila's account. It's nothing out of the ordinary: there are pictures of Laila with her friends, grinning at the camera, posed pictures with her family, and even a couple of shots of the Westbrook football team. I click onto one of them, smiling at the posed picture of the team in their matching kits, grinning from ear to ear.

But when I scroll down to the comments, my stomach drops.

Girls suck at football!!

THE PERFECT MATCH

Such an ugly uniform!
Are Muslims even allowed to play football?

All comments from what seems to be anonymous accounts. They're the same kinds of comments that I see about me, though some of mine are more personal. I guess I shouldn't be surprised. The internet can be a terrible place, especially when you're a woman. And especially when you're a young girl. It probably doesn't help that Laila is one of two brown girls on the team. An overwhelming feeling of sadness settles into my stomach.

I'm at even more of a loss now as to what I should do. How can I help Laila deal with internet bullies, when I can't even deal with my own?

My thoughts are interrupted when I spot a familiar figure in the distance. I blink, wondering if I'm seeing her because I've been thinking about her so much since the last time we ran into each other. But no, it's definitely Dina. She's dressed in a T-shirt and joggers, trying to shift a bag full of shopping into the basket of her parked bike.

I freeze on the spot, watching her for a little too long. I know that I should look away, make a run for it before Dina notices me, but it's like my legs have suddenly forgotten how to walk. All I can do is take Dina in, properly for the first time. How her black hair falls across her face, the wrinkle of her brow as she concentrates on budging everything into place.

As if she can sense me, her eyes snap up to meet mine. Surprise registers on her face. For a moment, the two of us just stare at one another, my heart beating so loud in my chest that I'm surprised everyone around us can't hear it.

A loud crash pulls me away from Dina's dark brown eyes,

and I realise that a jar has slipped out of the shopping bag and has splattered onto the ground. From the looks of the blood-red on the sidewalk, it seems like it was a jar of pasta sauce. Dina's eyes travel down to it, then back up to me. I step forward, as if I'm going to help her clean up or . . . am I going to offer to buy her another jar of pasta sauce?

All I know is that I should say or do *something*.

But Dina must want to avoid me even more than I want to avoid her. Because she's on her bike at the speed of light and before I can take another step forward, she's cycling away and out of sight.

'You're home late!' Amma says happily when I finally arrive home, still thinking about Dina.

'Yeah . . . practice ran late,' I lie.

'Have you finally caught up with some of your old friends?' Amma asks excitedly.

'No, I haven't. They're all . . . busy. They have lives and obligations,' I mutter, trying to make my way past Amma and up to my room. I hadn't expected her to ambush me just as I walked in.

'Are you seeing anyone then?' Of course, that's why she's suddenly so interested in my whereabouts.

I have to stop myself from sighing loudly and rolling my eyes. Instead, I just turn to her with a frown.

'Amma, of course I'm not seeing anyone. Where would I even get the chance to meet someone?'

'I don't know, you're out and about, reconnecting with old friends. I thought maybe there was someone . . .' She looks a little dejected and I feel a pinprick of guilt. She's just doing the things all desi mothers do – obsessing over my love life. I can't really blame her for it.

'I'm sorry, Amma, but there isn't anyone,' I say. There have been a few casual relationships over the last few years, but it was difficult to get into anything serious when I had a busy schedule full of practice and travel. I haven't met anyone that would make me consider really trying to juggle everything. The last person who I really connected with was . . .

I shake my head, trying to escape all of my thoughts of her. Because Dina and I are so far back in the past that we might as well be considered prehistoric. And there is no universe in which there is ever any possibility between us again, no matter how much seeing her has been affecting me.

'You know, your abba and I could find someone for you. Your Seema auntie has a son who's only a few years older, and he has a great job as an engineer,' she says, a little too casually. So it's definitely something she and Abba have discussed. Normally, this kind of thing would make me annoyed, but considering how weird things have been with Amma and Abba since I got back, it actually feels nice to have them trying to meddle in my love life.

Still, I wrinkle up my nose at the suggestion, because I remember Seema Auntie's son, Aashfaq. She always doted on him like he was some kind of golden boy who could do no wrong. It has been many years since I last saw him, but considering I've known him since I was a kid, the idea of dating him almost feels a little incestuous.

'I don't think so.' It's the nicest way I can think to turn Amma down. I know that if I don't nip this in the bud, she'll try to find even more prospects for me.

'Well, there's a dawat next weekend. Maybe you can reconnect with some old friends there, and meet someone through them.' Amma's voice is bright and optimistic, like it's just that easy to find someone you like these days. She definitely has not lived in the world of dating apps. She and Abba met in university and fell in love, and the way she describes it, makes it sound like some kind of romance movie. She must think that's somehow on the cards for me too.

'I don't know if I'm ready for dawats,' I say hesitantly. 'I mean . . . I might not want to see . . . I could run into . . . people that I don't want to.'

Dina's family and mine never exactly ran in the same circles and her parents were never big on dawats, but just being in the Bangladeshi community means that there's always overlap. I can't rule out that we'd run into each other.

Amma can read me a little too well, and she nods in understanding, even without me saying her name. 'The dawat is all the way in Wembley. I don't think you'll run into too many people that you . . . don't want to see.' Amma offers me a reassuring smile. 'But maybe some of the friends you've been trying to meet up with will be there. I know your old friend Zulaykha lives near Wembley now, so she's probably invited.'

Zul wasn't really my friend, so much as an acquaintance that I sometimes talked to at dawats. But I'm not in a position to pick and choose friends, considering everyone that I once knew here seems to have moved on. And maybe – and this is a thought that I definitely shouldn't entertain – she'll know what Dina has been up to these last few years, and who exactly she's dating.

'I guess it'll be nice to see Zulaykha again . . .'

Amma beams. 'Everyone will be so excited to see you.'

I smile back, but inside I wonder what I've let myself in for.

Chapter 11
Dina

'And who knows what she's even up to these days? She's probably just passing time before she starts taking sponsorships and becoming a celebrity influencer or something.'

Aisha doesn't respond to my lengthy rant. Instead, she just presses her lips together and looks at me silently for a minute.

'What?'

'Nothing. I was just making sure that you're finished. When you said you wanted to join me on my lunch break today, I just wasn't expecting it to be all about Maya. Usually you do anything to avoid the topic of her.' Aisha raises an eyebrow at me while taking a bite of her sandwich.

The two of us are sat at a bench in Victoria Park, which normally wouldn't set me off about Maya. But ever since bumping into her with Jen the other day, Maya has been running laps around my mind. And being here in front of the bandstand, where the two of us used to hang out after school, is bringing back too many memories.

'Sorry,' I mumble, heaping a forkful of pasta into my mouth. I don't admit to Aisha that I have been perusing all the online articles about Maya for the past few days. Since her retirement, she's racked up a lot of attention. 'Honestly, it's kind of weird that she's back. I'm not sure how I'm supposed to feel or act around her.'

I think about how I practically ran away from her the other day, with my tail between my legs. I've replayed that moment in my head a million times since, feeling more and more mortified.

'I feel kind of bad for her,' Aisha admits. 'I mean, retiring so young, and all that harsh media criticism? It can't be easy.'

'Yeah, I guess,' I mumble. I've seen some of the articles, calling her rude, and a bully, pointing out her 'attitude'. It doesn't sound like Maya, but I don't know her these days. 'I just wish that she didn't have to be *here*. Things are hard enough without dredging up our past.'

Aisha looks at me curiously. 'Would that be so bad?'

'What kind of a question is that? Of course it would be bad.' It already *is* bad. Being around Maya makes me act like someone I don't even recognise. A past version of myself who was quick to anger and apparently even quicker to run away.

'I just think that it might be nice to resolve whatever issues the two of you have and put it all in the past,' Aisha says.

Aisha sounds way too reasonable, so I just shake my head. 'Enough about Maya. Let's talk about something else.'

'OK. How's the job hunt going?' Aisha asks.

I make a face. It had been on the back burner since getting the assistant coach position, but I'd have to get out there again soon.

'You'll find something,' Aisha says encouragingly. But that's what she and Thea have been saying ever since I quit my job, and I've still got nothing. Because the problem isn't that I *can't* find a job, it's that I can't find the right one.

THE PERFECT MATCH

Aisha's lucky – she has two jobs that she loves: teaching, and art on the side. Even Thea, who grumbles about how hard she has to study, is still clearly passionate about becoming a lawyer. She might complain about her legal assistant job and all her co-workers, but I know she loves it all the same.

'You're still doing those catering jobs on the side, right? You remember my friend, Jana? She catered Khushi's wedding a couple of months ago? She's looking for servers. It pays pretty well.'

I only vaguely remember her, but I could definitely use the money. 'Give me her info, I'll get in touch.'

With Aisha's lunch break almost over, I offer to walk her back to her school. But then my phone buzzes with a call from Jen, and she waves me off, telling me that she'll see me at home later.

'Hey, Jen, what's up?' I ask.

'Dina, hey. I meant to call you last night, but it was late, and I thought maybe it wasn't such a good idea,' Jen says.

'Is everything OK?' Jen's serious tone makes a little tendril of worry burrow into my stomach.

'They will be. There was a little emergency with my family last night,' Jen says.

'Is everyone OK?' I ask, finding myself stopping in my tracks.

'My mum had to have an emergency surgery, so I had to drive to Manchester last night.'

'God, I'm sorry, Jen, that must have been scary,' I say, my mind reeling back to when Baba was ill. There were so many nights spent in hospital rooms waiting and worrying. I can almost see the cold, clinical hallways, feel the sense of panic and helplessness. I don't envy Jen right now.

'Yeah, yeah, it was. But I went to see her this morning. She's already doing a lot better. I'll probably have to stay here for a couple of days, just to make sure that she's recovering OK.'

'So, do you want me to . . . cancel practice this week?' But even as I ask this, I can sense what Jen actually wants from me. We may have only reconnected a few weeks ago, but I can already read the tone of her voice.

'Is there any way that you can – I know it's a lot to ask – but if you could hold the fort without me?' Jen asks tentatively. 'I know that they're a lot to handle sometimes, but you know I think that you're the perfect person for this job.'

'Yeah . . . yeah, of course I can hold the fort, I've got this, you don't have to worry. You just deal with whatever you need to.'

Jen sighs with audible relief. 'Thank you, Dina. Seriously. You don't even realise how much of a lifesaver you are.'

I find myself smiling, even though my tendril of worry has slowly grown into the size of a boulder, and it's weighing me down.

'I'm happy to do it, Jen.'

As I hang up the phone, my smile falters. I'm not sure what I've just signed myself up for.

It's not long until I find out, though. With Jen out of the picture, the team is even less enthused about training.

'If Jen isn't here, why do *we* have to be?' Sara asks. 'I mean, she's our coach. You're just like the assistant or whatever.'

'Well, with her gone, I'm the coach,' I say, trying to sound as authoritative as I can. 'And, Jade, didn't Jen tell you to make sure you've got your hair up when you come to practice?'

Jade glances up from her phone to give me a bored look, before quickly going back to her screen.

I obviously haven't come prepared like Jen, either. I don't have extra hair ties, or kits, or boots. I don't even have the cones that we use to do drills, and make a mental note to ask Jen about where she keeps her supply.

I try to remember what Jen said to me. She wanted me to be her assistant coach for a reason: she thinks I can do it, and I can't let her down.

'Guys, listen,' I say, trying to channel Jen's calm, cool energy. The way nothing seems to rattle her ever. 'I know that it's not fun to be up early to get to football practice in the morning on your summer holidays, but wouldn't it be great if we made the most of it? You're already here. If you came on time, dressed properly, enthused about maybe really giving football a shot, we could have a lot of fun. *You* could have a lot of fun.'

I stare at the blank faces of the team – and that's the select few girls who even bother to look at me. Half of them are whispering to each other, and a few of them are on their phones. This is clearly not working at all, which is unsurprising considering my attempt at motivation hasn't even managed to motivate me.

I decide to try something different.

'Tell me something, why did you guys decide to join football club?' I ask.

'Um . . . I wanted to do fashion club, but all the spots were taken by the time I got there,' Sara chimes in.

'I was going to do art club,' Jade says, nodding along.

'I needed to join something. I thought football looked OK.' Sophie shrugs.

Everyone else on the team mutters something similar

– there isn't a single girl here who actually has an interest in football. It shouldn't surprise me, and maybe it doesn't, but it also doesn't give me a lot to work with.

'OK, well. We're here now. So, why don't you tell me what you know about football? You must know some football teams, have watched a few matches, or maybe even played a little in the past?' I ask with tentative hope in my voice.

There's silence for a moment, and I worry that I'm not even going to get an answer to my question.

Then, Jade pipes up. 'I follow Colleen Rooney on Instagram.'

A couple of the other girls chime in to say that they do too.

'OK . . . good,' I say, mostly because I'm not sure how to respond to that. It's not exactly an enthusiasm for football – they could at the very least follow an actual footballer, but I'm going to have to take what I can get. 'Anyone else?'

'My brother's favourite team is Man United,' another one of the girls offers.

'I watch the World Cup with my family. Sometimes,' Sophie adds tentatively.

A few others mumble that they do too, though none of them seem particularly enthralled by the idea of it.

'OK . . . let's just warm up by running some laps.' I sigh, waving them forwards.

They slowly, hesitantly stand up and start to jog the length of the field. One of them pretends to pull a muscle, another checks her phone. All the while, my worry grows and grows. Because it's clear to me now that Jen has made a mistake.

And so have I.

'They can't be that bad, they're teenage girls,' Deen says to me later that night when I complain about everything over a late dinner at the restaurant.

'I just wish they actually *cared* about . . . well, anything. They don't know the first thing about football and they don't want to be there,' I say, moving around the rice on my plate with my fork instead of actually eating it.

'They said they don't want to be there?' Deen asks.

'No. They don't have to *say* it. I can tell from the fact that they don't even wear the right clothes, they don't have the right boots and they're constantly late. Most of them said that this was the only club available and that's the only reason they're there. Not to mention the fact that they're not tuned in to anything to do with football. Half of them have never even watched a football match. How's that even possible?' My voice gets higher and higher with every word, and I'm acutely aware of the fact that I probably sound a little crazed, but I can't stop myself. I took this assistant coach position because I was tired of doing absolutely nothing with my life, but going back to the days of lazing around the restaurant, job hunting and stuffing my face with Deen's cooking is looking attractive once again.

'Don't you think you're being a little harsh on them?' Deen asks with a raised eyebrow.

I frown at him across the table. 'How? Did you not hear all the issues that I just listed?'

Deen holds up his hands and starts counting on his fingers. 'Don't wear the right clothes or the right boots. They're late. This was the only club they had available, and they haven't watched a lot of football.'

'Or any,' I add.

'Remind me how into football you were before you

decided to try out for the school team,' Deen says.

I blink at him, taken aback by this sudden turn in the conversation. 'That's . . . different.'

'And remember how for all of your first year of secondary school you wore the wrong uniform because the real uniform was too expensive?' Deen continues, as if I haven't even spoken. 'If I remember correctly, Ma literally had to write you a note to make sure the teachers wouldn't give you detention every single day.'

'Not that it stopped them from trying,' I mutter under my breath darkly, remembering how some of those teachers seemed to take pleasure in anything they perceived as a slight from me. To Maya, though – perfect, teacher's pet Maya – they were always willing to give the benefit of the doubt.

'And how many times did you show up late to school?'

'That was . . . *not* my fault. It was Ma, and she was working all these nights at the time and Baba always had to be at the restaurant,' I say defensively.

'And do you remember the reason why you decided to try out for football in the first place?' Deen asks.

Of course I remember. How could I forget? I had ranted and raved to Deen about her even back then. Maya Alam, the bane of my existence.

'All of those cases are very different from this team,' I say instead.

Deen raises his eyebrow even further up – it almost disappears into his hair. 'Because you know them so well, after meeting them, what, a week ago? This club is run by the council so . . . yeah, it makes sense that they may not have the money to fork out on fancy football boots or football kit.'

I glare down at my plate of rice and chicken curry, moving my fork around even more aggressively so that it makes an unpleasant noise as it collides with the ceramic of the plate. Deen has a point, but I hate that he has a point.

'And they're young, of course they haven't had exposure to football. You didn't either until you actually got onto the team. And you joined the team for the wrong reasons too; doesn't mean you didn't end up loving it. But you didn't start off as a football fanatic,' Deen continues. He leans forward and gives me a small smile. 'Look. You and I both know how difficult it can be when you feel like the people who are meant to look out for you don't care about you. I mean . . . I felt like our teachers only saw me as a troublemaker and so that's all I could be. Do you really want to be like one of those teachers who made us feel less than we were?'

I shake my head. 'No . . . of course I don't. But—'

'I'm sure you're different from those teachers,' Deen cuts in before I can defend myself. 'But my point is that you should remember back to when you were just like these girls. When you didn't know anything about football, didn't have the right kit, maybe when you felt like people around you didn't really get you. What worked for you?'

The real answer is not one I can give Deen. It was Maya – it was my desire to do better than her. I was determined that anything she could do, I would do even better. I ran on sheer spite back then – maybe I still do, sometimes.

But I guess there were other factors too.

'Jen,' I say. 'She . . . cared about us. She didn't feel like a big, scary teacher who was out to get me. I felt like she actually wanted me to do well.'

'OK, so, start there,' Deen says. 'Inspire your team in

the same way that Jen inspired you. That's my final advice.' He gives me a grin, and I have to wonder how Deen went from the troublesome kid who I hated being associated with to someone who suddenly seems wiser than his years. He used to skip classes, get detention every other day, and by the time he got suspended in his last year of college, our parents were starting to worry he might not even make it to graduation. Now, here he is: stable, grounded, responsible. Taking care of our mum and our restaurant, while I am floundering.

He gets up from the table and begins clearing away our dishes.

'OK, enough about me. You want to finally clue me in on how your conversation with Ma went? Or did you still not have it?' After he cowed out of it during lunch with her last week, he's been putting it off again and again. But today was finally the day he was going to do it – so he texted me during practice – with many, many exclamation marks.

'No, we had the conversation,' Deen says. He comes back over to the table with a cloth, cleaning the surface and not meeting my eyes.

'And how did it go?'

'It was . . . I mean, as expected. Whatever.' He shrugs his shoulders like he doesn't care, but I can read the hurt in his words, in his voice. Of course, Ma wouldn't have approved of his ideas. It's not like she approved of my plans to go back to football.

'Maybe you just need to do it,' I say.

Deen stops his cleaning and looks at me. 'What do you mean?'

'I mean, you have so many ideas, so many plans. You already know what you want this place to be. I bet you have an entire menu in your head, and you probably have an entire Pinterest board full of decor ideas. Why don't you just do it?'

'Because Ma said it would be a mistake.' Deen speaks slowly, like he's talking to someone who has trouble grasping basic concepts.

'You don't have to listen to what she says.'

'But she's our mum.' Deen sighs. He sits down on the chair opposite me again – or, rather, slumps down onto it. 'I can't just go against her wishes. This place was started by her and Baba. It would be disrespectful – you know it would be.'

'Or would it be more disrespectful to let it fall to the wayside?' I ask. 'I know you don't want to go against Ma's wishes, but I don't know if she's ever going to come around. And you shouldn't just sit around and give up on your own dreams, just because she's too afraid of failure.'

Deen blinks at me, his expression unreadable. 'I don't know, Dina . . .' he finally says. 'Haven't I given Ma and Baba enough grief?' He smiles as he says this, but I can sense the heaviness behind those words. Like he's still holding on to all of his actions from when he was younger. Like he thought Ma was still holding them against him.

'Deen, you know Ma loves you. No matter what,' I say, looking him square in the eyes. 'And if you pulled this off, I think you'd be *saving* her from trouble. I mean, how much longer do you think this place is going to stay afloat?'

'Not much longer.' Deen sighs. He looks around the empty restaurant, like he's evaluating it.

'What do you think Baba would have said if he were here?' There's a certain sadness that clouds his words.

Baba started this restaurant when both of us were too

young to remember, but we've heard the stories. He saved up for years, banking on his dreams for this place. The day the bank approved the loan to rent the space, he brought our whole family here. Back then, it was a decrepit old place, but he told Ma to look past that. Ma said that he painted a picture with his words that won her over; she saw his vision. But by the time the restaurant was up and running, there were two Indian restaurants in the neighbourhood, which already had a regular customer base and were thriving businesses. Baba opened the doors to this place to a trickle of people, and though over the years he started to maintain at least a few regulars, business never boomed. The vision that he had, the one he described to Ma that day, remains unfulfilled.

'I think he would have told you to go for your dreams, the same way that he did,' I say to Deen. 'You know that he believed in us, no matter what.'

Deen smiles and nods. 'Yeah. Even when he probably shouldn't have.' He turns to me, and finally asks, 'If I do this, you're going to help me, right?'

My face breaks out into a grin. 'Yes, obviously. I'll do anything you ask me to do.'

Deen smiles too. 'OK. I guess I'll take a page out of your book and give this a shot.'

Chapter 12
Dina

'OK, come on, inside.' I wave the last of the students into the restaurant and shepherd them towards the chairs that Deen and I set up earlier this morning.

'Isn't this that place Jen brought us to the other week?' Sara asks, wrinkling up her nose as she looks around.

'Oh, yeah, it looks different now, though,' Jade says with a frown that indicates she's not a big fan of the differences. 'The food was good, I remember. I posted on Instagram to say 9/10 for the food, but, like, 2/10 for everything else.'

I try not to roll my eyes at that. Of course, the girls don't remember that it was me and Deen serving them at the restaurant last time they were here.

'We're not eating here today.' After ushering the last of the girls in, I flip the closed sign on the door and shut it behind me. I doubt many people will be filtering in here around this time of the day anyway.

'Hey.' Deen appears from the kitchen, holding a giant bowl of popcorn in his hands. 'I've got the popcorn.'

I grin. 'Great. That means we're all set.' Walking to the top of the room, I turn to face the girls, all of them sat in rows. 'We're not playing football today.'

'It would be pretty difficult to play here,' one of the girls says. I let the comment roll off me.

'Instead, we're going to watch a movie.'

As soon as I say that, all of their faces brighten.

'It's a movie about football.'

And at that, all of their faces fall again, and a chorus of groans fills the room.

'I thought it was actually going to be a *fun* movie.' Sophie sighs.

I frown. 'It *is* going to be a fun movie. It's one of the things that made me fall in love with football and you guys are going to love it. Plus, my brother, Deen, made us all popcorn.' I indicate to where he's set the giant bowl down and has set up a little tower of paper cones beside it. He waves at the girls, who give him an awkward smile.

The prospect of popcorn doesn't elicit the same excitement that the movie originally did, but at least they don't look that disappointed anymore.

'OK. Let's get started.' I bend down to where I've connected a projector to my laptop and hit the play button on one of my favourite movies of all time: *Bend It Like Beckham*. It was one of the first movies I watched as a kid where someone who looked like me was the main character. I fell in love with it for that, before football ever even came into the equation.

I make my way towards the back of the room and take one of the empty seats. A few minutes into the movie, Deen joins me, offering me a bowl of popcorn, which I take gratefully. For once, instead of paying rapt attention to this movie, which I've watched so many times that I could probably quote it off the top of my head, I watch the girls' faces for their reactions.

At first, none of them seem too into the movie, and a few of them are more interested in scrolling through their phones. But as time passes, they seem to slowly get into it. It's not long before they're laughing at the jokes, rooting for Jess and Joe, and cheering on the football matches on screen. It's probably the most engaged that I've ever seen this group of girls and I can't help the triumphant smile on my face.

Deen elbows me in the ribs. 'Don't get ahead of yourself. A movie can't solve all of your problems,' he whispers.

I elbow him back – a little harder than he did – and smile as he winces. 'Don't worry. I know what I'm doing,' I reassure him, though I'm not sure if I do, or if it'll work. But it's the only thing I have in my arsenal, and it was Deen who advised me to try to reach the girls through my methods. The only methods I know are what got *me* excited about football.

By the time the movie is over, a lot of my worries have dissipated. The girls are way more excited than I've ever seen them – they're practically bouncing in their seats as they discuss the movie. Out of the corner of my eye, I can see Jade taking a video for her Instagram followers. She's pulled some of other girls in to excitedly talk about the movie.

'Honestly, guys, I had no idea old movies could be *so* good,' Jade says as she records. 'And that football was actually not the most boring thing ever.'

I have to stop myself from wincing and try to count her comment as a win.

As I wave the girls off to go home for the day, I'm feeling pretty good about my plan. If nothing else, I've helped them get to know each other a little bit better.

'So, you think it worked? They'll all be star players tomorrow morning?' Deen asks as I put away all the chairs, and he unhooks my laptop from the projector.

'If only it were that easy.' I sigh. 'But . . . it's something. Maybe now they won't look bored out of their minds when I get them to actually *play* football.'

The next day at training, the girls show up *almost* on time. They're still not dressed the part, but as Deen pointed out, I can't blame them for that.

'Can we play a match like Jess and Jules?' Sophie asks before all the girls have even arrived.

I'm taken aback by the question. I thought the most I could get out of the team this summer was teaching them the basics of football. But the last thing I want to do is shoot down their excitement – especially when this is the first time I've seen them interested at the prospect of playing football.

'Um, well, we have to make sure we're ready before we can play any matches,' I point out diplomatically. 'And that means practising and getting our team into shape.'

'And then we can play matches?' Sophie says. 'Real matches?'

'I'll have to talk to Jen about how that would work, but if we practise hard then—' I don't get to finish my sentence, because the girls are already up and splitting themselves into respective teams for a practice match, without any prompting from me.

The next few sessions are the same – the girls show up *almost* on time, with only some stragglers a few minutes behind. They're almost dressed in the correct kit, and they're ready to jump into the game almost immediately. A couple of times I have to slow them down so I can explain the rules and put them in the right positions. Other times, I have to make sure that we warm up properly and do practice drills.

They're still not a real team, but it's definitely a start. And a huge improvement from the first day that I met them. I can't help the little glow of pride that I feel in my chest as I watch them practise day after day, knowing that I'm the person who helped them get here.

Well, me, and a little bit of *Bend It Like Beckham*.

'So, how's your mum doing now?' I ask Jen one evening when she calls to check in on the team.

'A lot better,' Jen says, sounding relieved. 'But . . . she's still recovering, and taking things slow.' Her tone is laced with guilt as she says this, and I quickly rush in to reassure her.

'It's OK, take your time, and take care of your mum. Things with the team are going a lot better. They have some interest in playing now . . . actually, more than some for a few of them.' I think about Sophie and Sara, whose rivalry has somehow brought out the best in them on the pitch. Whether they are playing against each other or with each other, they seem completely dedicated to outdoing one another. In some ways, they remind me of me and Maya. But I try to rid myself of that thought as soon as it comes to me – there's no point in dwelling over Maya, or sparing her even a single thought.

'I knew you could get through to them,' Jen says. 'You were always the most passionate player that I ever coached.'

I try not to beam at that compliment. Coming from Jen, it means all the more.

'They have been asking about playing real matches, though. I know it's a pretty informal team, but if we did have them playing matches, it would give them something to work towards.'

'Yeah, I've been thinking about that too,' Jen admits. 'There are quite a few teams in their age range, and they often play each other during the summer. I could speak to their coaches and arrange matches, but the other teams are a lot more experienced. I worry that playing against them could shatter their confidence. They're so new to football. But I'm up here, and you're the one there. What do you think?'

I chew on my lip, thinking back to today's session. They played well, but they are still getting the hang of things. We haven't even figured out positions for each of the players yet. They are a bit all over the place, constantly going offside, and I let it slide half the time because we aren't playing a real match. We would have to figure all of that out before we could play an established team.

'Maybe they need a little more time,' I say, even though I know the girls would hate me if they knew about this conversation. They are desperate to play some real matches, instead of just playing each other. It might not be long before they get bored once more, and I don't have an entire backlist of football movies to show them to get them inspired again.

'OK. I trust your judgement,' Jen says. She has more confidence in me than I feel in myself. 'And I promise I'll be back soon. My brother is supposed to come up any day now and then—'

'Seriously, Jen, don't worry about it,' I reassure her. 'I'm happy to hold the fort for as long as you need me to.' Especially now that I seem to have finally wrangled the team together to actually play the game.

'You guys are late,' I say to Sophie and Asha as they stroll in to practice. While there are always a few girls who are late, Sophie and Asha are two of the players who have been the most enthusiastic about playing since our movie night.

'Sorry,' Sophie mumbles softly, shuffling to where I've set up cones in order to do some passing drills to warm up.

I shrug it off and instruct them to find partners so they can practise receiving passes, before swapping over.

'You want to make sure that you receive the ball on the inside of your foot,' I instruct as I watch them attempt to take the ball and dribble it through the cones. A few of them fumble, but most of them manage to control the ball just fine. To my surprise, Sophie and Asha can't seem to get it right no matter what. Even Sara jeering on Sophie from the other side of the park does nothing to get her motivation up.

'OK, what's wrong?' I ask, stopping in front of them and looking between Sophie and Asha.

'Nothing,' Sophie says, not quite looking at me, but I can see the unshed tears in her eyes.

'Come on, I know something's up. You guys have been down since you got to practice. Did you guys have a fight or something or—'

'We ran into another team on the other side of the park. The Westbrook team,' Jade interrupts from a few paces away. I've realised that being an Instagram influencer means more than Jade always being on her phone – it means that she's weirdly attuned to everything that's going on all the time, and seems to know everybody's business.

'And?' I prompt. By now, all of the girls have stopped playing, and are watching our conversation unfold instead.

'They were just saying that they've seen us practise, and that we're rubbish.' Jade shrugs.

A strangely fierce defensiveness rises through me.

Westbrook used to be my old team, but these girls are my team now. We may not be winning any championships, but building a team, and skills in football, takes time.

'You shouldn't listen to them,' I say, trying to sound casual, even though inside I'm burning up with rage. 'I mean, who cares what they say? You don't even know them, do you?'

'No . . .' Sophie is the one who answers this time, though she doesn't look like she's buying my defence. 'But they're a proper team. They have matching kit, and they're really good.'

'They've even played matches against other teams . . . and won,' Asha says, sounding dejected. 'But we don't even have a team name, and you said we're not ready to play anyone yet. So they're right, aren't they? We *are* rubbish. We're not a proper team.'

I'm not sure who I should be angrier at – myself, for not having enough faith in the team, or this other group of girls who have clearly been antagonising my team without any thought.

'Look, don't listen to them, they don't know us or our team,' I say, but it's clear from the fallen faces of the girls that they're unconvinced. 'Besides, if the name and kit are what's keeping us from being a "proper" team, that's easy to fix. You guys come up with a name, and I'll sort out the kit.'

'Really?' Jade asks, clearly not believing that it can be that easy. And I'm not really sure what my plan is to figure out kit – I'm not exactly rolling in money since I quit my job – but I will have to figure something out.

'Yes. Let's do that now, come up with a name. *Not* the Lionesses. We can be more imaginative than that,' I say. 'And I'll be . . . right back.'

I turn away from the girls as they gather in a group, some of their enthusiasm back now as they excitedly discuss ideas for team names. I'm more interested in this other team, and why they've been badmouthing my girls. It reminds me of being back in school, having to deal with the mean girls, who would whisper about me and Deen, how our uniforms weren't right and how our books were second-hand. They didn't think we belonged in school with them, they thought we were less than them. And there is no way that I am going to let anyone make my team feel the way I used to when I was younger.

I march over to the other side of the park, my face set into a glare and my mind running through everything that I want to say to this team. I'll give them a rundown of what my girls said and demand an apology for their terrible behaviour. I won't leave until I have one – it's the least that my team deserve. And it's as I'm running through all of these thoughts that I see her: Maya Alam.

Chapter 13

Maya

'Maya.' The familiar sound of Dina's voice, loud and commanding, is not what I expect to hear during football practice. I half expect to wake up from some kind of dream. Not that I dream often about Dina (only sometimes). But I turn around, and there she is. Dina Chowdhury, in the flesh, glaring at me as if we're back in school and I'm back to being her worst enemy.

'Dina,' I say, noting her tracksuit, the whistle around her neck, the clipboard that she's carrying in her arms. I remember what Jen said when I ran into her and Dina in that cafe around the corner: Dina is helping Jen with coaching a football club. That must be why she's here. 'How . . . are you?' I'm at a loss for words, unsure of what to say or what to do.

'How am I?' Dina asks, like that's the stupidest question she's ever been asked.

'Well, it's been a while since—'

'Are you aware that your team have been harassing mine?' Dina interrupts.

I frown, glancing at my team, who have now stopped their game to look at us. 'What are you talking about?'

'I'm talking about the fact that I was trying to run a practice session with my team, but they're too demoralised to play, thanks to the crap that your team has been saying to them.'

I look at my team once more. Their usually happy and enthusiastic expressions have shifted into something resembling discomfort and nervousness. Of course, they would feel uncomfortable with a random woman marching up to me and accusing them of harassment.

I try to square up my shoulders as I turn back to Dina, meeting her eyes with a glare. 'My team wouldn't do that. They're a little too busy practising for their upcoming match to worry about some other team.'

'You must not know them very well then, because the girls from my team told me what happened.'

'Well, maybe the girls from your team were making it up.'

Dina's eyes never leave mine, and her glare intensifies. 'Or maybe the girls from your team are not the perfect little princesses that you think they are. They've been bullying my girls and . . .' At that, Dina takes a step back, looking me up and down like she's evaluating me. The action sends a flush of heat through me. 'I guess I shouldn't be surprised, considering who their coach is. They've clearly learned from the best.'

I step closer to her, refusing to back down. I can't believe she would stoop so low, go so far as to share the speculation and lies that gossip magazines have been spreading about me since I quit the Vikings. I thought Dina was better than that, but maybe I never knew her at all. 'Are you serious, Dina? You really think it's appropriate to come here and call me or my team bullies? Don't you think that's the real bully behaviour?'

'Well, I wouldn't know. I guess I'd have to ask your old

team,' Dina says. 'And maybe I should speak to Ms Jacobs, tell her the kind of stuff that you're really teaching the team that she entrusted to you.'

I scoff, at a loss for words. Of course, I know that Dina would never actually speak to Ms Jacobs. It's all just bluster – it always is with her. But that doesn't make it any less infuriating, doesn't make it hurt any less.

'At least I'm actually qualified to coach football. I have things to teach them. What are *you* doing as a coach?' I know the words are cruel even as I say them, but I can't help it.

There's a mix of guilt and satisfaction as I watch Dina's nostrils flare. She steps closer to me still, until the two of us are eye to eye, nose to nose, until I can't see past her, and everything else falls away.

It's me and Dina, fourteen years old again, on the school football team, arguing about kit, and matches, and anything and everything else under the sun. It sends a thrill through me that has nothing to do with football, and everything to do with Dina.

'What's going on here?' Jen's voice pierces through the tension. I blink, and suddenly the rest of the world comes into focus. The park we're in, where we're causing a whole scene. My team, and Dina's team, who have apparently followed her up here. All of us in the throes of some kind of a fight.

I step back from Dina, trying to ignore the strange feeling in my gut. I try to chalk it up to a case of nostalgia.

Dina looks away from me too, and ushers her team away. I try to wrangle mine away as well. We definitely don't need a physical altercation between our teams – or between us. Because surely that would get back to Ms Jacobs, maybe even the press. It wouldn't help my already-ailing reputation.

I really should know better than to let Dina get the best of me, but she's always been able to get under my skin in a way that nobody else can.

'Jen, what are you doing here? I thought you were still in—'

'Doesn't matter,' Jen cuts off Dina with a strict frown. This is not a side of Jen that we saw often when we were younger, but it did have to come out a few times – usually when Dina and I were on the verge of killing each other. 'You two need to explain what's going on. I leave for a few days and come back to a fight in the park?'

'Maya's team was antagonising us,' Dina says. She crosses her arms over her chest and meets my gaze, issuing some kind of a challenge.

'Dina came bounding over here making wild accusations about us,' I respond.

Jen looks between me and Dina, her frown deepening. 'You know, the two of you are supposed to be the adults here. The coaches, setting an example for your teams. You think any of this is a good example?'

Jen keeps looking between us, clearly expecting some kind of an explanation, but Dina just looks to the ground and says nothing.

The seconds tick by, the silence from us growing uncomfortable.

'We should have behaved better,' I finally mumble. I don't want to disappoint Jen, and I don't want the team, who have been stellar players and have never misbehaved, to think that getting into fights with people is OK. 'We could have . . . talked it out, instead of . . .' I wave my hands to indicate the argument and the stand-off between me and Dina that Jen witnessed just minutes ago.

'Dina . . .' Jen says, turning to her.

'Yeah, I guess I shouldn't have come over here all guns blazing,' she says drily, barely getting the words out. It's clear that she doesn't mean it.

'OK. Do the two of you have something to say to each other then?' Jen asks.

The reprimand from her is enough to make my face heat up. I really do feel like I'm a teenager again. Jen is using the same discipline tactics she used back then.

'I'm sorry, Dina.'

Jen and I both look at Dina now. She's still refusing to look up from the ground, and her arms are crossed over her chest. She's a far cry from the woman who marched over here a few minutes ago.

'I'm sorry too,' she finally mumbles, though it's clear she's struggling to get the words out.

'OK, good. Now, girls, why don't you apologise?' Jen nods at each respective team.

They mutter their own disgruntled apologies and, for a minute, it seems like that's that, and we can put this unpleasant interaction to bed.

But then, Hannah speaks up. 'I don't know why we have to apologise when we didn't say anything *wrong*. We're actually a proper team and they aren't. It's not a crime to say that. And there's nothing wrong with being amateurs, but they shouldn't be so sensitive about it.'

I can see Dina clenching and unclenching her hands into fists at Hannah's words.

'Hannah,' I say in a warning tone. 'Let's just leave it.'

'No.' Dina finally looks back up, her eyes meeting mine.

'Let's not leave it. If your team is so confident in their abilities, maybe we should put it to the test.'

I wasn't expecting this sudden challenge. Pitting our teams against each other is definitely not a good idea.

'Are you sure you want to do that?' I ask, raising an eyebrow. I haven't seen her team play, but I don't need to do that to form an opinion.

We have the support of the school behind us. We have kit and a team name. We've played matches and beaten other teams. We have access to the Westbrook football pitch for occasional practice sessions. Dina's team is run by the council, probably to give the girls somewhere to put their energy during the summer. They have no kit to speak of and practise in the park. From what I understand, they've never even played a match. The only thing they have going for them is having Jen as a coach, but I don't think that will help them beat us.

'Yeah, I'm sure. Let's play a match, see what a *proper* team can apparently do,' Dina says.

I know I shouldn't take the bait, that I should be better than this. Like Jen said, Dina and I are the adults here, the coaches who should be setting better examples. But even if I know better, I can't back down from a challenge issued by Dina. If I do, it's just going to confirm everything that she already thinks about me. And I doubt my team will be filled with confidence if I don't meet Dina's challenge head on. This is more than just about Dina – it's about proving my capabilities.

'OK, if you can handle us, then let's do it,' I say. 'We can play you tomorrow if you want.'

There's a flash of hesitation in Dina's eyes. She recovers quickly, but not quick enough for me to miss it.

'End of summer,' she says.

'Fine, end of summer,' I agree.

'Dina, Maya, I don't know if that's the best—' Jen tries to interject, but our teams are already excitedly agreeing to the match.

Dina gives me a wry smile.

I guess it's game on.

Chapter 14
Dina

Twenty days to the match
'I thought you said you didn't think they were ready to play against another team,' Jen states once we're away from Maya and her awful team. I can tell – even though Jen doesn't say it – that she's disappointed in the way I behaved. That it's reminded her of old times, when Maya and I were more obsessed with beating each other in any way we could than figuring out how to work together to play the best we could.

'I underestimated them.' My voice sounds a little too defensive.

'Hm,' is all Jen says.

The two of us round up the team, and Jen goes into a lecture about how she expects all of us to be better behaved, even when she's not around – *especially* when she's not around.

'Sportsmanship is something that all football players should know. We compete on the football pitch, not off it.' Jen looks at me when she says that, and I glance down at my feet, studying the colours of my boots, instead of dealing with her judgement. This is the tried-and-tested phrase she used to say to me and Maya all the time. Clearly, it wasn't one of the things we took away from Jen's coaching.

'We're still going to play them, aren't we?' Sophie asks once Jen is finished speaking. It's clear that that's the team's main concern.

'Well . . .' Jen looks between me and the girls. 'It's not until the end of the summer. And if we feel that we're ready by then, I suppose we could.'

'We can play some practice matches, against other teams. To . . . get ready,' I pipe up. 'You said you could arrange that, right?'

Jen's frown deepens. 'I could. But—'

'Yes, let's do that!' Sara interrupts. She's bouncing on her feet at the idea, and even the other girls seem excited.

'Did you guys come up with a team name?' I ask. 'Because we'll need that if we're going to play for real.'

'We did!' Jade is grinning from ear to ear. She looks to her teammates, and they nod, silently indicating that they are all in agreement. It's the first time I've seen them behave like this. Warmth radiates through me at the sight. They aren't just girls playing football for the council anymore – they are a team.

'The Divas!' Jade says excitedly. 'Because of Beyoncé, obviously.'

'Obviously,' I say. It's not the name that I would have picked, but it's not my team. It's theirs. 'I like it.'

I look to Jen. 'I guess the Divas are playing a few matches. And we're going to be in it to win it.'

'I don't understand why Ma has her heart set on going to this thing,' I find myself grumbling on Saturday afternoon. I'm hovering in the hallway of her house, dressed in one of my best salwar kameezes.

Deen glances at himself in the mirror, running his fingers

through his black hair, until it looks just tousled enough to not be picture perfect.

'You're the one who's always telling her she needs more of a social life,' he says.

I roll my eyes, because it feels like maybe Deen is the one who needs a social life, considering he spends so much of his time holed up in the family restaurant, still dreaming about making it his own.

'Besides, it'll be nice for you to stop overworking yourself with your new football team. Take a break or you'll wear yourself out before you even get to the match with Maya.'

I guess Deen is right about that. Since agreeing to the match with Westbrook, the Divas have been on overdrive. I've already started setting up matches for them, but to actually do *well* in them we have to practise. Even on days when we don't have practice, I've been suddenly looking through different plays and searching for teams who might match the Divas on their level – to give them a little confidence boost as they get started in competing. I have a feeling, too, that some of them have been making time to practise on their own. There have been a couple of times passing through Victoria Park that I've seen Sophie and Sara kicking a ball around between them. I feel a tingle of satisfaction at the thought of them falling in love with football, just like I did at their age.

I shrug now, because Deen is right. I don't want to wear myself out, and I don't want the team to be worn out either. The match isn't until the end of the month, which isn't a ton of time, but it's *enough* time. Or at least it has to be.

'Ma, we're going to be late!' I call up to her, just as she starts descending down the stairs. She's wearing a black-and-white sharee, and she gives me a frown as she takes me in.

'You couldn't have worn something nicer? The girls your age that come to these things wear nice sharees,' Ma complains.

I sigh. Sharees have never exactly been my cup of tea. Ma has had to drape mine the few times I've worn one because I can never quite get it right. Besides, the other 'girls my age' are newly-weds with wardrobes full of gifted sharees. I only have a couple of Ma's old ones, collecting dust in the back of my wardrobe.

'Look at your brother, so handsome!' Ma says, reaching up to pinch his cheeks like he's still a kid and not a grown man.

I roll my eyes. I've just had to accept the fact that Ma and Deen are closer than ever since Deen moved in with Ma after Baba's passing. It's not like Deen wasn't already a bit of a mama's boy to begin with.

Thankfully, Ma doesn't dilly-dally for long, and soon the three of us are piled into the beaten-up Toyota that used to belong to Baba.

Deen weaves us through the busy streets and in just an hour we arrive outside Isra Auntie's house. We're clearly late because there's already a pile of cars in and around her driveway, and we can hear the sound of music, talk and laughter drifting out through the window.

Deen parks the car on the kerb and we climb out, Ma complaining the entire time about how we're late.

'If we miss those shomuchas that Isra serves as nasta . . .' Ma says in a threatening voice, like it's anyone's fault but hers that we're late.

'I'm sure she'll have saved some for you, Ma. She knows you're crazy about them,' Deen reassures her.

We follow her to the front door, the noise getting louder

and louder as we approach. It's a wonder that anybody hears the sound of Ma ringing the doorbell, but only seconds later, the front door flies open. Isra Auntie stands on the threshold, her eyes lighting up as she takes the three of us in.

'Aminah bhabi!' she says, throwing an arm around Ma. She smiles brightly at Deen and me before ushering us in.

The dawat is already in full swing. I spot a few uncles in the sitting room loudly discussing the state of Bangladeshi politics. They smile and wave as we pass by, mumbling friendly greetings before going back to their discussion. I can't help but feel a little twinge of pain. If Baba were alive, he would be here with these uncles, discussing the restaurant, this country's economy, the upcoming Bangladeshi election and everything in-between.

I try to shake those thoughts off me as Deen and I follow Isra Auntie and Ma to the kitchen. Several aunties are standing around in groups, discussing kids' exam results, new jobs, promotions and wedding prospects. They barely even notice when we walk in, which is probably good because Ma seems less interested in them and more interested in the snacks laid out on the table. She immediately dives for the shomuchas. I smile at her antics, but there's a thread of worry there too. I wonder if she's so preoccupied with the shomuchas and the food because she can't exactly engage the aunties in boasting about me and Deen. Unlike their kids, Deen and I aren't succeeding at life, and unfortunately everybody knows it.

Determined not to seem antisocial, though, Deen and I mingle with some of the 'kids' our age – the few that still show up to these dawats and aren't too busy living their fabulous adult lives. Lina tells me about her recent engagement and invites me to her wedding in a few months' time, while Inam informs me about the new promotion at work, and how she and her husband are looking to buy a house, now that they can finally afford the down payment on a place. I smile through both conversations, trying to feign the appropriate amount of enthusiasm while feeling my insides contort a little with despair.

But it's not until I turn to speak to Zulaykha that I really start feeling despondent.

'Hey, Zulaykha, long time no see,' I say, approaching her after Inam dashes off to say hello to some of her friends.

Zulaykha turns to me, a smile crinkling her eyes.

'Dina, hey,' she greets me. And then the person next to her turns too – no trace of a smile in her eyes at all. Maya.

'Dina.' Maya's voice is clipped and terse.

I stop mid-approach, unsure of whether I should keep trying to make small talk with Zulaykha or if I should cut my losses and run, though it would be a pretty odd thing to do at this stage.

It doesn't help either that the sight of Maya makes my breath hitch, and my throat dry up completely. Because while I've seen Maya since she left for America, I haven't quite seen her like *this*. She's dressed in a lavender sharee that seems to cling to her just perfectly. The almost translucent material bares just a hint of skin where it skims across her midriff and rests over her shoulders; her long black hair hiding the rest. In all the years that I've known Maya, I've *never* seen her like this. She looks grown up, mature. She looks . . .

I gulp, trying to do away with the sudden dryness on my tongue.

'Maya . . . hey. I wasn't expecting to see you here.'

'Right? Me neither!' Zulaykha says, though, unlike me, she's clearly delighted by the surprise. 'I knew she was back, but I figured she was too much of a celebrity these days for the likes of us. You should hear her stories, Dina. You used to be into football, right? I bet you'd *love* them.'

I almost wince, and even Maya seems uncomfortable by the turn in the conversation from the way she ducks her head instead of looking at me again.

'I have to go find my brother. It was nice seeing you,' I mumble, knowing it's barely an excuse, and turn around. *That's enough socialising*, I think to myself, as I go in search of Deen. He's hovering by some of the uncles, awkwardly nodding and smiling as they loudly talk over him about what they think he should do with the restaurant. He catches my eye across the hallway, and it's almost like he can see the panic in me. He mumbles something to the uncles and sidles over to me.

'What's up?'

'Maya's here.'

Deen's eyes widen with the appropriate amount of surprise. 'You saw her?'

'I *talked* to her,' I say, though I'm not sure if that brief exchange could really qualify as talking. 'Honestly, maybe I should leave. I don't know why I came here anyway. I *should* be focusing on the football match coming up and I still don't know how I'm going to get kit for the Divas, because Jen says there's no funding for it, and if we don't have kit then—'

Deen's hand on my shoulder interrupts me. When I meet his gaze, he gives me a sympathetic smile. 'Dina, you are spiralling. And you can't leave, we just got here, and we haven't even eaten yet. We all drove together, remember?'

'Right.' I glance back to where I can now make out Maya and Zulaykha, still engaged in conversation, Maya's back turned away from me.

'There are a lot of people here. You can avoid her.' Deen sounds confident about that, so I nod, mostly because I don't really have any other choice but to try to avoid her.

'Yeah, I'll just stay away from her. Actually, I'm just going to go to the bathroom.' *And stay there for as long as possible*, I think but don't say out loud.

I stumble in my small pencil heels up the stairs and to the small bathroom on the right, closing the door behind me.

I don't actually have to use the bathroom, of course, but it's nice to be away from all the noise and hustle and bustle for even a moment. Up here, away from the rest of the dawat, the sound from downstairs is muffled. I close the lid of the toilet and sit down on top of it, trying to calm my heart, which has been beating a little too fast since I spotted Maya.

Maybe I should have expected to see her socially now that she's back. Of course, she would want to get back to her social life – see her old friends, go to the same dawats that her parents used to drag her to when she was younger. When we were kids, we didn't really attend the same dawats, but we had the occasional run-ins. In the beginning, it was always strange to see her away from school, though even at dawats she was always the image of perfection. While I always felt like I was on the outside looking in.

And then, for a while, I *wanted* to run into her everywhere and anywhere. We would use dawats to sneak off and find our own little corner; sharing secrets and giggling in hushed voices so nobody else would be privy to us. A shiver runs down my spine at those memories, as if that Maya is here right now, like I can still feel the heat of her body beside mine; the prickle of her touch making my skin break out into a fresh bout of goosebumps.

I shake my head, trying to rid myself of those memories, just as a loud knocking sound comes from outside. I guess that's as much time as I get to myself in the bathroom.

Getting up, I take a deep breath and unlock the door.

As luck would have it, the person on the other side of the door is none other than Maya.

Chapter 15

Maya

Eighteen days to the match

I almost recoil at the sight of Dina in the bathroom doorway. I wasn't expecting to run into her here at the dawat and I certainly wasn't expecting to run into her *here*. I thought I would be safe here from all the probing questions from everyone, about what I'm up to now, and how will I get a good job without a proper university degree? They weren't saying it with any form of judgement, but I could still see the sympathy behind their eyes with every word.

I'd had enough of it, and I needed to get away. But it isn't like there is a place to get away at a dawat. There are people around every corner. Apparently, even in the bathroom.

'What are you doing here?' Dina demands.

'I didn't know you were the only one allowed to use the bathroom,' I say.

Dina fixes me with a glare. 'I should have known it was you, hammering at the door like you're entitled to the bathroom or something.'

I scoff, because I certainly wasn't hammering at the door. And if I *was*, it's only because everything at this dawat has been much more overwhelming than I was expecting. Seeing Dina was just the last straw.

'I wasn't hammering, but I would appreciate it if you would move.' I make a motion with my hand for her to scooch out of the bathroom, but it's clearly the wrong thing to do.

'I'm not done, actually.'

'Are you serious?' I know Dina can be childish – but this is going a bit overboard.

'There are other bathrooms in this place. Go find one of those.' With that, Dina makes to close the bathroom door on me, but I step forward, pushing my way past her, so that the door shuts behind the both of us.

Dina shoots me another glare. 'Fine. Whatever. I'll go and find another bathroom then,' she huffs.

She twists the handle, but the door doesn't open. Dina's expression quickly shifts from anger to one of panic. She pulls at the door, desperation clear in her face.

'Don't tell me that—'

'It's stuck.'

Dina turns to me with another glare, like this is somehow my fault. 'It was fine before. I locked it behind me and I opened it no problem.'

'I didn't even touch the door.' I hold up my hands defensively, not that that makes Dina back up in any way. 'Here, let me try.'

I move past Dina, trying my best not to touch her, though this whole bathroom is filled with the familiar earthy scent of her and it's a little overwhelming. Twisting the doorknob, I pull, but it doesn't budge in the slightest. I try knocking on the door and calling out. 'Hello? Is anybody out there?' But all I hear is the ongoing muffle of noises drifting up from the party downstairs. 'Shit . . .'

'They're not going to hear us, unless they come upstairs,'

Dina says. She already sounds like she's given up, which is so typical of her that it makes a prickle of anger run through me. Dina has always been quick to give up. On everything, big or small.

I try banging on the door, louder now. But there's still no response.

I slip out my phone and try to call Amma, then Abba, but there's no response from either of them. By the time I turn back to Dina, she's sitting with the toilet seat down, studying me with a grim expression.

'If you hadn't tried to barge in here, this wouldn't have happened,' she says.

'Why don't you try calling someone?' I ask.

'I did. I texted Deen, but he hasn't replied. He probably doesn't even have his phone on him, I don't know.'

'Well, it's not my fault. You were being ridiculous.'

Dina stands up suddenly and starts walking towards me. I feel my face flush as she advances, unsure of what exactly she's doing.

'If you have to use the bathroom, I'll turn away,' she says, stopping just a few paces ahead of me.

My face heats up even more at that idea. I shake my head quickly. 'I don't actually have to use the bathroom,' I admit. 'I just . . .' I pause, unsure of what I should even say . . . 'needed a moment to myself.'

Dina frowns. 'Oh.' She pauses for a beat and adds, 'Why?'

'I don't know. Just a little overwhelming, being here, seeing everyone.' I shrug. I definitely don't want to get into it with Dina. I'm not sure I want to get into it with anyone. I came up here to try to get away from all my spiralling thoughts and anxieties, not to ruminate on them further.

'I would have thought you'd be loving all the attention.

The prodigal daughter returns,' Dina says, her voice bitter.

I wonder if that's what Dina really thinks of me – that I'm someone who is obsessed with attention, who loves to live in the limelight. I shouldn't be surprised. Back in school, she thought that I was a teacher's pet who would do anything to have the attention of the teachers over her. There were years of bitterness between us before she admitted that was why she hated me so much – she saw me as someone who had everything but still wanted more. It was getting to know each other that had shattered those illusions about me, and I guess she'd had to shatter some of the illusions I had about her too.

It had felt brave back then, opening myself up to Dina. Sharing things with her I'd never shared with anybody else. And she'd seen me, understood me. Or at least I thought that she had.

Because when things had gone wrong – when Dina didn't get what she wanted – she turned on me so easily, it felt like she just flicked a switch. Then, opening myself up in the way I had felt foolish: like I had offered my heart to Dina on a platter, ready for her to break it into a million pieces.

'I don't,' I reply simply. I turn away from her and go for the door once again. It rattles stubbornly against the doorframe. But it doesn't give even an inch, and I sigh, collapsing against it.

'Are you going to Zul's wedding next month?' Dina asks suddenly. 'I'm guessing she's invited you, now that you're back.'

'I don't know, I haven't decided.'

Dina sighs. 'Well, let me know. If you go, then I can't.'

I look at Dina once more, pressing my lips together as I

study her. 'Is this really what it's going to be like? We're just going to avoid each other, and when we can't, we're going to snipe at one another?' I ask.

Dina looks surprised by the question, though I don't know why she should be. Ever since I've known I was coming back, I've been going over everything about our past, obsessing over when I'd inevitably run into her again, what I'd say, what she'd say. Never in a million years did I expect things to be the way they are – I couldn't have predicted us suddenly finding ourselves to be rival football coaches. But it doesn't mean that I don't want to find another way.

'Do you have a better solution? Because it's not like we can be friends.' She says it so matter-of-factly that it sends an ice-pick through my heart.

I still remember when the two of us couldn't bear to spend any time away from each other. When we weren't hanging out at school or practising football in the park, we were at each other's places. But now we're strangers to one another. I don't even recognise this Dina, with her air of defensiveness and bitterness. A Dina who barely deigns to give me a passing glance.

'I'm not leaving, Dina. I'm not going back to America, and my parents are here. We're going to run into each other at dawats, weddings, on the streets . . . who knows where else? Wouldn't it be better if we weren't always glaring at each other across the room? I don't know why we can't at least be civil with each other now.'

Dina finally looks up at me properly. If I thought her glares from before were bad, this is ten times worse. It seems to go through me, sending a chill down my spine.

'You *do* know why we can't be civil with each other,' she says. 'Don't pretend that we're just two people who broke up or drifted apart. Do you even know what I've been doing these past few years? I've been working in fucking finance, hating every minute of my life, but just trying to make ends meet. All the while, I've been thinking about the fact that things could have been different – I could have had what you had, if only you hadn't taken it all from me. And now you're back here, pretending that you're somehow the wronged party. Like I'm the bad guy because I'm not smiling and laughing and embracing you with open arms. Did you even think about me once when you were gone?'

I'm so stunned that I can only blink at Dina for a moment. Her anger and bitterness is not something I'm alien to. I still replay the moment when she marched into my house all those years ago and ended things, blaming me for everything. And now she's here again, doing the exact same thing. It's like no time has passed at all. I'm still the one to blame, I'm still the villain who ruined Dina's life. But that's not even what hurts the most.

'You really think I haven't thought about you since I left?' I ask.

A flash of surprise appears on Dina's face, but I don't give her a chance to respond. Suddenly, the words are pouring out of me.

'I thought of you every day when I was gone. I tried so hard to stop, to forget you. But . . . it's easier said than done.' I let out a small, humourless laugh. The sleepless nights I spent after our break-up, reconsidering everything and anything, aren't something I can forget. I don't know how Dina can even entertain the idea that I've spent all these years *not* thinking about her.

Dina stares at me, unblinking, like she's looking through me. It makes my mouth dry up like a desert. 'That doesn't . . .

change anything,' she finally says, her voice slightly hoarse. Like even she doesn't fully believe that.

I want to ask her if she thought about me too, but I know it will come out pathetic and sad. Thankfully, that's when the sound of marching footsteps from outside the door interrupts us.

'Dina? Are you in there?' a familiar voice asks.

The next minute, the door is flung open from the other side, and Dina's older brother is peering in at us from the doorway.

'Maya . . . hey,' Deen says, sounding and looking confused as his eyes flick from me to his sister. 'Dina, I got your text. How long have you guys been stuck up here?'

'Too long,' Dina grumbles. She's already pushing past me, past Deen, and down the stairs. I can only watch her go, feeling my heart squeeze in my chest with the same pain that she left me with nine years ago.

Chapter 16

Dina

Sixteen days to the match

I somehow manage to avoid Maya for the rest of the dawat, but that doesn't mean that my mind doesn't circle the last question she asked. *You really think I haven't thought about you since I left*? She asked it with so much earnestness that it took me by surprise. I've always assumed that Maya was too busy living the life of a famous footballer to even remember me. I've imagined that she was making new friends, dating other football players . . . living it up and forgetting all about me, while I was the one left to pick up the pieces of our relationship.

But now, I wonder.

Still, I don't want to spend any more time thinking about Maya than I have to. No matter what her life looked like when she was gone, she still *left*. So, instead of obsessing over Maya and our conversation, I decide to throw myself fully into the football team. We still have our upcoming match, and the days are counting down fast. We finally have a name, but no kit to speak of. Which is one of my first major problems to solve.

Deen suggests trying to find some kind of a sponsor who would fund our kit, but considering we've never played a match, I doubt that anybody would consider sponsoring us.

Aisha, finally, suggests the best idea: if I could find some plain T-shirts, we could paint over them to resemble kits.

I end up calling Ma, hoping she can give me a list of discount shops where she used to get our cheap clothes back in the day.

'Did you know Maya Alam was at the dawat the other day?' Ma asks almost as soon as she picks up. Leave it to her to be late on the news cycle, despite literally being at that dawat.

'Yeah, I saw her there. Ma, I called because—'

'And she's now retired. Who retires at twenty-eight?' Ma sounds scandalised by the idea.

'Well, football players retire early. They can't play until they're sixty-five.'

'What's she going to do now? She doesn't even have a degree.'

'It's not like a degree got me and Deen anywhere,' I say.

That must make Ma consider her words because she's silent for a full minute, during which I finally get a chance to ask about her discount shops.

'I can text you a list. Why do you need it?'

'Cheap clothes. I'm not really flush with cash these days. Thanks, Ma. I'll—'

'You haven't come home for dinner the last few days,' Ma cuts me off, like she can tell I'm trying to hurry her off the phone. 'I wanted to hear about . . . your new job.'

That surprises me. I was sure that Ma was happy that I hadn't come home, that she had an excuse to avoid talking about my coaching position, which she definitely did not want me to take.

'I've just been busy,' I explain.

'And Deen is apparently so busy these days that he barely

eats at home anymore,' Ma grumbles, and I can read the sadness behind her words.

Just a few weeks ago, Deen and I were spending all our time with her, probably far more than was normal. Now, he is busy with the renovations, and I'm caught up in this football match. Meanwhile, Ma is home all alone, no Baba to keep her company these days.

I sigh. 'Do you want to come to some of the discount shops with me? You could show me where they are and—'

'Yes!' Ma says enthusiastically before I can even finish my invite.

That's how I find myself shopping with my mother the next day. Something I haven't done since I was thirteen years old.

'I'm looking for T-shirts. Plain ones!' I say for the umpteenth time, while Ma holds up a floral dress to me, revelling in how great the colour would look against my skin tone. The two of us are in one of many charity shops we've been to today. This one has a mish-mash of decor; from painted masks on the walls, all the way to rainbow-coloured bunting.

'Why do you need so many plain T-shirts? You already have five.' Ma nods at the shopping bags in my hands.

'It's for . . . a project,' I lie.

Ma sighs, squeezing the dress back onto a rack brimming with clothes. 'It's for your football team, and you don't want to tell me. Like Deen doesn't want to tell me about how he's renovating the restaurant without my permission.'

I freeze halfway through sifting through the clothes rack. Ma has always been astute; I don't know why Deen and I thought we could get away with lying to her and avoiding her.

'We just . . . don't want you to be upset. Deen knows how you feel about the restaurant, and I know how you feel about football.'

Ma studies me for a second and I brace myself for one of her signature reprimands about how she's our mum and she knows what's best for us. Stuff that Deen and I have heard a million times over the course of our lives.

'I know your baba was the dreamer in our family, but I don't want you and Deen to shut me out,' Ma says, her voice soft. 'The three of us are all we have.'

My cheeks burn with shame. Ma is right – we have been shutting her out. I can't even imagine what that must feel like. Especially when I know she has her reasons for warning me and Deen away from football and the restaurant. Ma struggled with her own aspirations of being an actress. She knows what it feels like to have your dreams crushed.

'Sorry,' I mumble.

Ma smiles, before turning back to the clothing rack as if our conversation hasn't even happened. 'So, how many plain T-shirts do you need?'

'It's for a full team, so I need eleven. We're . . . going to paint them to make them into a kit.'

'You're going to paint?' Ma asks with a chuckle.

'Aisha and Thea are going to help, don't worry.'

By the time we've found all the T-shirts that we need, we've been going from shop to shop for hours. I'm exhausted and starving, but Ma somehow still has a spring in her step as we lug our shopping around. We end up trudging into Buttons, one of the restaurants that we used to go to all the time when Deen and I were younger. It's one of the few restaurants in the neighbourhood that has stuck around and, of course, Baba used to be friends with the owners.

The place is packed, but we manage to find a small booth in the corner. It's only when we squeeze in and I'm looking around that I spot the familiar face of Maya on the other side of the restaurant. She's with both of her parents, the three of them laughing and joking without a care in the world.

'Shit,' I mumble under my breath. I shouldn't be surprised – Maya used to come to this place all the time. We even dragged our parents here to meet each other properly back when we were dating.

'Don't curse, Dina,' Ma says, almost automatically, flicking through the menu.

'Maybe we should go somewhere else,' I say. 'This place is too crowded and way too noisy.'

Ma just frowns, not even looking up from studying her menu. 'You can go if you want. I'm eating here.'

I sigh, slinking down in my seat and ducking my head so Maya won't spot me. Maybe we can eat and leave without her even knowing I was ever here.

But when Ma finally looks up from the menu, her frown deepens. 'Why are you slouching?'

'No reason.'

'And who are you looking at?' She turns all the way around and her eyes light up when she sees Maya and her family across the restaurant. She starts to wave wildly – so wildly that I'm sure half the restaurant sees her. And, of course, Maya and her parents do.

'Ma, leave them alone,' I say, but it's too late. I can only watch in horror as Maya shuffles over, a hesitant smile pasted on her lips.

'Hi, Auntie,' she says, her eyes quickly flickering over to me before travelling back to Ma. 'It's nice to see you.'

'Maya, I missed you at Isra's dawat the other day. And Dina never told me that you were back.'

I groan. Ma has always been obsessed with Maya, and I've never really told her how bad our break-up was. She still thinks that Maya moved away and so it made sense for us to stop seeing each other.

'I've only been back for a few weeks,' she says. 'I'm coaching our old school's football team now.'

'Wow.' Ma actually looks impressed. 'Dina's coaching a football team too, did she tell you?'

Maya gives me another fleeting glance. 'Yeah. We're actually going to be playing each other. Our teams, I mean. In a few weeks. It should be . . . fun.'

Definitely not the word I would use, all things considered.

To my absolute horror, Ma stands up. 'I should go say salaam to your parents. I'll be right back.' She offers me and Maya a bright smile, before hurrying away.

I expect Maya to scurry after Ma, but she just stands there in front of our booth, shifting from one foot to another.

'I didn't expect to see you here,' she finally says.

'Yeah, I didn't expect to see you here either.'

'Did you go shopping?' She nods to the bags beside me in the booth.

'Yes.' I pause for a beat, then add, 'It's for a makeshift kit for my team. We don't have fancy school funds to get us stuff like that.'

'Oh.' Maya actually looks surprised, like she expected a council team gets all of the support that a team like Westbrook does. She looks over at where Ma seems to be having a lively discussion with her parents, before sliding into Ma's seat and giving me a serious look. 'Can I ask you something?'

I almost want to say no, afraid of what she might ask me. The last time the two of us spent more than five minutes with each other, things became too much too fast, and I'm not sure if I'm ready to dig into our past. Especially not here, in this crowded restaurant, with our parents so close by. 'Um, I don't—'

'It's about my students. Do you really think they're bullies? Like . . . were they really being awful to your team?'

I blink at her for a moment, trying to digest what she's just asked. When I had marched up to Maya at the park, it had been adrenaline pushing me forward. I'm not even sure I totally remember everything that I said.

'I don't know. I haven't met any of the girls from your team. All I know is they were mean to some of the girls on mine, and I . . . wasn't going to tolerate that,' I say. 'If you're still offended about—'

'I'm not. There's this girl on my team, Laila. I think . . . she's being cyberbullied,' Maya sighs. 'I *know* she's being cyberbullied. I brought it up to Ms Jacobs, and she talked to her parents earlier today. Their solution was to make her get off social media, which feels . . . unfair. I was just thinking maybe it was some of the other girls on my team, or maybe it's just nobodies on the internet.'

'Sorry,' I offer, but a tendril of warmth tugs at me. I remember what it feels like to have Maya care for you.

Maya gives me a tight smile. 'I just wish I could help her.'

'You looking out for her is already helping,' I say. 'You know . . . there's this girl on my team. Jade. She's a social media influencer. Maybe she and . . .'

'Laila,' Maya says when I look at her searchingly.

'Right, Laila. Maybe she and Laila can talk; she could give her some advice. Jade has so many followers, I'm sure she's seen her share of hate comments online.'

'You think she'd be OK helping someone from the opposing team?' Maya asks.

'I guess we'll find out. I'll talk to her.'

'Thanks.' Maya smiles, before slowly standing up. 'I should probably get back to my parents.'

Maya heads off and, in a few minutes, Ma comes back, looking happier than I've seen her in a long time. The two of us order, and as we chat and eat our dinner, I occasionally look over at Maya, noticing her looking at me too. The two of us had a normal conversation – one that wasn't about our past and didn't erupt into an argument.

Maybe it will be OK to have Maya around here again.

Chapter 17

Maya

Fourteen days to the match
Nadine is already sitting at a table in the restaurant when I arrive. She waves me over and I nod to her when the waiter asks me if I have a reservation, before making my way to her. She looks different from when we were younger – way, way different. Her hair, which used to be dyed a different colour every couple of months, is back to her natural shade – a deep chestnut colour. There are bags under her eyes and smile lines around her mouth. Back in school she used to experiment with all kinds of make-up, but she seems to have foregone most of that now.

'Hey!' Nadine jumps to a stand as soon as I'm in front of her, wrapping her arms around me. At least she still seems to have her fervour.

I hug her back and when we pull away from each other, I take the seat opposite her. She smiles, seemingly studying me in the same way I've been studying her. She doesn't say anything, though, and I wonder what she thinks about the ways I've changed and the ways that I haven't.

Ever since the dawat at Isra Auntie's house, I've decided to try to reconnect with old friends again. Despite feeling overwhelmed at seeing so many people and being accosted with so many questions, it also feels like the first step to really figuring out my life again. Because it has to be more than quiet dinners with my parents and coaching the girls on my football team. Nadine has been the only one who's managed to find some time in her busy schedule to suggest a meet-up, and I jumped at the chance. After all, we were best friends once. For a long time. Even if we lost touch when I moved to America.

'So . . . what have you been up to?' Nadine finally asks.

The question feels elusive. How do you condense nine years of life into a single conversation?

'Oh, you know,' I say. 'Just . . . this and that. Playing football and then not playing football. And now I'm coaching a team for the school. Ms Jacobs asked me to.'

Nadine's eyebrows shoot up. 'You've seen Ms Jacobs? Recently?'

'She basically forced me to give an impromptu speech to the entire school, and then asked me if I'd coach the school team for the summer.'

Nadine's eyes widen, and she lets out a quick, short burst of laughter, which makes me grin. 'Ms Jacobs was always a character, wasn't she?'

'I guess she was.' I'd forgotten how Nadine, Gwen and I used to roll our eyes at Ms Jacobs' antics sometimes. How she'd try to mimic any slang that we used to say at the time and act like she was in the know. She definitely seems a lot more comfortable with herself now.

'It must have been weird being back in school,' Nadine says.

'That's one way to put it.' I shrug. 'What about you, though? What have you been up to? I can't believe it's been so many years since we last saw each other.'

'You're the one who jetted off to America,' Nadine says,

teasingly. She doesn't sound bitter about it, the way Dina did a few days ago. At first, Nadine and I had tried to keep in contact, but it was difficult with the time difference. It didn't help that, in the beginning, I felt so overwhelmed with everything, and I was still reeling from what had happened with Dina, that the thought of staying in touch with anyone felt painful. It wasn't long before our messages had trickled down to a few times a year, for birthdays or special occasions. And then complete silence.

'Well, yeah, but I'm back now and I want to know everything that's been going on with you.'

'Nothing too exciting.' Nadine shrugs. 'I mean, no jet-setting around the world, or becoming kind of a celebrity.' She gives me a smile. 'I went to university for a while, did a bullshit business degree that didn't take me anywhere. I hated every job that I had afterwards, and I'm actually doing a nursing degree now.'

Nadine and I used to stress out about what we even wanted to do with our lives after school. I'd never seriously considered football, it always felt like too much of a risk. I used to say that maybe I'd study medicine, or engineering. The kind of fields that I felt my parents might be able to brag to aunties and uncles about. Nadine used to float around between different things she wanted to study; one day it was psychology, the next computer science. I vaguely remember when she'd finally applied and got her offers. Even vaguer are the memories of when she started university; she'd text me about her classes, lecturers, the people she met. I was too busy with my own life to pay too much attention to what was going on with her. I'm sure she was just as overwhelmed as I was.

'Do you like nursing?' I ask.

'Yeah.' Nadine smiles, and it makes her eyes light up. 'My aunt got sick a couple of years back and I got to see how hard the nurses worked. It made me appreciate it and helped me realise that I wanted to do something like that with my life, instead of working for some firm that's pretty much destroying the world.'

She sounds so sure of who she is now, so proud of her work. I'm happy for her, but there's this quiet whisper of envy inside me too. I want to feel like Nadine does: happy with where I am, satisfied in my career. Instead, I still feel unmoored and unsure. After my summer of coaching, who knows what I'll do? Maybe I'll be back to moping around my bedroom, feeling sorry for myself.

'I'm really glad that you found something that you love,' I say.

Nadine's smile widens. 'Do you like the coaching gig? Do you . . . miss playing professionally?'

I hesitate to answer. I haven't really asked myself either of those questions. *Do* I like coaching? I think so, but I still second-guess myself, still question what I'm teaching the team half the time. I still feel a little bit like an imposter who just walked onto a football pitch – not unlike how I felt the first time I played a match for the Vikings.

'I like coaching,' I say finally. 'I mean, I learned so much while I was playing in America, and it's nice to be able to do something with all that knowledge.' I chew on my lip, not wanting to answer the second part of her question, even though Nadine is looking at me expectantly. Because if I answer honestly, then I know the question that comes next, and it's not one I want to answer. 'Playing professionally was nice. It was . . . kind of a dream come true, but . . .' I pause, shrugging my shoulders. 'It's behind me now.'

Nadine studies me for a moment, and I inwardly wince, awaiting the dreaded questions about why I quit my dream job, about the things that the newspapers have been saying about me. But she doesn't. Instead, she picks up the menu and says, 'Should we order then? The fish here is really good, by the way.'

I let out a breath, feeling my shoulders relax a little. 'Yeah, let's order.'

It's strange how quickly Nadine and I manage to slip back into conversation after we've ordered. It almost feels like no time has passed at all – that there was never a hiccup in our friendship for nine years. Nadine tells me about the professors at her university, and the other nursing students. She tells me about the things that she likes about it, and the things that she doesn't. She fills me in on what her family have been up to, and some of the old friends from school that she still keeps in touch with. Gwen, apparently, met a guy in Paris and decided to move there and get married. Now she works as a teacher there and is a fluent French speaker despite failing French GCSE in school.

Meanwhile, I tell Nadine about my old teammates, living in America, travelling around with the team to play matches. I leave out the bad stuff, only because I don't want to think about it, and I don't want to invite questions. Still, it feels nice to talk about it. It reminds me that my time on the team wasn't all bad.

By the time Nadine and I are finished with our lunch and finally ask for the bill, hours have passed by. Outside, the sun is on its way down, and it's shocking that the waiters haven't kicked us out.

Nadine and I stand up and make our way outside together.

'So, where are you living these days?' I ask. Back when we were in school, Nadine's house was only a fifteen-minute walk from mine. We spent a lot of time at each other's places, and our parents were probably sick of it.

'I have an apartment in West London,' Nadine says. 'It's near the university, and I share it with a couple of other nursing students. It's pretty intense; we pretty much spend all of our time studying.'

'I'm back in my parents' place,' I say.

'My parents are still in the old house. Maybe I can come around to see you next time I visit them,' Nadine says.

'Yeah, that would be nice.' I smile. I've been nervous that seeing Nadine again would feel strange. Unlike Zul, Nadine and I were *really* friends. We shared everything with each other. I was worried that reconnecting with her now would do away with our past somehow. That it would feel like meeting a stranger who you have vague memories of. But it hasn't felt like that – it feels like old times and I'm glad that I did it.

I pull Nadine into a hug as a form of goodbye, but just as the two of us are about to go our separate ways, Nadine calls me back.

'You know, if you ever wanted to talk about stuff, I would listen,' she says. Her voice is sincere, but it surprises me that after our casual conversation she says this at all. When I look at her questioningly, she sighs and adds, 'I could tell that you were holding stuff back, about your time in America. Which is fine, it's not like everything in life has been rosy for me in the last couple of years either.' I guess I shouldn't be surprised. It's been so many years since Nadine and I last saw each other – of course she's had struggles too.

'Thanks. Maybe next time we meet we could talk about the not-so-rosy stuff,' I say.

Nadine smiles as she waves goodbye.

As I walk to the tube station, I wonder about telling Nadine. I imagine filling her in on everything that's happened, telling her the reason why I quit the team. I'm sure she would listen with rapt attention, that she would give me a sympathetic smile or hug. But she wouldn't really understand. There's only one person who would get it, and she's the one person that I can't talk to. She's the one person who doesn't want anything to do with me.

My phone buzzes with a notification and I slip it out of my pocket to see a new email from Isabel. Frowning, I click onto it. I'm not sure why Isabel would email me, when we usually just talk on the phone.

> Subject: Fundraiser Info
> *Nina is so excited that you agreed to speak! The fundraiser is on the 14th (I know that's soon, but I'm guessing you've already been preparing the speech), and Nina says you can speak as little or as much as you want! It's really just about sharing your experiences so that the attendees can see the importance of women's football, supporting youth clubs for girls, etc. Location of the hotel attached! Nina is so excited to see you again!!*

My stomach sinks more and more with every word. What the hell have I signed up for? I vaguely remember a call with Isabel where she mentioned Nina, but I was too preoccupied with coaching to hear exactly what she said. I have half a mind to email Isabel back and say absolutely no way in hell am I going to be doing this. But I can feel the enthusiasm in her email, and it will be nice to see Nina again.

Maybe it won't be the worst thing in the world, going to this fundraiser.

Taking a deep breath, I click on the attachment.

Chapter 18

Maya

Thirteen days to the match

I stare at my phone screen, the words that I've written for today staring up at me. They feel disingenuous – like I've written out a bunch of lies to parrot.

Now that I'm sitting on the tube going into central London, to a big, fancy hotel, wearing a dress that clings to me a little too tightly, I'm reconsidering everything.

Technically, I could just turn back around and go home, but I know that both Isabel and Nina are counting on me. So, I stare at the words on my phone screen again, silently mouthing the speech about how important football has been to me, and why it's so vital that we encourage more women to get into the game. But the speech feels phony, like it belongs to a past Maya rather than the one of today.

Sighing, I put my phone away just as the tube pulls into my station. I step off and navigate my way towards the hotel. I stand in front of the entrance for a moment, contemplating if I really want to go in, when a familiar voice calls my name from behind.

'Maya?' I turn around, to come face to face with my old teammate, Terri Calahan. 'Oh my God, it really is you!' Her face breaks out into a smile when she sees me. She ambles forward and pulls me into a hug. I feel like I'm frozen in place, unsure of what to say or even do. I let her hug me for a moment, before quickly pulling away and trying to put on a smile of my own.

'It's good to see you. I didn't know that you would be here,' I say.

'Yeah, I got the invite a couple of weeks ago. I've been back here for a few weeks, because of my knee injury, so I thought, why not?' She shrugs. 'Well, come on, let's go in.'

'Right.' I follow her through the front doors. I guess there's no turning back now.

The fundraiser is already in full swing, and as soon as I walk into the hall, I spot half a dozen people that I recognise. Players from teams that I've played against, their coaches and managers. I even spot some of the reporters that were constant nuisances when I was playing. The whole scene unfolding in front of me makes my heart beat faster.

I take a deep breath and turn away from the crowd, hoping that none of the people here recognise me. Instead, I focus on the events hall itself. It has been decorated in football paraphernalia, though somehow the hotel has managed to make football-themed decorations and finger food look upscale instead of like a ten-year-old's birthday party, which is pretty impressive. I see football-shaped macarons going around, along with glasses of wine, while the whole room has been decked out in the colours of the England women's football team. I also notice several photos on the walls of various girls' football clubs. The photos show the girls beaming at the camera with their arms slung around each other.

'Wow, they've really gone all out with the fundraiser,' Terri chuckles. 'I shouldn't be surprised. Nina Hall organised this. Remember her?'

'Yeah, Isabel mentioned that. Nina was always on top of everything,' I say.

'So, how have you been anyway?' Terri asks.

'Good, yeah,' I say, at a loss for how to respond. I could tell Terri about coaching, but it feels so lacklustre all of a sudden.

'Honestly, I'm kind of surprised to see you here. I mean, when you quit, we thought you were done with football for good.'

I frown. I never gave a real explanation for why I made the decision that I did. They wouldn't have understood; everything they had done, or not done, had showed me that they wouldn't, even if they wanted to. But I still don't know why they would assume that I would be completely done with football simply because I had quit the team.

'Isabel invited me,' I explain, trying not to let my annoyance seep into my voice. 'I'm actually speaking. I guess Nina and Isabel thought that I could talk about how important football is for young girls, since I've been playing since I started secondary school. And it turned out . . .' I drift off, because we both know how it turned out.

'We wondered why you—' Terri begins.

I knew that this was coming, the wondering, the questions. I don't have any answers. I'd rather chew my own arm off than continue discussing this.

'I'm going to get something to drink,' I cut Terri off, turning around and launching myself towards the crowd. I look around for one of the waiters that I've seen floating around with trays of food and drink. Finally, I spot a black-and-white tux in a sea of sparkly dresses. I weave through the guests, trying to get the waiter's attention, but there are a few too many people. Someone jostles me as I'm passing by, and I run right into the waiter, whose tray full of food goes splattering to the ground.

'I'm so—' But when I look up and find familiar liquid brown eyes, my words catch in my throat. It's not just any waiter that I've run into.

It's Dina.

For a moment, I'm not even sure what to think or feel. My heart is beating a million miles a second, and my mind is a jumble of thoughts that I can't make head or tail of. Dina must be just as surprised to see me here as I am her, because we can only hold each other's gazes. And I'm a little too aware of the fact that Dina is also holding *me*. Her arms are wrapped around my waist in a bid to keep me from tumbling to the ground, while my arms are clasped around her shoulders.

As if we both realise the position that we're in at the same time, we step back. Dina retrieves her arms as I stand up straight. Still, I feel the absence of her touch like a missing limb. Just in the few seconds she was holding me, I remembered what it felt like to be held by Dina.

And I've started missing it already.

It takes me another moment to come back to reality – one where Dina and I aren't the only people in the room, or in the world. Where we're surrounded by my football peers, at a charity fundraiser, and Dina is wearing a waiter's uniform.

'What . . . what are you doing here?' I blurt out.

Dina takes a step back, trying to clean off her uniform, which is smeared with some of the entrées on her tray. 'You should watch where you're going,' she mumbles, just as a host of other waiters appear, helping her clean up and mopping the floor around us.

When I look around, I realise that the world didn't stop when Dina and I ran into each other. Instead, the whole thing has turned into a little bit of a spectacle. It's not just other waiters who saw what happened, but the attendees of the fundraiser too, their eyes shifting from me to Dina. Heat floods through me. If people weren't paying attention to me before, they definitely are now. I want to apologise to Dina for causing such a ruckus, and I still want to know why – of all the places in the world – she's here. And why she's waitressing, when the last time we spoke, she told me about some job in finance. But it's not the right time. Here, especially, the differences between us feel marked – with me dressed up with my peers and Dina in a uniform. This is definitely not the time and place for any kind of conversation, if that time and place even exists.

I retreat, mumbling an apology that I'm not sure Dina even hears. There are still curious onlookers watching me, though many have turned away. I move through the crowd again, trying to find some kind of reprieve from all of these people. The idea that I've made a mistake by coming here is growing stronger and stronger with each passing moment. I've left this life behind, that was my choice. Dipping my toes back into it is a terrible idea.

But then I spot Nina in the distance, waving me over. She looks the same as I remember – with her shoulder-length dark red hair framing her heart-shaped face. She's surrounded by a few women that I don't recognise.

Though it's the last thing I want to do, I make my way over, joining them with a smile.

Nina leans forward, pulling me into a hug. 'It's so good to see you again. Are you OK? I saw that little tumble over there.'

'Yeah, I wasn't watching where I was going and . . . it was totally my fault,' I say, feeling like I have to defend Dina.

'These things happen, especially when there's so many people around.' Nina waves her hand like she's seen it a million times. 'Besides, sometimes these catering companies hire new servers who don't always have the hang of things; it takes them a while to figure everything out.'

Nina speaks like someone who has organised a lot of these events, and I wouldn't be surprised if she has. Ever since she left her coaching position, I thought that she would be relaxing and settling into a life back home. But she has always been a bit of a go-getter. Even back when she was coaching, she used to run a mentoring programme for young girls in football.

'You guys remember Maya, right?' Nina asks, turning to the other women.

I immediately recognise Claire and Louise, former players from Nina's team.

'It's been ages, Maya,' Claire says as she pulls me into a hug, and Louise gives me an enthusiastic pat on the back. The last time we saw each other was when the Vikings beat the Royals in a match. But they were good sports about it, and we all went out for drinks afterwards.

The other women shake their heads. I've never seen them before either, though I'm not exactly surprised. They look young and shy, and I realise they must be new recruits. Seeing them makes me feel a little nostalgic – I remember being the new recruit, being filled with hopes and dreams. Unfortunately, it only carried me so far in the end.

'This is Charlotte,' Nina points to the girl with black hair and a bashful smile. 'And Emilie.' The girl with the blonde bob waves. 'They've just started with the Knights football team here. And Maya used to play as a forward for the Vikings.'

'Who do you play for now?' Emilie asks curiously.

'Um, I don't play anymore, actually. I . . . retired.'

'Oh.' Emilie looks taken aback by that response, and I feel myself flush.

'Oh, I remember they did a story about you on *The Warm Up*,' Charlotte says.

That elicits an awkward silence from the entire group. Like they've all watched the show, the one pointing out how it was probably my prickly personality that resulted in me leaving football. Standing there, surrounded by these women, I realise that they've most likely been hearing all the news stories. They've probably been on Twitter, seen the viral tweets calling me out for being a bully. Maybe they've been scrolling through the same subreddits where people are pointing out every single flaw that I have, marking out every mistake that I've ever made.

I'm trying to think of excuses to exit the conversation without seeming rude and regretting the decision to even come here at all. But Nina chimes in before I can say anything.

'I think *The Warm Up* was so unfair to you. Just perpetuating rumours without any kind of citations. I thought sports journalism was better than that,' she says, offering me a sympathetic smile.

I'm not sure if I should feel touched by her support or mortified that she thinks I'm so pathetic I need it.

'The newspapers in general have been terrible,' Louise says, nodding in agreement.

'Sports journalists used to have respect for the game back

when I played. These days, it's all about sensationalising everything. I mean, it's pathetic that a player can't just retire without it having to be a whole big thing. There doesn't have to be a story to everything.' Nina's voice takes on a tone of righteousness.

And while I appreciate her support and understanding, this is the last thing I want to talk about. I don't want to know what news articles and talk shows my peers have watched. I don't want to know what they discuss about me, what they believe and what they don't believe.

'Did you injure yourself, or something?' Emilie asks with a frown. She obviously hasn't been keeping up with the news cycle.

Claire shoots her a glare, but I've had enough of this conversation.

'Sorry, I should go. I told my friend that I would . . . and, yeah, I have to . . .' I turn around, though my excuse was barely formed. I can feel the pinprick of tears behind my eyes, the blood rushing in my ears. The room around me begins to blur as I push past throngs of faceless people, who all seem to peer at me like I'm some kind of animal in the zoo. I'm not a person, I'm a curiosity, and it feels like these questions will never stop.

I should never have come here.

Chapter 19
Dina

By the time I traipse back into the kitchen, my head is spinning, but I'm trying to keep everything under control.

'Dina, everything OK?' Jana, the catering supervisor, asks, eyeing the mess that is my shirt.

I take a deep breath, trying to calm myself down and put on a smile before replying. 'Fine. One of the guests bumped into me and my tray went flying.'

Jana frowns. 'You didn't get anything on the guest, did you?'

'No, I don't think so.' My voice sounds more clipped than I know it should. Because Maya *is* a guest here and I'm a server.

Ever since Aisha mentioned this catering job several weeks ago, I've been waiting to get a call. The pay is good – enough to help me keep up with my rent and bills at least for a little while, until I find something permanent. Jana had said that we would be catering a fundraiser. It was only when I arrived, several hours ago, that I realised what exactly it was a fundraiser for. I couldn't duck out then. I needed the money. Besides, it wasn't like I had a valid excuse anyway. I could barely even justify it to myself.

But running into Maya? That was just the tip of the iceberg. The whole thing makes me feel like the universe has some kind of sick sense of humour and is determined to make me the butt of its joke.

'There's some extra uniforms in the back over there. Try not to run into anyone else.' Jana points to a corner with a rack of identical uniforms.

I want to tell her that it wasn't *my* fault, it was Maya's, but that would just make me look incompetent. So I give her an appreciative nod and move towards the rack, stripping off my shirt and putting on a new one.

I grab a tray of drinks from the kitchen counter and move out into the events hall once again, though this time my eyes are already looking for Maya. So that I can avoid her. At least that's what I tell myself. Somewhere, though, in the back of my mind, I want to see her again. There was a moment before when we both felt frozen in time. She had looked at me with that deer-in-the-headlights expression. There was something about her – there has been something about her ever since she came back. She's different than she used to be, but I can't put my finger on it. I want to write it off as haughtiness because she's some kind of celebrity football player now, but that isn't what it seems like.

Back when we were in school together, Maya was always so sure of herself. She always had her hand up first when any of the teachers asked a question, she always wanted to be one of the captains when we chose teams. She always wanted to prove that she was better than anyone else, and most of the time she *did* prove it. But now I realise that that spark behind Maya's eyes is what is missing. That surety of herself. Instead, she seems more vulnerable now. Like she wants to hide herself away, instead of rise up to the challenge. Definitely *not* the Maya that I used to know.

But it isn't any of my business. At least that's what I tell myself while roving through the crowd once more.

I smile at guests and offer them drinks, all the while with my mind constantly drifting back to Maya. It's not my job to worry about her, I tell myself, but she seemed off when she ran into me.

Finally, I spot her on the other side of the room. She doesn't look like a deer in headlights anymore. She looks distraught as she pushes past people, her face a curtain of worry as she stumbles out of the room.

I look back at the host of servers walking around. I know that I shouldn't follow Maya. I've already made enough of a scene and I need this job. But it's like my mind and legs are in an ongoing battle, because without even thinking it through, my legs begin carrying me towards Maya. Soon, I'm following her out the door of the events hall.

For some reason, I'm expecting her to be waiting on the other side of the door, but of course, she isn't there. In fact, she's nowhere in sight. For a moment, I wonder if she's left completely. A little thread of worry worms itself into my chest. There was definitely something wrong with her. It wasn't like at the park. She didn't have that determination, that passion and righteousness that always got under my skin. She didn't seem like the Maya that I know.

Then again, I haven't known Maya for a long time now.

Still, my worry niggles at me enough that I lay down my tray on one of the tables and step towards the lobby of the hotel, looking around for Maya's familiar form. But she's not there.

I walk to the exit, pushing the door open and peering around the corner. She's not there either. There's no sign of her. The little thread of worry grows bigger with every passing second.

I would call Maya if I had her phone number, but of course I don't.

Just as I'm about to give up my search, I spot the hem of her dress, peeking out from a corner hidden behind a large fern. She's tucked herself into the furthest nook of the hotel lobby. Clearly, she doesn't want to be found. And maybe if I hadn't seen her walking out, looking the way she did, I would have left her alone.

Instead, I stride towards her. She's sitting with her back against the wall, her knees pulled up to her chest, and her head buried in them. She looks so small sitting like that; like half the person that she is.

I sit down next to her. Maya's breathing is shallow and fast. I put an arm on her shoulder, and she looks up. A flicker of something passes in her eyes as she takes me in, but I'm not sure what that something is. All I see is the panic behind her eyes, the way her fingers shake, even as they're wrapped around her knees.

I'm not alien to panic attacks – Ma used to have them all the time right after Baba passed away. Deen and I would sit with her back then, not sure what to do, how to take away her fears and anxieties, how to bring her back to reality. We've learned since those early days.

Now I rub my arm up and down Maya's shoulder, trying to soothe her. I tell her to count her breaths in and out, slowly, and she actually listens to me and follows my lead. After a few minutes, her breathing is back to normal, her fingers have stopped their shaking. She brushes away a few tears that have gathered on her cheeks, smudging a little bit of her make-up away, and sniffles.

'Sorry,' Maya whispers, sounding completely unlike herself.

'For what?'

'I don't know. Being a mess, or whatever,' she says. She's not looking at me anymore. She's looking at the floor.

'If being a mess requires an apology, then I'm in trouble,' I say with a sigh. When Maya barely reacts to that, I bump my shoulder against hers. I do it so she stops miserably staring at the floor. What I don't expect is that spark of electricity that the moment's touch sends through me.

Maya finally looks at me, but there's no humour in her eyes. 'You don't have to do this, you don't have to be here. You don't . . . owe me anything.'

'If I didn't want to be here, I wouldn't be,' I say. 'And if you want me to leave, just say the word.'

Maya doesn't look away and neither do I. She parts her lips, but initially all that escapes from them is a sigh.

'I don't want you to leave.' Her words make my pulse race, but I try not to read anything into that.

'So, you want to tell me what's wrong?' I ask.

She sighs again. 'I don't even know where to begin.'

'The start is usually a good place,' I offer.

At least that gets a smile out of her, even if it's fleeting.

'When I was in there, in that room, it felt like . . . the walls were closing in on me or something. And it felt like everyone was looking at me and talking about me, and like it was inescapable, their judgement.'

I frown. 'OK . . . you know that none of those things were happening, right?'

'Some of them were.' She shakes her head like she's trying to clear her mind of the things she heard said. 'You know what the press have been saying about me. Everyone knows. And I'm expected to go up there and say, "Hey, it's great to be a woman in football," so that we can raise money for all these youth clubs. But the truth is, it kind of sucks sometimes, especially if you're me. You have all these hopes and expectations, but all people see is what they expect you to be. You're brown, so you're not good enough, so you're aggressive and angry; you're written off. You can be twice as good as everyone else, but it feels like you're still behind. And your teammates, they don't understand, even though they see it all. They keep saying, "It's fine, it'll blow over, they say stuff about me too." But not this stuff, not this constantly. It chips away at you until, until . . .' Maya's eyes have filled with tears, her voice wavers, her lips tremble. She sniffles, rubbing at her face until her mascara and eyeliner are smudged.

'Until you decide to give up?' I finish for her.

'Yes,' she says softly. 'And of course you'd get it, you're the only person who would. You're the only person who ever did.'

My insides twist at her words – with guilt, anger, remorse? I'm not even sure what it is I feel anymore. Because she's wrong – I didn't get it. Not until now anyway. This must have been why she came back, why she retired. I'd never even thought for a second that she wasn't living some glamorous life, but here Maya is in front of me. Telling me a truth that I haven't even considered.

'Have you tried telling everyone else?'

Maya turns to look at me in bafflement. 'Yes, of course I have. But they don't . . . they think they get it, but they don't. It's not the same, you know that. And now I have to go up and speak about women in football, as if my reality is not my reality.'

'So then don't.'

'But I have to. I told everyone that I would.'

I shake my head since she clearly doesn't understand

what I'm saying. 'I mean, don't pretend that your reality isn't your reality. You were asked to speak, not sugarcoat or lie. Be honest. Not everybody gets an opportunity to speak in front of a group of people who are so entrenched in this field and say what they have to say.'

'But . . . I can't,' Maya says, though it looks like she's seriously considering it.

'Why not? What are they going to do? Kick you off the team that you already quit? Or maybe speak about you in the press, even more than they already do? Maybe tell people that you're difficult to work with, in the same way that they already have been?'

'I don't know.' Maya still seems hesitant, like she really thinks she still has more left to lose.

I sigh. 'You're Maya bloody Alam. If anyone can do this, it's you.'

And my words seem to have the desired effect. Her face becomes more resolute and she scrunches her eyebrows together as if in thought. The motion is so familiar to me that I have to look away. It makes me remember that jolt of electricity that passed between us just minutes ago. It makes me remember our past, and the fact that the two of us don't just get to exist in this moment – that we have a history that I can't shake, no matter how much I want to.

'Yeah. You're right. I don't have anything to lose.' Maya nods. She wipes away the remnants of her tears and tries to stand up, stumbling and nearly toppling over on me. I take hold of her shoulders, helping her balance herself. And she looks up, meeting my gaze once more. There's that electricity passing between us again, charging the air.

I pull away, ignoring it, and clear my throat. 'Are you OK?'

'Yes,' Maya says, taking a deep breath. 'And I'm ready to do this.'

After fixing her make-up in the mirror, Maya has her game face on, even if she's wearing heels and a dress instead of a football kit. I follow her as she marches back into the events hall, trying not to breathe in the earthy scent of her, even though it's a little overwhelming and heady.

The speeches have already started when we arrive. A woman in a shimmery black dress speaks about the difficulties of getting women into football and then getting the funding to sustain them. Her eyes land on Maya and she brightens, as if she was just waiting for Maya to make her appearance.

'Which really is the perfect segue into announcing our next speaker. She's someone who has absolutely killed it on the football pitch, and even my team have taken a beating from her.' At this, the crowd bursts into an appropriate titter of laughter. 'You all may know her as the former striker for the Vikings. Let's have a round of applause for Maya Alam!'

Maya doesn't march towards the stage, though. Instead, she turns to look at me as the room breaks out into applause. It's almost like she needs me to go up, and that makes me feel a confusing jumble of emotions that I can't even begin to decipher. I offer her an encouraging smile, reach forward and squeeze her hands. That simple touch sends jolts of electricity through me. But it must be enough for Maya, because she takes a breath, smiles back and turns to weave through the crowd.

She makes her way up to the podium, her smile still on, if a little practised.

'Hi, everyone, and thanks, Nina, for asking me to be

here today,' Maya says, her voice a little shaky as she begins. She takes another breath and meets my gaze even through the throngs of people, before looking away again. 'You know, I want nothing more than to speak today about how great women's football is and how many strides we've made, but . . . I don't feel like that would be honest. Women's football *is* great, and we *have* made strides, but that doesn't mean that things aren't difficult – haven't been difficult. I mean, there are all the usual things that we all know about: how we're underfunded, how we're paid less than the men. How, no matter how many matches we win or how many viewers we draw, we're never taken seriously. But there are other things too. Some of you – maybe all of you – know that I recently made the decision to quit the Vikings, and retire from football. And there are so many rumours going around about why I made that decision.'

Maya looks at me once more, and I give her an encouraging nod. I'm barely aware of the fact that there are other people here. It feels like only me and Maya, our gazes meeting across the room. And my chest tightens with every word that she speaks. It almost feels like she's speaking directly to me. Like she's telling me about how things have been for her, now that I'm finally being forced to listen.

'Everyone tells me that I should ignore the things in the papers, but it's strange that nobody asks me about why they say those things, or why they make up lies about me. They don't ask me if I'm OK after everything that's happened, if I'm OK after making the difficult decision to leave football – something that's always been important to me, that's been my life for the past nine years. For longer, probably. And the truth is that it's hard to be a woman of colour in football. Ever since I started playing professionally, I feel like I've been called things like a bully and aggressive more than I ever have in my life. The double standard became clear to me from my first few months playing. One of my teammates got into a screaming match with the captain of a rival team after my fifth match and she was celebrated online for her actions, while the same people seemed to take glee in criticising every single thing I did on the pitch. At times, it felt relentless, inescapable. Even now, it seems like I can't escape it.

'My teammates would be celebrated on the field, while there would be jeers about me. I watched so many of my teammates become hot commodities within women's football; they would move up in the world quickly, being traded between teams as they improved. But it felt that no matter how well *I* did, nobody seemed to see me as worthy. The more opportunities they got, the more I was passed over for. Maybe if it was just the press, or the crowds, or the ignorant teammates, I could have taken it. But it was everything all together, and at some point I realised that it always would be. It felt like I was fighting an uphill battle since I started, and every time I improved, every time I scored a winning goal, or helped us win a championship, I thought *surely* they'll see me now for who I am, for what I can bring to this team, to women's football. But . . . it was as if the goalposts were always being moved. And, eventually, I realised that it would always be that way. And I wasn't sure if I wanted to keep fighting. I wasn't sure if I had it in me.'

I've avoided everything to do with Maya for the past nine years, so it's not a surprise that I missed so much of this. And, clearly, it has affected her in ways that I can only ever imagine.

But there's still a part of me starkly aware of the fact that

Maya and I are in different positions at this fundraiser. She's giving a speech, while I'm dressed in a server's uniform. Maybe neither of us quite belongs, but it's in drastically different ways. I can't help the thread of envy still burrowed inside me.

As Maya finishes up her speech, there's stunned silence in the room for a moment, before the place breaks up into thunderous applause. She's spoken well, I'm not surprised that the people here connected with it. Maybe now, Maya will finally feel understood. She breaks out into a smile on stage too, but I can't look at her anymore.

I duck through the crowd, and back into the kitchens. The event will come to a close soon, so most of the trays have already been circulated. Staff are busy washing up and reorganising.

I think for a moment about finding Jana and making up an excuse to leave. I could feign sickness, and with the event so close to being over, maybe she won't even be too angry about it. But I discard that thought as soon as it comes. This isn't the fundraiser for women's football; it's just a kitchen and this is just a job.

I roll up my sleeves, and get busy.

Chapter 20

Maya

It's a strange feeling going from keeping all of my feelings bottled up inside of me for the past few years to suddenly being pressed for more by everyone. The few reporters at the event are eager to score exclusive interviews about the real reason that I quit the Vikings, and I'm torn over allowing them to share my story after everything they've been writing about me. The most surprising thing is when Erica Hadley strolls up to me, handing me her card as if I don't know exactly who she is.

'I'd love to interview you on *The Warm Up*,' she says. 'Give me a call sometime.'

I take the card from her hand, at a loss for what to say. I half want to challenge her for all the stories she's run on me over the past few months – the ones that had never held back on besmirching me and spreading unfounded rumours about my 'attitude'. But Erica disappears back into the crowd before I've mustered the courage to say anything.

Taking a deep breath, I look around the room, trying to spot Dina. I lost sight of her sometime during my speech, and even now she's nowhere to be found. There's a hollowness in my chest at the thought of her being gone.

'You were amazing, Maya!' Nina says, appearing over my shoulder. She's beaming from ear to ear. 'I knew that things were difficult for you, but I had *no* idea. I just know that everything you said will stay in people's minds for a long time. I know it's definitely made me re-evaluate a lot of things.'

'Thanks, Nina. And thank you for letting me speak here. After I retired, I . . . kind of felt like I had to say goodbye to football in every way. I thought maybe there was no place for me in a space like this.'

Nina's eyes widen. 'Maya . . . there will always be space for you here. I think you're exactly the kind of voice that we've been missing in football. You're an amazing player, and it's our loss that you've retired. That you felt like you had to.'

The genuineness in Nina's voice tugs at my heart, makes tears pinprick on the edges of my eyes. I blink to keep the tears from falling, because that doesn't seem like a great way to end the night. I doubt that Nina wants to be comforting a tearful ex-football player either.

'That means a lot,' I say instead, meaning it with my whole heart.

Nina pulls me into a hug and soon we're saying our goodbyes. But just as I'm about to turn and leave, I pause, calling out to Nina one last time.

'The caterers. Have they already left?'

Nina's eyebrows shoot up, like that was a question she wasn't expecting. 'I'm not sure. They might still be in the kitchens. Why?'

'I just . . . I ran into that server earlier and I feel bad. I wanted to, um, apologise,' I say.

Nina smiles. 'If only the press could see you now, huh?'

'I'm sure they'd find a way to turn it around on me.'

Nina lets out a small laugh. 'They are very good at that.'

She points me towards the double doors leading into the kitchen, before waving goodbye.

I hesitate in front of the doors. I can hear sounds coming from inside: talking and laughing, the clatter of plates and glasses and cutlery. If Dina is in here, would she really want to see me now? But after what she's done for me, it doesn't feel right to leave without saying anything either. Especially since she disappeared in the middle of my speech.

Hesitantly, I push the door open. Compared to the quiet of the events hall now, the kitchens are utter chaos. There are servers everywhere; people rushing to and fro. I almost get knocked down by someone carrying a stack of dirty dishes as soon as I enter, only managing to swerve to avoid collision at the last second.

'You're not supposed to be back here,' a woman says from beside me. She's carrying a clipboard and pins me with a small frown. 'The exit is on the other side. The double doors there.'

She must really think I'm a dolt who can't tell the kitchen from the exit.

'Sorry . . . I was looking for one of your servers,' I say. 'She, um, she was really great. I just wanted to pass on my thanks.'

'To one of the servers?' The woman narrows her eyes at me. Like she can't possibly imagine what a server needed to have done in order to garner a thanks from me.

'Yes. Her name was Dina Chowdhury, and I . . . knocked into her, but she was so great about it. I just wanted to—'

The woman holds up a hand to silence me, scanning her clipboard. She taps on it with her pen, before her eyes flick up to me once more. 'Yes, I have a Dina here. She's new. I'll make sure to pass on your message. But I really can't have you here. Everybody's busy working.'

She steps forward and holds open the double doors, waving me out. I take one last look around the kitchen, hoping to spot Dina. But when I don't, I'm forced to admit defeat.

I step outside and towards the other side of the events hall, spotting Dina's familiar figure in the distance. She's at the drinks table on the edge of the hall, collecting used glasses and throwing bottles into a rubbish bag. I feel a tug in my heart. What was it Dina said to me? That she had been hating every moment of her life, trying to make ends meet. That was about working in finance, but I doubt that working as a server is part of her dream life either. I remember when we were young and bright-eyed with hopes for the future. We traded these grand dreams of being star football players. When we went to the football museum in Madrid for our school trip, we even talked about how one day our football shirts would be displayed there, because that's how successful we would be.

But it seems that neither of our dreams were meant to be.

'Hey,' I say hesitantly as I approach Dina.

She jumps a little, before turning towards me. She looks more surprised to see me now than she did when I ran into her.

'What are you still doing here? I thought everybody had left.'

'I was looking for you. I think I spoke to your boss, in the kitchen.'

Dina frowns, before turning back and throwing a bunch of bottles into the rubbish bag. I dive towards the other side of the table and begin collecting dirty glasses and bottles too.

'You don't have to do that,' Dina says. Her voice is grim, and she doesn't look at me. I can't tell what she's thinking. Whatever moment we had before, where I actually opened up to her, where she seemed like she still cared about me, seems to have passed swiftly.

Maybe that realisation should deter me from trying with Dina now, but I'm not sure if I can stop. It felt like there was still something between us earlier, and I'm not willing to give up on that so fast.

'I just . . . wanted to say thank you.'

Dina pauses in her work and her eyes snap towards me. 'For what?'

'For helping me earlier. I would never have been able to go up to that podium and speak if it weren't for you. I probably would have just had my panic attack and cried in the bathroom and gone home. And Nina would have been down a speaker, and I would have felt . . . well, humiliated.'

'You would have figured it out, even without me.'

I shake my head. 'No. I don't think I would have. I needed someone to say the things that you did. I needed . . . you. You were the only one who could push me in that way. The only one who understood me about so many things.'

Dina seems to study me, her eyes roving over me as if she's looking for something, but I don't know what it is. 'I didn't know things were so difficult for you,' she finally says. 'I'm sorry that you've had to deal with so much.'

'Yeah, it's been . . . It hasn't been easy.'

Dina sighs. 'I thought you were living some dream life, that you were about to announce that you'd be playing at the next World Cup or something.' Dina almost seems shamefaced as she admits it, but I feel a smile tug at me. While others in the football world overlooked me, Dina always saw something in me. Even if it was tainted with envy.

'I wish.' I toss some empty bottles into the bag. They land with a loud clink.

'Maybe now that people are finally hearing your side of the story, things will change,' Dina says.

'Maybe. I wouldn't hold my breath.'

I reach for some of the empty glasses scattered around the table at the same time that Dina does. I freeze as our fingers brush, and fresh goosebumps erupt across my skin. Our eyes lock for just a moment, across the table. The dark brown of her irises pulling me in. My cheeks flush.

Then, all too soon, Dina looks away. I pull my hand aside and watch as Dina ducks her head, gathering the glasses and lining them up on a tray to take back to the kitchen.

'Thanks,' Dina mumbles, her voice soft. 'You didn't have to help me with this.'

'I wanted to. I can help with the other—'

Dina cuts me off with a shake of her head. 'Jana would probably kill me if she saw a guest helping me clean up, and I kind of need this job. The assistant coach position is only part-time, and this job pays better than the other catering gigs I've been doing.'

This is the most Dina has given me since I came back, and there's a part of me that's bursting with questions to ask her. About her job in finance that she must have quit, her other catering jobs, about what her life has been like for the past nine years. The curiosity of it all gnaws at me, but I simply nod.

'Yeah, sorry.'

'It's OK.' Dina offers me a smile that quickens my pulse. 'By the way, I talked to Jade. She said she got in touch with Laila.'

'Really?' Dina has come through for me twice now, in ways that I couldn't have even imagined. 'Thank you.'

'You should thank Jade, not me,' she says. 'And wait until she actually does something to help Laila out. For all we know, they're at each other's throats.'

'I can definitely see that,' I say with a chuckle.

A door squeaks on the other side of the hall, and Dina freezes for a moment, her smile dropping.

'I should go, right? Before your boss catches me here,' I say.

'Probably . . . I'll see you around?' Dina says it like she hopes that will be the case, but I don't know if I'm just reading my own hopes into her words.

'Yeah. See you.'

I turn around and head out of the double doors, feeling lighter than I have in a long time.

All this time, I've thought that Dina hated me with every fibre of her being, but now I wonder if there's still some part of her that cares about me. It may be a part that's buried down deep inside of her, but maybe, just maybe, it exists. And maybe there's a chance that the two of us could go back to what we once used to be.

Chapter 21

Maya

Thirteen years ago
Ms Nichols checks her watch, and then her register. Not that she needs to. Not that any of us need to. We *all* know who's missing from our group: Dina. Once again, she's late. Except, this time, it's not just for class, it's for our once-in-a-lifetime trip to Spain. The one that we've been counting down the days to for what feels like forever. And now that it's finally here, we're all waiting just inside the airport for Dina to show up.

'Who's friends with Dina? Can you call her and see if she's almost here?' Ms Nichols asks, eagerly looking around for people's hands to shoot up. I look around too, but everyone looks as annoyed as I feel. Which actually makes me feel a little less annoyed. It also makes me feel a pinprick of guilt. Nobody raised their hands because Dina doesn't really have many friends – maybe not any. She's always at the outskirts of everything. Sure, there are a few girls that she hangs out with here and there, but she doesn't have her group, like me, Nadine and Gwen.

'Maybe if she had friends she'd actually show up to things on time,' Gwen says, a little too snidely for my liking. I can't even say anything because I would have said the same thing only moments ago.

Thankfully, a car pulls up outside just then, and Dina's familiar figure climbs out of the passenger seat. Followed by her older brother, Deen. From the driver's side, her dad emerges, and all three of them rush towards the entrance.

I heave a sigh of relief. It isn't that we are massively delayed. Ms Nichols has made a schedule that has accounted for the fact that there are thirty of us going on this trip, which means that things won't always be running smoothly.

Dina doesn't immediately run towards us though, instead she has an entire, rambling conversation with her dad, before she finally makes her way over. Her face is a little flushed, and I don't know if it's from running from her dad and brother towards us, or embarrassment. Maybe a little bit of both.

'You've finally made it, Dina,' Ms Nichols says. She sounds a little chiding, and Dina doesn't respond. That niggling feeling of guilt grows in me, even though I haven't done anything.

We get through security and to our gate, and by the time we're boarding our plane an hour later, my strange sense of guilt has faded away. When I get to my seat and see Dina seated next to me, I expect to feel annoyed. But I don't. I stuff my backpack underneath the seat in front of me and sit down, buckling my seat belt. Dina gives me a scathing look before turning to stare out of the window.

Her hand grips the handrest with a little too much intensity, nails digging into the foam so hard that I'm surprised she hasn't torn into the handrest.

'Are you OK?' I find myself asking, against my better judgement.

'Fine.' Dina doesn't even turn to look at me.

Rolling my eyes, I sit back. I shouldn't have asked. What else did I expect from Dina?

But as the plane starts to move, Dina seems more on edge. Her grip on the handrest tightens — if that's even possible — and her legs go up and down, like a nervous tic.

'Is it your first time flying?' I ask.

'That's none of your business.' And that's Dina's way of saying *yes*.

'Don't be nervous. More people die from car crashes every year than plane accidents, so . . . you really have nothing to worry about.'

Dina finally turns to me. 'You really think that's helpful? And I'm not nervous. I didn't even say it was my first time flying.'

'I'm just trying to help.'

'Well, don't.'

I huff, crossing my arms over my chest as the plane turns into the runway and slowly starts picking up speed. It's not a big plane, which means that I can feel the rumble of the engine alongside my own heartbeat. Beside me, Dina closes her eyes, and I can sense her breathing becoming shallower. She's definitely not doing a very good job of pretending not to be nervous.

I study her closed eyes, the shallowness of her breath. This is maybe the only time I've seen her actually look vulnerable. Like for this one moment in time, she's let some of her walls down. Looking at her like this, my heart seems to still. I haven't quite admitted it to myself before, but when Dina isn't scowling at me and trying to beat me at anything and everything, she's really quite beautiful.

Gently, I place my hand over hers, fitting my fingers into the gaps in hers. Her eyes fly open, but I turn away before she can look at me. I fully expect that she'll pull away from me, grumbling about how she can take care of herself. But she doesn't. Our hands stay like that as the flight takes off and the ground gives way from underneath us. My stomach lurches, and I'm not sure if it's because of Dina squeezing my hands with hers, or because of the plane taking off.

'How come you're always late to class?'

'What?' Dina asks through gritted teeth.

'If you talk, it'll make the flying easier.'

'*This* is what you want to talk about?'

I shrug. 'I'm just curious.'

Dina glances out of the window, seems a little terrified to see a tiny, sprawling London underneath and quickly turns away. She takes a deep breath.

'My dad, he works all the time.'

'What?' I don't know if that's just information she's offering to change the subject. Because that's what it feels like.

'He has a restaurant. It's open until late, and he's there even later. It's not doing so well, I don't think, so he's stressed about that and he's tired in the mornings. It's difficult to get him up and drive me to school. So I'm late sometimes,' Dina explains.

'What about your mum?'

'What about her?' Dina frowns.

'Can't she drive you?'

Dina shakes her head. 'She works a lot. She's a nurse, she's always doing night shifts and double shifts, and then she comes home and helps with the restaurant in whatever capacity she can. She's even more tired than my dad most of the time.'

Dina glances at me with a flicker of worry in her eyes, like she's afraid she's revealed a little too much of herself.

But I'm finally starting to understand Dina, for the first time since we met. All this time, I thought she was someone who just got away with stuff that the rest of us would never be able to. That she had everything come easy to her. In reality, it's the exact opposite. She's just good at hiding her insecurities. Really good at it.

'I like the food at your dad's restaurant.'

Dina raises an eyebrow. 'You've had food there?'

'My parents have ordered from there a couple of times.' I shrug. 'And they've even invited your parents around for dawats, they said. But your parents say they're always busy.' After the first couple of times they turned down the invite, Ma and Baba started complaining about how Dina's mum and dad must think they're too good for us, since they never wanted to come around and they never invited us around either. Dawats are a big part of Bengali culture, and turning down so many invites is definitely a huge social faux pas.

'I mean . . . they *are* always busy,' Dina says, a little defensively.

'I didn't know that. My parents didn't either. Your mum and dad just say they're busy, they don't explain any of the other stuff.'

'What are they supposed to say? That they have to work 24/7 to make ends meet?' Dina snaps.

I slink back in my seat, not quite wanting to look Dina in the eyes. All this time, I really thought she believed she was above the rest of us. In reality, she was just trying to get by.

'No . . . sorry. We just didn't know.'

Silence washes over us for a few minutes. Even through the rumbling of the plane, and the sounds of all the people around us, the silence between the two of us feels heavy.

'You can get a lift with us sometime if you want,' I finally offer.

Dina turns to me with a frown. 'What?'

'I'm pretty sure your place is on the way to school. My mum could pick you up.'

'I don't need your charity,' Dina grumbles, finally pulling her hand away from mine. I'd got used to the warmth of her fingers in mine. Our hands seemed to fit together a little too perfectly. I try not to let on how unsettled I suddenly feel without her touch as I pull my hand away from the armrest too.

'Giving you a lift is not charity. I'm just offering. You don't *have* to accept. We'd be going that way anyway.' I try to sound casual about it.

'I'll think about it,' Dina says, and I know it's probably the most I'll get from her right now.

Things are different between me and Dina in Madrid. Maybe it's the fact that we're away from home. Or maybe it's the conversation we had on the plane, but we don't bicker over everything. In fact, we barely even speak to each other. It doesn't help that every time I so much as look at Dina, I feel my heart start to beat faster and my skin prickle with heat.

Even Gwen and Nadine pick up on the weirdness, though thankfully they don't ask too many questions. Because if they did, I would probably have to tell them the truth. And the truth is that, against all the odds, I'm pretty sure that I've developed a crush on Dina. I want to blame it on the heat of Madrid, or the overexertion of walking across the city in the ceaseless sunshine, but if I'm being honest with myself, my feelings for Dina probably started way before this trip. But it's difficult to have feelings for someone that you find just a little bit intolerable. Though with Dina's new revelations on the plane, she seems softer, more vulnerable. Herself, in a way that she never has before. Like I'm finally seeing Dina as a full person; not just the prickly, ever-tardy girl with the wrong school uniform and the haughty attitude.

Still, it's not like I can do much about my crush. I already know that there's no universe where Dina returns my feelings. She tries to one-up me still whenever Ms Nichols asks a question about Madrid, and utilises her Spanish conversational skills at every opportunity, always followed by a cursory glance at me, like she's challenging me to try to show her up. For once, I don't.

After two days of sightseeing, we get a free day to ourselves to do whatever we want. Nadine and Gwen are desperate to hit the shops, but I've already got my outing planned. So I say goodbye to them at the hotel lobby and make my way to the football museum that Jen told our team about a couple of days ago. It feels nice to be away from Ms Nichols's watchful gaze.

I queue up in line to get my tickets when a familiar voice makes my stomach drop.

'What are you doing here?' I turn around to find Dina a few people behind me in the queue. I should have known she would come here.

'Same thing as you, I'm guessing,' I say, trying not to look at her too directly.

'I didn't think this would be your thing,' Dina says.

'Because we're not on the same football team,' I reply drily.

She frowns. 'Well . . . fine, but if you're going to be in there, don't bother me.'

'Fine, as long as you don't bother me either.' I was already planning on trying to stay out of her way anyway. But once we get into the museum, the two of us constantly run into each other: we arrive at the display for Messi's original jersey at the exact same time, frowning at each other across the clear display case, and somehow, we find ourselves alone in the audiovisual room as they talk us through the various World Cups. I can barely pay attention because I'm a little too busy studying Dina. She's wearing a dark green T-shirt and jeans, her hair pulled up in a short ponytail, out of her deep brown eyes. Eyes that seem to keep flickering towards me, making me turn away and pretend to be concentrating on the audio narrator. One thing I do pick up on is the fact that the narrator has told us about five different men's world cups, but absolutely nothing about any women's world cups.

'Isn't it ridiculous that this is an entire museum about football, but there's not a single thing about women's football?' I blurt out, finally looking at Dina properly. Dina takes so long to respond that I'm sure she's going to pretend that she didn't hear my question at all and that'll be that.

But then she says, 'Right?' with so much indignation that it feels like we're on exactly the same page. It makes my heart leap to my throat. 'I mean, it's like women's football doesn't even exist. An entire movie about world cups, but not a single video about the women's World Cup?'

'And all of these legendary players, but not even a mention of a female player!' I say, throwing my hands up. 'Where is Marta's jersey, or any mention of Homare Sawa's legendary hat trick at the last World Cup?'

'You'd think that women didn't even play football,' Dina grumbles.

'I really thought there'd be . . . something. Especially since Jen recommended it.'

'I like the shirt room,' Dina admits. 'I mean, it's cool to see all of these players and their shirts. I bet when they started playing most of them had no idea how much they'd be admired around the whole world.'

'Yeah, I bet they couldn't imagine something they wore being in a museum one day,' I add.

'Being gawked at by teenaged football fans,' Dina says with a smile that makes my stomach do somersaults. Dina barely ever smiles, which means that when she does, it lights up her whole face.

'Do you . . . want to get some food?' I ask, trying to sound as casual as I can. 'I'm starving.'

Dina stares at me for what feels like a full minute, like she can hardly believe I've asked that question. I can hardly believe it either. I'm preparing for her to turn me down with one of her signature scowls.

But then she says, 'Um . . . OK. Sure.'

And I feel my stomach twist again. But not with hunger this time.

We end up buying calamari sandwiches from a food truck and eating in a nearby park. I scarf mine down in a matter of minutes, not sure if it's the hunger or the fact that I'm so nervous I needed something to do. But then I'm left to fill the time with conversation as Dina nibbles at her sandwich slowly and carefully. I try not to stare at her lips the whole time, which is easier said than done.

Surprisingly, our conversation doesn't veer off into an argument. We talk about football, the museum, our team, Jen. Everything and anything. It feels like a conversation between friends. Conversations that we've been bottling up all this time that we've been needlessly competing against each other.

'Are you being nice to me because of what I told you on the plane?' Dina suddenly blurts out when the two of us are on our way back to the hotel.

I can only blink at her, taken aback. I wonder if this is what's been running through her mind all this time. I remember what she said on the plane: that she didn't want my charity.

'No,' I say decisively, not stopping in my tracks.

Dina frowns. 'Then why are we suddenly not fighting?'

I shrug. 'Because we realised how much we have in common.'

'Liking football is the bridge between our rivalry?' Dina asks.

'Maybe. Can't it be?' I ask.

Dina looks at me closely, like she's thinking about it. It feels like she's looking through me, seeing every part of me. It makes heat flood through me.

'I guess. As long as you admit that I'm better at football than you,' Dina finally says. Normally, that would elicit a glare from me, but Dina says it so playfully, so – well – flirtatiously that it just makes me laugh.

'Yeah, I'll admit that when you admit I'm smarter than you,' I counter.

'Please. I knew way more about the history of Madrid during this entire trip *and* my Spanish is better than yours.' We're stopped in the middle of the street now, staring each other down. And I'm definitely not backing down from her challenge.

'I won the Spanish speech contest last year.'

'Yeah, but I'm the only one in our class who's managed

to have an entire conversation in Spanish with a native this entire trip.'

'I bet I can do that too!' I say.

'I would take that bet, any time, any day!' Dina says. I know she means it – and she'll hold me to it.

I smile at that, suddenly realising that the two of us have inched closer and closer to each other during this whole conversation. There's barely any space left between us. When Dina speaks, I can feel her breath on my skin, and I can smell the sharp, sweet scent of her.

'OK, let's bet on it,' I say.

Dina takes a breath, and I can see it up close. The quiver of her lips, the soft sound of it. She's staring at me the same as I'm staring at her. And I think that she'll step away from me, put some distance between us. But she doesn't. It's just the two of us on this street, the world melting away, like it doesn't even exist.

And then, without even thinking about it, I lean forward, my eyes flickering up to Dina's for only a moment. Asking her for permission. She leans forward too and my heart leaps up, twists and turns. My stomach tumbles, doing more somersaults than I ever thought was possible. Our lips meet somewhere in the middle and just like that, Dina and I are kissing.

Never in a million years would I have thought that this is how our trip to Madrid would end.

Chapter 22

Dina

Eleven days to the match
The Divas are on a streak. Unfortunately, it's a losing streak.

Since agreeing to the match with Maya's team, we've played three teams, and have even increased our weekly practise sessions. The team has been getting better with every match. Today, they were tied with the other team until the second half of the match, when things fell apart. It's the best they've done so far, and I'm proud of them, even if there is that thread of worry that they will never be good enough to beat Maya's team.

Since we set up this match between us, I've been thinking about Maya as this person I have to beat. An obstacle in my way. And this match as my chance to show her once and for all what I am capable of. But the fundraiser has changed things. I'm now thinking of her as *Maya*, the girl I used to date, who was my first love, who betrayed me and everything that we were. Who I might still have feelings for.

It didn't help that I came home from the fundraiser to look Maya up, trying to find the truth of what she had confessed to me. For the first time, I'd understood what she must have been going through over the past few years. I started noticing the snide tones of the articles about her, the dismissiveness of videos. And even when Maya was being lauded with praise, the comments below were tarnishing her; calling her names and telling her that she was less capable than the other players. Just a few minutes of reading those comments was enough to make my blood boil.

All of these thoughts are swirling around my brain when I enter the restaurant after losing yet another match.

Deen is waiting for me at one of the tables, studying the place intensely. He invited me over because he said he wanted my opinions on some things. Since Ma still refuses to help with renovations at the restaurant, I've been Deen's one and only confidante when it comes to what he wants to do with the place.

'I feel like I can already see it,' Deen says when I approach his table. He doesn't greet me, doesn't even turn to look at me.

I slump down on the chair next to his. 'What can you see?'

'The way it's going to look after a renovation. We'll get new tables and chairs, and we'll have a big, fancy sign up on that wall' – he nods to where he's looking – 'that'll say the restaurant's new name. Nobody'll even know what this place used to be, and we can have a relaunch to celebrate the new place.'

'You're going to rename it?' I ask. I'm fully onboard with all of Deen's renovation plans, I always have been, but the restaurant's name is something that Baba picked out: Ekushey. If you translate it literally, it just means twenty-first, but in reality, it means the day we honour the martyrs of the Bengali language movement: the twenty-first of February. After our victory day, it's probably the most celebrated occasion for Bengali people. Baba lost one of his uncles on that day; he had more reason than many to want to commemorate it and so he had, in the form of this place. His dreams; for his uncle and for his people.

'I know the name meant a lot to Baba . . .' Deen says slowly, carefully. 'But people don't know what it means unless they're Bengali. I thought something more catchy would help attract people, you know? Maybe something like Calcutta Kitchen.'

'We're from Bangladesh, not West Bengal,' I point out drily.

'You know what I mean,' Deen says. 'Besides, Indian restaurants do better than Bengali restaurants. Maybe that's what the rebrand needs to be.'

'Hm,' is all I say, because while I get what Deen is trying to do, I don't know if I want him to do those things. It feels like he's stomping all over Baba's dreams.

Deen finally turns to me with a frown. '*Hm*? What is that supposed to mean?'

'Just hm,' I say.

'Since when do you reserve your opinion from me?'

'I'm not reserving my opinion, I'm just . . . thinking about it.'

Deen clearly doesn't believe that I'm taking my time to think about it, but he still humours me, talking me through his vision for the restaurant. How he would redecorate, what the new menu would look like, the dishes that he would have on it.

'Is this really what you want?' I ask finally, once he's done.

'Yeah, obviously. Aren't you the one who talked me into it?'

'I talked you into doing something with the restaurant, not *this* specifically. It's just that this is your chance to make this place what *you* want it to be. Not what Baba dreamt of, or what Ma wants to maintain it as. But, also, not what other people want, or what you think they want,' I say. 'Your food is good, Deen. Some of the best food ever, you know that. So make this place your vision. Not someone else's. And if that includes changing the name and calling it an Indian restaurant, then OK, I'll support you. But if that's not what you want, don't throw away this opportunity.'

I feel better after saying my piece.

Deen sighs and sits back on his chair. 'Yeah, you're right. I don't know. I was doing all of this research into the restaurant business, and I feel like I got caught up in this idea of wanting this place to be a success. I mean, I *do* want this place to be success, but maybe . . . that doesn't mean I have to take away from what makes it special.'

'I agree.' I give him an encouraging pat on the shoulder. 'Instead, think about all of the things we've talked about in the past. All of the wild ideas we've had for this place.'

'Right, they never involved changing the name or advertising ourselves as not being Bangladeshi. Just being . . . more,' Deen says. He has a faraway look in his eyes and I know that he's already envisioning something – the dreams that he's told me about for the past few years. I can see them too, unfolding in front of me in this restaurant. I want to have hope for my brother that this place will be successful soon, that it will be brimming with customers. But even if that doesn't happen, I'll still be proud of him for giving his dream his best shot, and not compromising.

'I might need to dip into my savings to do everything that needs to be done,' Deen says after a moment. He's always been scrupulous with his money, something that I would never have expected from him. But after Baba passed away, Deen was stuck with the responsibility for what felt like everything, and it made him more careful. Far from the kid in school who got detention every other day and almost got suspended on more than a few occasions.

'It'll be worth it,' I say encouragingly. 'And whatever happens, I'll be here with you. Just tell me what I need to do and I'll do it.'

Deen gives me a smile. 'So, how are things going with the team?'

I groan. That's the last thing I want to talk about.

'Another loss, huh?' Deen asks.

'We got closer this time,' I say. 'I'm proud of them, but I just wish they could magically become superstar footballers overnight.'

'They'll get there eventually.' And I know Deen is right, I just worry that eventually might be too late for the match against Westbrook – which will send a whole slew of disappointment through everyone on the team. There's less than two weeks left until the match, and we still have a long way to go until we're ready to beat them.

'You had that catering job Aisha got you this week, right? How did that go?'

'It was fine.' I shrug. I haven't told Deen about the fundraiser, running into Maya there and what transpired between us. Because I know that he will read more into it than he should, give me hope about something that I don't even want to think about.

'Just fine?' he probes.

'It was a job. I was a server. That was it.'

'What was the event?'

'It was boring, do you really want to hear about it?' I ask the question with a roll of my eyes, but clearly Deen isn't buying my lies.

'You're being weird about it, so yeah, I want to hear about it. Was it for something weird? Was it like . . . a furry convention or something?' Deen grins.

'No, it wasn't a *furry* convention. It was . . . a fundraiser.'

Deen keeps looking at me expectantly, so I know I have to say more.

'For . . . women in football.'

'Seriously?'

'Yeah. I know. Just my luck, right?'

I expect Deen to drop it at that, but he tilts his head to the side and studies me. 'And what else?'

'What do you mean?'

'*Dina.*'

'I think you and I are too close. It's not very healthy.'

Deen gives me a poke in the ribs and I pull away from him, groaning.

'OK, OK. Maya was there.'

'Really?' Deen's eyebrows shoot up. 'So . . . did you guys talk?'

'Why would you think that?'

'Because the fundraiser happened a few days ago, and you haven't been talking my ear off about how much you hate Maya. You haven't even mentioned it.'

I guess I'm more of an open book than I thought.

I know that Deen isn't going to let up, so I spill about everything that happened. How she ran into me, how angry I was. Then, seeing her upset and following after her. Her panic attack and how I calmed her down. Her speech. And our conversation afterwards. The one proper conversation we've had in nine years that hasn't erupted into a fight. That felt like being back to the old us.

'Wow. So, what are you going to do?'

'What do you mean?'

'I mean . . . you guys actually had a conversation with each other. She even thanked you for helping her. You're not going to try to reach out to her? Talk to her again?' He's studying me a little too closely and I worry that he can see everything in my expression – my confusion, my desperation, my longing. But I don't even know what any of it means.

I would be lying if I said I hadn't thought about it. That I hadn't spent the last few days thinking about barely anything but Maya. I even asked Jen for her phone number, pretending I needed it to make arrangements for our match. But I haven't called or texted her. I'm not sure what it would look like to open up a line of communication with her again. I'm not sure how to be around Maya when I still feel angry about everything that has happened in the past.

'Look, Maya is . . . She's . . . We've always been . . .' I keep stopping and starting, trying to find the right words to describe things but coming up blank. But finally, it just spills out of me, like I've been holding it all in; a dam waiting to burst until this moment. 'Maya and I have always been complicated, but I obviously have thought about her over the past nine years. I've thought about her, like, every single day, no matter how many times I didn't want to think about her. And her being back is just . . . weird. But not even weird bad. It's just . . . I don't know. It feels like I finally have something now, you know? With the football competition and going up against her again. It feels right, like this is what I was missing in my life.'

Deen just shakes his head, chuckling like I've told him some kind of joke instead of spilling my heart out to him.

'None of this is funny,' I say angrily.

'Actually, it's all kind of hilarious. Dina, you and Maya have a pattern.'

'How can we have a pattern when we haven't seen each other for the past nine years?'

'Because it happened before. When the two of you were so obsessed with each other, all you could do was compete in whatever you could compete in. If it wasn't trying to outdo each other in your classes, it was trying to outdo each other on the football pitch. And now you're doing the same but with the teams that you're coaching. The writing is on the wall, Dina. You like her, she likes you. Now what are you going to do about it?'

And when Deen says it like that, it almost sounds that simple.

'But too much has happened between us. She . . . betrayed me. And she left,' I say.

'Overdramatic.' Deen gives me a pointed look. 'Dina, you can hold on to the past and refuse to forgive Maya, if that's what you want. And if it was, then I would support you. But I don't think that's what you want. Because you wouldn't have thought about her for the past nine years, or avoided anything to do with her during that time, if that was the case. Maya obviously means something to you – she meant something to you then, and she means something to you now.' He looks me square in the eye as he repeats his question again. 'Now, what are you going to do about it?'

And even though I don't want Deen to be right, I know that he is. I'm the one who is in the driver's seat and I have to do something.

I have to make a choice about Maya.

Chapter 23

Dina

Nine years ago
I have my eye on the ball, and I'm ready to take it from my opponent. I weave around some of the other players, feeling the rush of wind around me with every step. I step forward, my foot angled towards the ball, about to manoeuvre it right towards me.

And then suddenly I'm falling face first on the ground, and there's a searing pain running up my leg and all I see is red, red, red.

'Dina, Dina, are you OK?' Jen's face is suddenly in front of mine, concern etched on it.

'I'm, I'm . . .' I look down at my leg. It's bent a different way than it should be, and I can feel the ache, throbbing and burning. I close my eyes and shake my head. 'Shit. I don't think so.'

'OK, come on, let's get you to the school nurse.' Jen waves over Baba, who is on the touchline as he always is. He rushes over, his panic clear, and Maya appears right beside him, a twin expression on her face.

Jen and Baba put their arms around me and I try to balance myself with their help while trying my hardest to work through the pain that seems to be getting worse and worse with every passing second.

They help me all the way to the nurse's office, where they sit me down on the bed. Maya must have silently followed behind because she hovers in the doorway.

'What happened?' Nurse Gail asks, looking from me to Jen to Baba to Maya.

'Just an accident during football practice,' Jen says. She offers me a smile like she's trying to tell me that it's no big deal. But we both know it's a big deal. Next week, the under-18s league have organised for a scout from a professional team to watch us play. It's the last match of the season and Jen told me that the scouts were specifically interested in me, and that I could have a chance at a real team if I played well.

And now, I've somehow injured myself while practising for the school team.

Nurse Gail pulls up a chair near me and examines my leg carefully, but every time she touches me, a fresh wave of pain goes through me. I try not to wince, but it's difficult.

'Is she going to be OK?' Maya asks. She's hovering close to me, looking like she wants to reach out and soothe me, but she doesn't.

'She'll be fine,' Gail says. 'It's better than it looks, you're lucky.'

I certainly don't feel lucky with this excruciating pain. 'So, I'll be fine to play next week?'

Gail's expression drops. 'Next week? No, honey, you'll take a little longer than that to recover. It's a sprain; you'll need crutches for at least two weeks, probably three.'

'But I have an important match next week. I have to play,' I say, as if Nurse Gail can somehow magically heal my leg. I look to Baba, expecting him to say something about how I have to play too, but he just gives me an encouraging smile.

'Dina, you need to recover. That's more important than a match,' he says.

'But—'

Maya rests a hand on my shoulder, and I cut myself off. When I look at her, the deep brown of her eyes makes me feel a little calmer. She has a way of making me feel more at ease, less angry. Which is ironic considering she had been the source of my anger for so many years.

'Let's make sure you're OK. That's the most important thing right now. We can worry about the other stuff later.'

I want to worry about that stuff now, I want to make sure that I'm not going to miss my chance at my dream because of a stupid sprain. But I know that Maya is right. I'm not going to get anywhere by trying to argue my case in the nurse's office while wincing in pain.

'OK, yeah.' I sigh.

I'm on bedrest for the rest of the week, and I take it seriously. I'm hoping that if I don't use my bad leg at all, I'll be well enough to play by match time. But the game is approaching fast, and my leg isn't much better. It still hurts to put any pressure on it. No matter how much I wish for some kind of a miracle, there's no way that I can play, I know that.

'Jen said she told the scouts that you weren't playing,' Maya tells me when she comes over to visit me the day before the match. I try not to be hurt by this – it's what Jen should have done as soon as I was injured. She'd postponed because I'd asked her to, probably knowing full well that there was no way that I was going to be able to play.

'I guess that's it then.'

Maya frowns at the dejection on my face. 'Hey, it'll be

THE PERFECT MATCH

OK. I bet Jen can reschedule and they'll come and see you play another match. This isn't your only chance, I promise.' Maya obviously can't promise because she doesn't know what's going to happen. This feels like my only chance, especially since I rarely ever get chances anyway. But football has been like a lifeline from the beginning – something that could maybe change things for me. And this opportunity has felt like a start. Finally, a chance to prove myself, to try to achieve my dreams.

I should have expected that everything would come crashing down.

'Yeah, maybe,' I say.

Maya scoots closer to me from the end of the bed where she has been sitting. She brushes my hair away from my face, and even though it does nothing in reality, it calms me down a little. At least, no matter what happens, I have Maya here with me.

'Look, you don't even know what was going to happen with these scouts. I know you're sad about missing this opportunity, but there will be others,' Maya says. 'And you're like the best football player ever. Trust me, someone is going to scoop you up before long, and then the only place I'll ever see you is on my TV screen, killing it on the football pitch.'

I smile at Maya's faith in me. 'Please, you'll see me on that pitch when we're on competing teams.'

Maya's smile widens. 'Yeah, and I guess I'll have to beat you. Maybe I'll take pity on you and let you score a goal.'

I roll my eyes. It sounds silly to say it aloud, but I can almost imagine that life. Me and Maya both making it onto professional teams. We'd be like a football power couple.

I lean forward and plant a kiss on her lips, and she smiles against me for a moment.

'Thanks, Maya,' I say. 'You're right. There'll be more opportunities. For both of us.'

'I told you we'd be late,' I grumble to Deen as he turns the car into the car park. We've already missed half the match, thanks to my brother.

'Hey, I'm doing you a favour by driving you. You shouldn't even be here,' Deen says.

Technically, I'm still supposed to be on bedrest, but I didn't want to miss the match. The least I could do is come out here and support the team, and Maya. Especially when Maya has been making sure I've been taken care of since I got injured – both emotionally and physically.

'Just find a parking spot!' I say, not wanting to be any later than we already are.

Deen rolls his eyes, but quickly parks the car, before opening my door with my crutches in his hands. I take them when he offers them to me, and it takes a second for me to find my balance. I haven't had to use them much since I've mostly been in bed for the past week and so I'm still getting used to them.

'You need some help?' Deen asks, raising an eyebrow.

'I'm fine,' I say, hobbling towards the football pitch.

I hear Deen sigh behind me as he starts to follow. I know that he would rather be hanging out with his friends today, so I appreciate that he actually agreed to drive me here. With Ma at work, and Baba busy with the restaurant, he was my only choice.

The match is in full swing and I spot Maya on the pitch. She is laser-focused, and I know that she probably won't even notice me until the match is over and she doesn't have tunnel vision anymore.

'Dina.' Jen notices me from her position on the touchline. She comes over, frowning. 'What are you doing here? How's your leg?'

I'm sure Maya's been giving her daily updates about me.

'It's OK, a little better,' I say. 'I thought that I'd come and support the team.'

'You should really be at home, getting some rest,' Jen says.

'But it's the last game of the season,' I reply.

'Well, take it easy,' Jen says. She's about to turn back towards the match, but I stop her.

'I'm sorry you had to cancel with the scouts,' I say. 'I know it wasn't easy to arrange them coming.'

Jen gives me a flickering smile. 'You have nothing to be sorry about. And, actually, I did tell them that you wouldn't be playing, but they still wanted to check out the match. They want to see what the team is capable of.'

'Oh.'

'Yeah, and they're really impressed with the team, actually,' Jen says. She doesn't quite meet my eyes as she says this.

'It's a good team,' I reply, a sense of dread building in my stomach. What is Jen not telling me?

'They've offered the spot on their team to someone else,' Jen explains.

The feeling in my stomach grows and I can feel the pinprick of tears behind my eyes, even though it's silly. I shouldn't be upset that someone else on the team got this great opportunity. It's just that if I was here, if I had played,

I would be the one they would be offering that spot to. I just know it.

'Who did they offer it to?' I try to keep my voice steady as I ask. And before Jen says her name, I already know from the guilty look in her eyes.

'Maya,' Jen says. 'And don't worry, Dina, there are other teams and other scouts. Even though this is the last match of the season, I'm sure that we can . . .'

Jen keeps talking, but her voice drowns out for me. All I can hear is the rush of blood in my ears, all I can feel is the well of tears building behind my eyes. I look from Jen to Maya's distant form, through a blurry vision.

How could she have dreamed with me about my future just yesterday and then turned around and betrayed me like this? How could she have told me all about these opportunities that I would supposedly have, and then taken mine right from under me?

'Dina? Are you OK?' Jen's voice finally grounds me back in reality.

'I'm fine. Sorry, Jen, I'm feeling a little . . . sick. I should go home,' I say, turning around before Jen even gets the chance to respond.

I find Deen in the crowd of spectators.

'Let's go home.'

'What? We just got here!' Deen says. But when he catches my eye and sees the look on my face, he doesn't argue any further. 'OK, let's go.'

Back in the car, Deen and I sit in silence as he drives out of the school gates. All the while, though, rage is building inside of me. So fast and so hot that it feels a little suffocating. I wish that I could have just marched up to Maya on that football pitch and demanded what the hell she was thinking, what she was doing. But instead, I just have to sit here in a car with Deen, and stew in my anger, while Maya gets to live out her dream – *my* dream.

'OK, what happened?' Deen asks finally, breaking the silence.

'Doesn't matter,' I say, crossing my arms over my chest and looking out of the window. All the while, I'm trying not to cry, feeling the injustice of it all, the fact that Maya always seems to get what she wants while I end up with nothing.

'Dina, come on. Something clearly happened. Was it the scout? You know that just because you showed up at the match didn't mean you would be able to play. You knew that, right?'

'Yeah, it was stupid. Going to the game,' I say. 'It doesn't matter anyway. I'm done.'

'Well, good,' Deen says, clearly not understanding what I mean. 'Because, honestly, Ma would probably kill me if she knew I took you to the game when you should be resting.'

'No. I mean, I'm done with football. It's about time anyway. I'm too old to be in the under-18s league next year.'

Deen turns to give me a concerned look. 'I mean, you could join another team, you could—'

'No. I'm never going to be a professional football player, so what's the point? It's stupid and a waste of time. I'm done. For good.'

That thought follows me all the way to the next day when I show up outside Maya's house. I know that I probably look terrible; I haven't slept, tossing and turning all night, thinking about the fact that, in just a few weeks, Maya will be going away to join a football team in the US. That Maya betrayed me. That Maya is leaving me.

I feel like in the blink of an eye I've lost control of

everything, and all I know is that I have to take control of something. Even if it's not in the way that I want.

I press my finger on the doorbell and I can hear it ringing out sharply. A moment later, I hear the sound of footsteps inside, bounding down the stairs. And then the door is open and Maya stands in front of me.

She looks jubilant, her eyes bright, her long hair loose and free behind her. The sunlight casts a light on her that almost seems to make her glow. She looks *happy* to see me, like she didn't break my heart yesterday.

'Dina!' Maya leaps forward, throwing her arms around me.

For a moment, I close my eyes, take in the scent of her, luxuriate in the feel of her arms around mine, the warmth of her skin, the familiar embrace of her hug. This is the last time that we'll have this, and as much as I hate her right now, I savour it. Then, I'm pulling away, wrenching her fingers off me. I don't want to give her the satisfaction of knowing that, when she's gone, I'll miss this. I'll miss her.

'You took my spot.' I spit the words out, and Maya's expression changes.

She shakes her head, but I know that she can't deny it. 'I didn't – it's not like that Dina. They offered me the position. I couldn't turn it down. But that doesn't mean—'

'How could you sit there and tell me about how I'll have so many opportunities? How we'll both be on football teams in the future? Were you planning on taking my spot the whole time? Was it all some sick joke?'

Maya's eyes widen. 'Is that really what you think? That I was sabotaging you?'

'You knew how important this match was for me. What else am I supposed to think?'

Maya's face hardens. It reminds me of the first day of secondary school when I walked into class late and interrupted her. The way she zeroed in on me. It's like we've gone back in time, like everything that's happened between us since then has suddenly been erased. 'Did you ever think that you're not as amazing a player as you think you are? You made a stupid mistake and got yourself injured for your big match. Maybe even if you *had* played they would have picked me. Maybe it's the best player who got that position.'

If there's one thing Maya knows how to do, it's twist the knife in deeper. I feel her words in my chest, like a stab to the heart. But I don't let her see just how much she's hurt me.

'Fuck you, Maya,' I say, my words soft, but I know that she hears them. I know that's all she needs to hear, that's all I needed to say. Then, I turn around and walk away. Some part of me wants Maya to call me back. Wants her to take back her words, so I can take back mine too.

But Maya doesn't call me back, and I don't turn around.

This is it, then. I'm done with football, and I'm done with Maya.

Forever.

Chapter 24

Maya

Ten days to the match

'Wow, you guys are really good,' Nadine comments, as the two of us watch the latest match between Westbrook and St Totnes. She texted me a few days ago, saying she'd be in the neighbourhood, but the only time we could make work was during the match. Surprisingly, Nadine actually seemed excited about it.

'We've been practising a lot,' I say. And we have been. Ever since we agreed to the match with Dina and her team, the girls have stepped up their game. Their focus has been razor sharp and they are playing better than ever. Even Laila is doing better, especially now that she and Jade are hanging out. We had two matches lined up before this one, and Westbrook won both with ease. Instead of making me happy, the whole thing makes my stomach clench with worry.

I have been trying to keep Dina out of my mind after the fundraiser, if only because thinking about her constantly is driving me a little mad. But it's proving to be increasingly difficult, especially with our match on the horizon.

'Why do you look so down?' Nadine frowns at me. It's weird how the two of us have barely talked in the past nine years but now that we're back in contact, it feels like nothing at all has changed. Like she can still pick up on my little ticks, and almost read my mind.

'I'm not down.'

Nadine just raises an eyebrow at me, and I sigh.

'It's . . . a long story.'

Nadine nods at the time on the scoreboard. We haven't even hit half-time yet. 'We've got a lot of time.'

So, in-between watching the match, I end up filling Nadine in on everything. The match with Dina, the fundraiser and everything else.

'I can't believe Dina is back in the picture.' Nadine shakes her head in disbelief. She was my confidante during our break-up. When I was heartbroken and devastated, with no Dina to speak to anymore, I turned to Nadine. And as any good best friend would, she told me about all of Dina's faults and all of the reasons why I was far better off without her. I knew she was just saying it because she was my friend. Of course, she liked Dina, the way everyone liked Dina.

'I know, I know.' I sigh. 'I shouldn't even be thinking about her after everything. I just feel weird about the match. I mean, our team has so many advantages compared to hers. It doesn't feel totally fair.'

Nadine frowns, considering my words. 'Dina's the one who proposed the match.'

'Because she's headstrong, not because she thought it through,' I point out. 'I wouldn't be surprised if she's regretting the whole thing. I mean, I've seen them play. They aren't . . . I don't know.'

'Dina isn't your responsibility,' Nadine says, drawing my gaze away from Laila and back towards her. 'Neither is her team. You shouldn't worry so much about her, and you shouldn't get too bogged down by her either. You . . . already got hurt once.'

I sigh. Nadine is right, but that doesn't stop me from worrying.

When our match finally wraps up and I've said goodbye to Nadine with promises to see each other again soon, I pack up and start heading out of the park.

Of course, that's when I spot Dina. I've been hoping to run into her since the fundraiser, but it's today of all days that I see her. When I look totally dishevelled, and when Nadine has already warned me about being careful.

Dina's sitting on a bench, her legs pulled up and crossed beneath her, and there's a woman sitting right next to her. The two of them are so engaged in conversation that they don't even notice me.

I could probably hurry along and avoid Dina altogether, and the speed at which my heart is beating makes me think that I should. But there's a voice in my head that reminds me of the way Dina looked at me at the fundraiser. That moment when our hands touched. It reminds me of how she stayed with me through my panic attack, that she listened to me, was there for me, when she definitely didn't have to.

I don't get the chance to decide what to do because – as if they can sense me watching – Dina and the woman look over to me.

Automatically, I paste on a smile and raise my hand to wave. For an excruciating moment, Dina just stares and I wonder if this is going to be another incident like outside the park, where she rode off on her bike at the speed of light. Instead, Dina raises her arm reluctantly. Just that simple action makes my stomach do a somersault.

Nadine would be so disappointed in me right now.

I approach Dina, trying not to sound too eager as I greet her. 'Hey,' I say.

'Hi.' Dina doesn't exactly smile, but she doesn't glare either so that seems like a win.

For a moment, we just look at each other in awkward silence. Then, I hear the sound of someone clearing their throat, and I remember the woman that Dina is with.

Dina seems to remember her too because she quickly turns towards her and says, 'Uh, this is Thea. Thea . . . you know Maya.'

My heart almost stops at Dina's words: 'You know Maya,' as if she's been talking about me. I try not to read into it too much. It could just be because I used to play football professionally. Maybe Thea knows me from that. Or maybe Dina has been talking shit about me for so long and to so many people that anybody in her life would know me as that girl who killed her chances at football. Knowing Dina, it's probably that last one.

'Hey.' Thea smiles at me.

I study this girl, Thea. She's tall and lean, with chestnut-brown hair that falls around her shoulders in curls. I try to gauge if that's Dina's type, but it's difficult to say. For all the time I've known Dina, *I've* been her type. But the way the two of them were sitting, close together, face to face, doesn't dissuade me from thinking that maybe she's Dina's girlfriend.

'It's nice to meet you.' My voice comes out sounding a little more clipped than I want it to. It's none of my business if Thea *is* Dina's girlfriend, but I feel a tug of envy in my chest, hot and uncomfortable.

'You were at football practice?' Dina asks, though it feels like a taboo question.

'We had a match. I was just . . . heading off,' I say.

To my surprise, Dina stands up, giving Thea a cursory glance.

'I'll walk with you. Thea has to get back to her studies,' Dina says.

Thea scrunches up her face. 'Never get into law.' She shoves a few heavy books into her backpack and then, with a wave, hurries towards the other side of the park. Leaving me and Dina all alone.

There's a lump in my throat that I try to swallow as the two of us fall into step. We're not exactly brushing up against each other, but I'm all too aware of the heat of Dina's body next to mine; the soft sound of her breathing, the sharp scent of her.

'So, how's your player doing? Laila?' Dina asks.

'Better, I think. Jade helped. I don't know what advice she gave her, and Laila isn't back on social media or anything, but . . . she seems more focused,' I say. I wish Jade would give *me* advice, because clearly she's cracked something that I didn't when it came to being in the public eye.

'And . . . how have you been?'

I feel myself flush at the question. She's clearly thinking about the breakdown I had at the fundraiser.

'OK. It's weird. I'm getting all of these interview requests now to talk about the racism I faced while I was a player. But the same journalists were all OK spreading lies about me just days ago.' I sigh. When I told Isabel about everything that had happened, she suggested I talk to some of them, but I'm still not sure. It finally felt like some of the media attention had been dying down, and the fundraiser has just put me back in the public eye.

'Hypocrites.' Dina shakes her head. 'But . . . maybe you

should talk to them. I mean, this time you can control the narrative, right?'

'I wouldn't be the one writing the articles, so . . . not exactly.'

'Right.' Dina frowns and there's a beat of silence, only broken by the sound of our walking. 'You could find a way to control it, though, couldn't you? You could write your own article? Or you could give an interview or something? Then it would be you speaking, not someone speaking for you.'

It isn't a terrible idea. Erica Hadley's card is somewhere in the bottom of my purse and *The Warm Up* is a big show. Maybe if I reached out to her, I *could* control the narrative.

'Maybe. I'll think about it.'

The two of us descend into silence again. The entrance to the park appears in sight, and I know that in just a few minutes, we'll be going our separate ways.

'You didn't have practice today?' I ask, wanting to spend more time with Dina. I look to her, expecting her to bristle at the question, but she doesn't.

'Not today. I had to give them a break. I feel like . . . I don't know, they've been working so hard over the past few weeks. Ever since . . .' She glances at me hesitantly, leaving the sentence hanging there.

Ever since we set up this competition between our teams. I wonder if she has the same worries as I do.

'Yeah, it's the same with my team.' I sigh. 'Honestly, they're so dedicated to football, and even more so now that they have something to work towards. I don't remember being like that when we were on the school team.'

Dina raises an eyebrow. 'Really? Because we didn't practise day and night when we had a match coming up?'

'That was different,' I insist.

We pause by the entrance to the park, turning towards each other now, neither of us making a move to end the conversation or go our separate ways.

Dina chuckles. 'In what way, exactly?'

'That wasn't about football. It was about . . . I don't know.' Spending time with *you*, I want to say. All those practice sessions right here in this park, or in our back gardens. I wonder if I would have been so intense about things if Dina wasn't around. It wasn't that I didn't – don't – love football. Of course I do. But with Dina there, my love for it felt even more real, more palpable. Because Dina and I understood each other, we shared the same dreams, the same goals. It was like football and Dina went hand in hand. I guess, in some ways, they still do.

'I'm just saying, we were pretty obsessive about football back then,' Dina says after a beat. 'Besides, you should be happy that your team are so intense about it. It took me a while to get my girls to even care about football.'

That surprises me. When Dina had marched up to us in the park, it definitely felt like they'd all cared. 'What do you mean?'

'I mean . . . they didn't really join the team because they watch football matches in their spare time. I'm pretty sure some of them had never watched a match before, or even kicked a ball. They signed up because they needed to sign up to something.'

'So . . . how did you get them so invested?'

Dina shrugs, and there's a blush creeping up her cheeks, tinging her skin with the slightest hint of pink. 'I barely did anything.'

'You must have done something.'

'It's . . . kind of silly.' Dina actually sounds embarrassed as she speaks. 'I made them watch *Bend It Like Beckham*.'

A laugh bursts out of me.

'I told you it was silly,' Dina mumbles, her blush even more evident now.

'Sorry, I didn't mean to – it's not silly. It's just so you.'

Dina almost looks offended. 'So me?'

'You were obsessed with that movie. We used to watch it like every single week. You could quote the whole thing.'

'Yeah, because you never wanted to watch it, right?' Dina asks sarcastically, rolling her eyes.

'Only because you did!'

'I wasn't the one who had the poster in my room because I had a huge crush on Parminder Nagra. I bet you even took that thing to America with you,' Dina retorts.

Now my face heats up with a blush because I *did* take that poster with me, carried it around from state to state. I was too embarrassed to put it up anywhere, but I kept it. It wasn't because of Parminder Nagra, but because it reminded me of the good times with Dina. We had both felt so seen by that movie. Even if it hadn't been about football, I think we would have watched it obsessively. We shipped Jess and Jules like nobody's business, and it was one of the rare things that felt perfectly made for just the two of us.

'Shut up,' I say to Dina now, at a loss for anything to say.

Dina grins, clearly knowing she's got the best of me. I don't even feel annoyed about it like I might have at one time. Because this feels like going back in time, to before I went away, before everything went wrong with us.

'You were always so sensitive about that crush,' Dina teases, poking me lightly in the ribs.

'At least I could admit it, unlike you reading your smutty fan fiction of Jess and Jules in secret,' I say accusingly.

'I have *no* idea what you're talking about. And if I *did*, I would say that you didn't have a problem with fan fiction when you were asking me for recommendations.'

I'm suddenly aware of the fact that the two of us have moved dangerously close to each other in the midst of all of our teasing. That the rest of the world has somehow faded away into nothing. It's just me and Dina, her dark brown eyes boring into mine. And I'm sure that she can hear the thud of my heart thumping in my chest.

Dina inches an arm forward, her finger grazing my cheek as she brushes a strand of hair away from my face. Just that one single touch sends a tingle down my spine.

And even though this is the last thing I should be thinking of, my eyes automatically travel down from the dark depths of Dina's eyes to her lips. The ones that I have kissed a hundred times, the ones that I haven't kissed in many, many years. I wonder what it would be like to kiss Dina now. If I just stepped forward and closed the gap between us . . .

When my eyes flicker up to Dina's once more, I realise she must be thinking the same thing. She takes a step towards me.

I lean forward, my breath caught in my throat.

And then a ringing sound pierces the space between us.

Dina steps back immediately, the spell between us broken too fast. Even though she's still just there, the distance between us already feels monumental as she digs a phone out from the pocket of her jeans.

'This is Jen. I should take it,' she says, her voice soft.

'Yeah, you should. And I should probably get going.' I

try to meet her gaze again, but Dina is looking away, down at her phone. Anywhere but at me. 'See you around.'

'Yeah, see you,' Dina says.

I take a deep breath, trying to get my heart beat back to normal. Then, with one last, fleeting glance at Dina, I head off.

Chapter 25

Dina

Eight days to the match

Maya has been running circles around my head. I think about reaching out, but I'm not sure what I would even say to her. Not when I almost kissed her the last time we were together. I can't help it – being around her feels like taking a time machine back to when we were together. When things were good.

It helps that Deen has saddled me with a whole list of things that need to be done before the restaurant relaunch. Since we're doing it on a budget, everything has to be done by the two of us, and any friends that we can rope into the endeavour. In-between football training and matches that the team is still losing, and more catering gigs, I have been making Pinterest boards and trying to design a new restaurant menu. I don't have *time* to think about Maya.

'Have you slept in the past week?' Thea asks when she peeks into my bedroom one afternoon. I've only just come back from yet another match that the Divas lost and am poring over my computer, trying to figure out which printer will be able to print our new menus on a tight schedule and even tighter budget.

I turn to face Thea, rubbing at my eyes. 'Yes, of course I've slept,' I grumble, though, if I'm being honest, my sleep has not been great. If I'm not worrying about the football match that's creeping up faster and faster, then I'm worrying about the relaunch. And in-between I'm wondering if I've thrown myself into all of this work just so I can avoid my feelings about Maya and doing something about that.

'Recently?' Thea asks, tilting her head to the side.

'Yes,' I scoff. 'I just haven't slept . . . great. But once Deen's relaunch is done and the match is finished, things will be . . . easier. I just need to get through the next couple of weeks.'

'Maybe you need a little bit of a break?' Thea says.

'I don't know, I have a lot to do.' Though a break does sound pretty nice. For the past few days, I feel like I've been drowning in everything: my thoughts, my feelings, my work. And maybe I need to come up for a little bit of air.

'Aisha's convinced me to take a break from my studies tonight and go out. You should come with us,' Thea says. She is very dedicated to becoming a solicitor, and when we aren't watching football matches together, she's pretty much always at her assistant job or holed up in her room studying. Now, with her exams coming up in just a few weeks, it's really crunch time for her.

'Dina, you *have* to come with us.' Aisha pops up from beside Thea in such a timely fashion that I know they must have planned this.

I look to my open laptop, and then back to Thea and Aisha.

'I guess one night out can't hurt.'

Aisha beams. 'Yes, we're going out!'

An hour, half a bottle of cheap Tesco wine and an outfit change later, Aisha, Thea and I find ourselves in a new club in Shoreditch Thea has heard about. The three of us grab a corner booth, but it's not long before the two of them are dragging me onto the dance floor. I go along with it, because I can't even remember the last time I went out.

'You need to stop thinking about all the work you have to do,' Thea says, shouting over the thumping music. It's like she can read my mind.

'Easier said than done,' I shout back, but I know she's right. There's no point in being here if I can't even take a few hours to relax. I might as well be at home, staring at my laptop with bloodshot eyes.

I take a break from the dancing, weaving through all the bodies on the dance floor to the bar. Just the few minutes of dancing have made my breath come short and fast, and I'm sure there's a sheen of sweat across my made-up face. Still, as I try to catch the bartender's eye, the actual eye I catch is of the woman on the other side of the bar. She has dark brown skin, red hair that stops just past her shoulder and striking eyes that are taking me in. I feel myself flush under her gaze.

I look away at first, leaning against the bar, but after a moment, my eyes drift back to her. She hasn't looked away from me.

I consider turning back to find Aisha and Thea, because I'm here with them after all, but I also know what they would say if they were here now. They'd tell me to go up to her, they'd tell me that this is what I'm here for – to blow off steam and have fun – and flirting with a gorgeous woman at the bar who seems to be checking me out unapologetically definitely counts as blowing off steam *and* having fun. Besides, I haven't been with anyone since Anu and I broke up a few months ago.

So, instead of running back to my friends with my tail between my legs, I approach the woman at the bar. She positively beams at me when I'm close enough to be within earshot.

'Hey,' I say.

'Hi.' She smiles. 'It's impossible to get a drink here, isn't it? I've been trying to get that guy's attention for like ten minutes.'

'If a beautiful girl like you can't even get a drink, then the rest of us have no hope,' I say. I'm trying to sound smooth, but my throat is so dry that my words come out raspy.

'Cat got your tongue?' she asks, with a smirk in my direction. I guess she heard me even if my words barely made it out.

A flush crawls up my skin. 'Now you know why I need a drink.'

She lets out a chuckle, which makes me feel at least a little satisfied. I've managed to get a laugh out of her, even though I clearly have no game anymore.

'It didn't seem like you were interested in talking to me,' she says.

I clear my throat, really wishing I'd been able to get a drink before trying to have this conversation. 'Well, I'm over here, aren't I?'

'I'm Lora,' she says.

'Dina.'

'Nice to meet you, Dina.' She glances at the bartender for a moment before heaving a sigh. 'Want to join me for a smoke outside?'

Getting imbued with smoke isn't my idea of fun, but I'm not about to turn down Lora, especially not when I've already got this far.

'Sure.'

She leads me away from the bar. I glance back, trying to find my friends, but it's too dark and there are too many people. I'm sure it'll be fine, though.

A few people are huddled in the smoking area. There's a chill in the air despite it being the summer. Lora and I go to a corner, and she doesn't take out a cigarette. Instead, she leans dangerously close to me, staring at me with her dark brown eyes. For a moment, I'm reminded of Maya, the way she looked at me wide-eyed when she ran into me at the fundraiser. It had sent a jolt of lightning through me. I'd thought that I would never feel anything like that for Maya again. That we had moved past the point where she could make me feel anything at all. That's how things should work. When someone betrays you, breaks your heart, you should be able to put away your feelings. Lock them up and be done with them forever.

'Are you OK, Dina?'

I blink, and realise that it's not Maya's dark brown eyes staring at me. It's Lora, a woman I've just met. A woman who is looking at me very differently from how Maya used to. She's looking at me with a vacant kind of hunger, like I could be anyone in the world. And that's who I want to be for her – someone who is uncomplicated, someone who is disposable, at least for the night.

'I'm fine,' I say. 'Sorry.'

'Do you come to this club a lot?' Lora asks.

I raise an eyebrow in her direction. 'Seriously? You're really asking me if I come here often?'

Lora laughs again. 'I didn't mean it as a line. I've never been here before. I like it, though.'

'It's my first time here. One of my friends heard about it,

and . . . we all needed a night away from . . . life, I guess.'

Lora gives me a questioning look. 'Life has been troubling lately?'

I shrug. The word troubling doesn't exactly cover it. It's been messy and complicated and confusing. 'My ex moved back to town and it's been . . . weird,' I explain. It doesn't feel like a good enough explanation, but it's all I can give.

Lora smiles sympathetically. 'You still have feelings for her?'

'No.' But the word comes out pathetic and hollow. We both know it. I sigh. 'Maybe . . . I still have some feelings. I don't know. It's complicated, and I wish I was over her.'

'I can help with that,' Lora says. She inches closer to me.

For a moment, I think about stopping her. But then I'm leaning towards her too, trying to put Maya out of my head for good.

But I'm hyperaware of the fact that the two of us are surrounded by a crowd of people; the music thumping in the distance, the bitter smell of smoke all around us. I should be feeling somersaults in my stomach, the quickening of my pulse, blood rushing to my cheeks. Instead, I just feel a strange mix of hot and cold, and I can't stop thinking about the fact that there's sweat pooled over my upper lip.

Still, Lora clearly doesn't care about any of that. Our lips meet and she kisses me as hungrily as she looked at me just a moment ago. She pulls me close to her, and I lean towards her. Her hands are on me in a second; her fingers running up my back, threading through my hair.

I feel every touch like it's alien. I can't lose myself in the kiss, in Lora. Instead, all I can think about is Maya. Maya, Maya, Maya, like she's imprinted on my brain and no matter how hard I try, I can't get rid of her.

I pull away from Lora, and she brushes away strands of her hair, still smiling at me. Whatever wrongness I felt in the kiss doesn't seem to have bothered her.

'You want to come back to my place?' Lora says.

I don't know what's wrong with me, but I shake my head. 'I'm sorry, I don't think so.'

Lora seems completely unfazed by my response. She shrugs and takes out a pack of cigarettes, lighting one and offering me another. I shake my head again.

'I should go, my friends . . . they'll be looking for me.'

'OK,' Lora says, raising an eyebrow in my direction.

I don't wait for any goodbyes, I just turn around and head back inside the club. Back to the booth where Thea and Aisha are having a spirited debate about *Love Island*.

'Where'd you go?' Thea asks when she spots me.

'Nowhere, but I have to get going,' I say, grabbing my purse from the booth.

'Where?'

'I'm going home. I'm just . . . tired. I need sleep,' I say.

'Let us come with you,' Aisha offers, giving me a worried look.

'No, it's fine. I'll be fine,' I reply.

Once I'm outside in the chilly night air, though, I wish I'd taken up Aisha's offer. There are too many people on the street for this time of night, and I'm still a little too buzzed. My head feels woozy, and I'm cold.

Somehow, I manage to walk all the way back to our apartment. It's on muscle memory alone because for most of the walk, I'm still thinking about Maya. Remembering the first time that we kissed, walking back to our hotel in Madrid. Remembering the last time we kissed, the day before the match that changed everything. I miss those days so potently that it hurts. All this time, I thought that what I missed was football, the possibility of what I could have been. But I'm realising that I've missed Maya more than those things. I've missed her most of all.

It's only when I'm back in my apartment building and start rooting around for the keys in my purse that I remember I didn't bring them out with me. I hadn't been able to find them as we were leaving the flat, and Thea and Aisha had theirs, so I thought it wouldn't matter.

'Shit, shit, shit,' I mumble. I could call Thea or Aisha, but I know that would ruin their night, and I've already put a dampener on it. I could call Deen, but he has enough stress on his plate. I'm pretty sure his sleep has been worse than mine the past couple of weeks.

I pull out my phone, trying to figure out my best option. And then I see Maya's name on my contact list.

Before I know it, I'm hitting call, my heart beating a little too fast.

The phone rings. Once, twice, three times. I'm sure that it's too late at night and Maya is asleep and won't pick up. I'm almost feeling grateful for it, when I suddenly hear her voice.

'Hello?'

'Hi . . .' I say.

'Dina?' She recognises me almost instantly.

'Yeah. Um . . . I'm locked out of my apartment.'

There's silence on the line for a minute. If I were her, I would have already hung up. Here I am calling her out of the blue to tell her that I'm locked out of my apartment when we've barely managed to have two civil conversations since she's been back. I don't know what's wrong with me today.

'I can come get you. Give me your address,' Maya says finally.

'You don't have to do that.'

'Yes, I do. Just send me your address,' Maya says.

I rattle it off to her, and she firmly tells me to stay put before hanging up the phone. I go down to the ground floor, and my head feels a little less fuzzy. The cold night air and the phone call has sobered me up a little.

The more time that passes, the more it dawns on me what I've done.

'Shit, shit, shit,' I mumble again.

Chapter 26

Maya

I find Abba's keys in the bowl by the front door. He and Amma are already asleep since it's almost 2 a.m. The house is dead silent. I consider leaving them a note, just in case they wake up and freak out about me being missing. But considering how they both sleep like they're dead to the world, I decide against it. Besides, I'll be back in just a few minutes.

I pull out of the driveway, entering Dina's address into the car's navigation. I still know the address of her old house. I could probably drive there with my eyes closed, considering how often I used to go there when I was younger. It's strange that I don't even know where Dina lives now.

As I drive, my mind starts going into overdrive. I don't know why Dina called me, and I don't know what it means. Maybe I'm just a last resort, I try to tell myself. That would make sense, and maybe in a way it would be the best-case scenario.

The navigation tells me that the apartment complex on the left is my destination, and I pull up. I can already see Dina pacing back and forth through the glass front doors. Her eyes widen when she spots me, and she lets herself out of the door. I notice then that she's dressed like she's going out – or was out. She's wearing a black dress that accentuates every curve on her body. Her hair is loose, and even though it's a little wind-blown and messy, it frames her face perfectly. She's even wearing make-up. There's slightly smudged eyeliner and mascara on her eyes; her cheeks are tinged a rosy pink, and her lips are ruby red.

The sight of her lights my insides on fire. I have to look away as she climbs onto the passenger seat. I grip the steering wheel, trying not to look at her out of the corner of my eyes.

'Hey,' Dina says softly.

'Hey.'

I turn the car around, pulling onto the road back to my house.

'I'm sorry for making you come all the way out here.'

I shrug. 'It's fine. And you were locked out. Did you lose your keys or something?'

'No. I didn't even take them with me. I went out with my flatmates, so I thought they have keys and so it doesn't matter that I don't have mine and . . . well.' She stops there, though it doesn't feel like the end of the story.

I glance at her out of the corner of my eye, even though I know I shouldn't. She's half hidden by the shadows, but that doesn't stop my heart rate from increasing at the sight of her.

I grip the steering wheel more tightly, until my knuckles are white.

'How come your friends didn't come home with you?' I ask after a beat of silence.

'I was tired, so I decided to leave. They're probably still having fun,' Dina says.

'You weren't having fun?' I ask.

'I . . . was just tired,' Dina says after a moment's hesitation.

'Hmm.' I can tell there's more to it, but I don't press it.

I can feel Dina looking at me, and my face warms. I can't look at her, though. I won't look at her. I know that if I do, I won't be able to stop myself from looking at her, and I need to concentrate on driving, instead of the rising beat of my heart, instead of my mind flooding with thoughts of Dina.

Finally, I pull into our driveway. Dina stumbles out of the passenger's side as I close my door and lock the car.

She blinks up at the house, like it's a place of wonder. 'It's been so long since I've been here,' she says.

'Nine years.' The words slip out of me, though I don't mean to say it.

Dina casts me a look over the roof of the car, and even though neither of us says it, I know we're both thinking about the day that she came here to confront me.

'Let's get inside,' I say, turning away from her and towards the door. This definitely doesn't feel like the right time to think back to the past. And definitely not to that day.

The door unlocks with a click, and I push it open, waving Dina inside as I put Abba's car keys back in their place.

'Are your parents home?' Dina asks in what's supposed to be a whisper but is still a little too loud.

I crack a smile, though I should really be worried about Abba and Amma waking up and wondering why Dina is here in the middle of the night, and jumping to conclusions that I definitely don't want them jumping to.

'Yes, so we have to be quiet,' I reply in an actual whisper.

Dina nods, and follows my lead as I head up the stairs and to my bedroom. As Dina looks around, I feel a strange sense of vulnerability overwhelm me. It's been a long time since Dina has been in here, and I don't even want to know her thoughts. Is she thinking about the fact that I'm back in my teenage bedroom? That I'm a failure who is stuck back where I started? Is she thinking about the fact that nothing in this place has changed at all? Is she wondering if even I have changed at all in the past nine years, or if I'm stuck as the same eighteen-year-old who she broke up with on the doorstep of this house nine years ago?

'Sit down, I can find you some clothes to get changed into,' I instruct.

Dina does exactly as I tell her, plopping herself down on my bed and looking around wide-eyed.

'Thanks . . . for helping me tonight,' she whispers slowly. Like it's a struggle for her to say thank you. I guess it always has been a struggle, considering how Dina prides herself on being so self-sufficient. On not needing anyone but herself.

I smile, sitting down on the bed next to her. 'How come . . . you called me tonight?'

'My brother is too stressed, my mum would murder me if I called her,' she says, ticking off the apparent list of people she could have called.

'What about your girlfriend?'

Dina whips her head around to stare at me. 'My what?'

'You know, that girl I saw you with at the park the other day.'

'You thought Thea was my girlfriend?' Dina knits her eyebrows together in confusion. 'Did we look like we were dating?'

'I don't know.' Though now that I think about it, they definitely didn't. If it wasn't for the bouquet I saw on Dina's Instagram page, I probably wouldn't have given them a second thought.

'Why would you think I was dating Thea?' Dina asks. She's grinning now like she finds this whole thing funny. I would too, if it wasn't embarrassing. If it didn't reveal that I was thinking about Dina in that way when I definitely shouldn't be.

'I saw this photo on your Instagram. It was this bouquet of flowers and I thought . . .' I shrug.

'I must be dating someone.' Dina chuckles. 'Maya Alam, were you stalking my Instagram?'

'I wasn't.' My face is hot now from all the blushing and I'm sure Dina can see it. We're sitting close enough for her to make out the pink tinge on my cheeks, but she doesn't comment on it.

'It's OK. It's not like I haven't stalked your online presence,' Dina admits.

I blink at her, surprised. 'Why would you do that?'

'I don't know,' Dina says, her voice getting softer with every word. So soft that I have to lean forward to hear her, until the two of us are a little too close to each other. I can feel her breath with every word that she speaks now. 'I guess I missed you.'

'Oh.' I don't know what I'm supposed to say to that. I'm not sure if I can even say much at all.

My eyes travel down to Dina's lips, even though that seems like a bad idea. This whole thing seems like a bad idea, especially when I had so thoroughly convinced myself that I was done with Dina. That I was ready to move on.

But now here I am again, sitting in my bedroom, face to face with Dina. Thinking once more about what it would be like to kiss her.

Dina's eyes seem to glitter when the light catches them. She leans towards me, agonisingly slowly, tilting her head to one side. Something draws me forward too; it's almost like a pull of gravity. I can't help but go towards her, studying the honey-brown of her eyes; how they shift and shimmer in the light, how they darken and lighten, as if by some magic.

I reach out a hand, touching the corner of her lips where the red of her lipstick has smudged into a streak of pink. I wipe it away, and I can feel Dina's sharp breath at the touch more than I hear it.

Then, all at once Dina presses a kiss to my lips. It's feather-light, hesitant; almost like she's asking permission. I pull her close to me, already losing myself in the heady scent of her, and circle an arm around her waist. As if this was all that Dina needed, she deepens our kiss, and suddenly it feels desperate and hungry. I kiss her back with this same kind of desperation, like Dina is sand between my fingers and if I don't kiss her now, I might never get the chance again.

'I've been wanting to kiss you since we first ran into each other. It's all I've been thinking about doing,' I mumble into her lips.

'Me too.' Dina sighs against me. She tugs at the buttons of my blouse, and surprisingly quickly and smoothly, she manages to pull it off me.

I move back on the bed, until I'm against the headboard, pulling Dina with me. She hesitates for only a moment, before she climbs on top of me, her legs straddling me. Her thumb caresses my bottom lip for only a second before she's kissing me again.

Her kisses are different from how I remember. Before, it was like neither of us knew exactly what we were doing. We would fumble and bump noses, and laugh and kiss. We were each other's firsts, still learning. But now, things are different. Nine years have taught both of us a lot, clearly, I think as Dina presses herself flush against me, running her fingers through my hair, skimming my ear, my cheeks, my neck, leaving a trail of goosebumps that seem to be sending pools of desire through me.

All of my thoughts about this being a bad idea, about moving past Dina, melt away. Because how could *this* be a bad idea? How could Dina ever be a bad idea?

We pull apart, breathless, but Dina doesn't let go of me and I'm not sure if I want her to.

'Are you OK? With this?' Dina asks, her eyes boring into mine.

'Yes,' I say, without even thinking about it.

We're both breathing hard and my whole body is flushed with heat. Dina brushes a lock of hair behind my ear before her teeth nib at my neck, my jaw; her lips trail kisses down to my collarbone. I feel like a livewire everywhere Dina touches. And as much as I know that I should stop her, that we should stop, period, I don't want to.

Then, a creak pierces the silence of the night. Dina stops and leans back, and suddenly it feels like the rest of the world rushes back into focus. I can hear Abba's soft snoring in the other room, the creak of the bed as Amma tosses and turns, the rush of wind outside, creating a soft hum as it passes through the trees.

Dina and I are still staring at each other, but the moment is gone. Even if the ache of longing in my chest isn't. Dina swiftly clambers off me and I sidle off the bed, trying to comb my hair into something more than a restless tousle.

Dina sits on edge of the bed now, her hands pressed against the duvet, knuckles a little white from how hard she seems to be pressing down. She's staring at the ground, like she can't look at me now. I can't look at her either.

I have a million questions. I want to know why Dina kissed me and why now. But, mostly, I'm still feeling the ghost of her fingers caressing my neck, her phantom kisses still on my lips.

'We should get some sleep,' I say, not looking directly at Dina, and instead ducking past her and opening up my wardrobe. I can feel her staring at my back, but I don't turn around. I busy myself rooting around for a set of pyjamas, like I should have before. Maybe if I hadn't sat down next to her on the bed, if I hadn't told her about that photo I'd found, we wouldn't have felt emboldened to kiss each other and things wouldn't feel even more complicated than they were before.

When I finally find the pyjamas, I toss them in Dina's direction, and she catches them perfectly, like she had been expecting the throw.

'You can change in the bathroom,' I say.

She nods, and softly opens the bedroom door to head into the bathroom.

I close my eyes for a minute and take a deep lungful of breath, trying to calm my heartbeat. The kiss had been just a kiss. A spur-of-the-moment thing. After all, Dina only called me because she was locked out of her apartment with nobody else to call. I tell myself all of this, no matter how much I desperately want to hold on to that kiss as the start of something between the two of us again.

Once my heart has stopped racing, I quickly change into my own pyjamas, and make up a bed with pillows and sheets on the floor.

'You can take my bed,' I say to Dina once she comes back to the room. She frowns between the bed and the makeshift one on the floor.

'It's fine, I can sleep on the floor.'

'Just take the bed,' I say firmly.

'Fine,' Dina agrees in a disgruntled voice.

She climbs onto the bed, while I turn off the light. Shuffling to the makeshift bed, I lie down. I stare up at the ceiling, trying not to think about the fact that Dina is lying down only a few feet away from me. It's difficult when I can hear the sound of her soft breathing, when I can hear the rustle of her blanket every time she turns. I don't turn on my side, afraid of catching a glimpse of her and it sending my heart into a panic.

'Does it feel weird being back?' Dina asks in a whisper after a few minutes.

'A little,' I say.

'What was your room like, over there?' she asks.

We're veering into dangerous territory, but in the darkness of my room, it feels easier to talk.

'I shared an apartment with two of my teammates,' I say. 'It was pretty small. My room was, like, half the size of this. But it was fine, because we travelled a lot and I was barely ever home.'

'Did you miss being home?' Dina asks. I know which home she's talking about.

'Sometimes. I missed . . .' *You*, I want to say, but I can't. That would be admitting something too vulnerable, revealing too much of myself. 'My parents.'

The room settles into silence. After a few minutes, I think that Dina must have fallen asleep. But then she breaks the silence again.

'Things are too complicated.' She sighs, like she's been thinking about that for a long time. 'I mean, for that to happen again.'

A lump forms in my throat when I realise what Dina means. She already regrets kissing me, while I was thinking about how everything finally felt like it was slipping into place.

'Right. Yeah,' I agree, my voice throaty and rough.

'I just mean – I don't regret kissing you. But there's so much history and so much we haven't sorted out. I don't even know how I feel about . . . anything,' Dina says. 'It would be a bad idea, for us to start something.'

I want to tell her that she's wrong. That if we wanted to, we could figure it out. But maybe she's right. I don't even know who I am now that I'm back home, or what I want out of life. I've just been caught up in my messy, unresolved feelings for Dina. Feelings that would only get me into trouble.

'Yeah, we shouldn't let that happen again,' I say.

'We should sleep,' Dina whispers. 'Goodnight, Maya.'

'Goodnight, Dina.'

Chapter 27

Dina

Seven days to the match

I'm woken up by the light peeking in through the gap in the curtains. Trying to avoid the glare, I turn around, but I see the figure lying on the floor, and nearly jump out of my skin.

It takes me a moment to remember last night. The club, the girl I met there, the walk home, calling Maya. Kissing Maya.

Shit.

Embarrassment surges through me as I run through the events of the night. I have no idea what was going through my head, what I was doing. Clearly, I wasn't thinking.

I rub sleep out of my eyes, wondering how I look before remembering that I shouldn't be wondering that at all.

I glance down at Maya's sleeping form on the floor, trying not to think back to the kiss from last night. She had kissed me back. The memories of it all flood back fast; the feel of her lips on mine, the way she looked at me, like she wanted this as much as I did. But then the moment had passed and we'd barely spoken about it. I can't even imagine what she thought of me. Probably she thought I was a total mess, and she wouldn't be wrong.

I slip out of bed, looking for my clothes. I find them in a

crumpled pile on the bottom of the bed and quickly change. I'm afraid that Maya's going to wake up and we're going to have to go through the events of the night. That I'll have to explain everything even though I have no explanations to offer her.

I consider leaving Maya a note. Instead, I decide I'll send her a text when I'm out of the house and well on the way home. That's the only way I can think to deal with this situation. So I quietly slip out of her bedroom and hurry down the stairs. It takes me a minute of trying before I finally manage to get the finnicky front door open, but just as I'm about to step outside, a camera flashes in front of me, blinding me.

I blink, not sure what is going on. A moment later, when my vision clears, I finally see the spattering of reporters on the street, their cameras propped up in front of them.

'Dina Chowdhury!' one of the reporters – a woman that I'm sure I've seen before – hurries towards me, a bright smile on her face. 'What an unexpected sight. So, am I right to assume that you're dating Maya Alam?'

I can only blink at her, my jaw open. Why the hell are reporters here? And why are they asking me about my love life?

Another reporter hurries forward. 'What does it feel like to be dating your rival coach, Dina?' he asks enthusiastically.

I can barely even make sense of the question before a hand grips my shoulders, pulling me back into the house.

Maya is frowning, her eyebrows scrunched together. As soon as she's pulled me back in, she leans forward, glaring at the reporters. 'You really need to get out of here, this is private property,' she says, her arms outstretched over me as if she's protecting me from their prying eyes.

'Maya, maybe you can tell us how it feels to be dating a rival coach?' the male reporter says, his eyes alight with excitement.

'Ten minutes, and if you're not out of here, I will call the police,' Maya says firmly, barely even looking the guy in the eye before slamming the door shut.

She presses her fingers to her forehead, like the whole thing has given her a headache.

'Are they . . . always at your doorstep?' I ask. I don't remember seeing any reporters last night, but maybe since Maya has come back this is her morning routine. Maybe this is what it's like being a professional footballer – I wouldn't know.

'No, of course not!' Maya exclaims. 'I have no idea what they're doing out there. And what were they even talking about?'

That question brings me back to earth. They'd been asking about Maya and me dating, about us being rival coaches.

'They were saying . . . we were rival coaches. How would they know that?' I ask, frowning. 'They knew my name. How the hell did they even know who I was?'

Maya shakes her head. 'I don't know; they must have found out from somewhere.'

She takes out her phone and begins typing into it. After a moment, her face falls, and she looks up at me hesitantly. She turns the phone towards me, and I see what has made her face fall.

Former football star Maya Alam caught up in EXPLOSIVE match with rival coach.
Maya Alam vs Dina Chowdhury: the football rivalry of the decade?

The websites they link to aren't the *Guardian* or the *New York Times*. They're just local papers, some that get delivered to our door for free every once in a while. But the fact that even local papers would know about me, or Maya, or the match, is so baffling that I don't know what to say.

Maya turns the phone back around and clicks into one of the articles. I watch as her eyes scan it, her frown growing deeper with every passing moment.

'It says that apparently there was some viral Instagram video talking about the match,' Maya says.

Cold dread spreads through me.

'Oh no . . .'

Maya looks up at me questioningly. 'What?'

I don't know how to explain it, or if I'm even right. I just take out my own phone and search for the one and only Instagram influencer that I know of personally: Jade. Her account comes up as soon as I search for it, and the pinned post on her profile is a video of her in her football kit.

I click onto it, and Maya comes close, looking at the video over my shoulder. I flush at the memory of the two of us this close last night in the dim light of Maya's bedroom, trying to ignore the heat of her body, the familiar scent of her, as the two of us watch Jade on my small screen.

'We're playing the match of the century. The Divas vs Westbrook. And *we* are in it to win it!' As Jade finishes speaking, the video transitions to a montage of the team sprinting, passing and scoring goals. It certainly makes the team seem a lot more competent than they are half the time in practice.

'This isn't the only video,' I say, as I scroll down, seeing multiple videos where Jade is talking about the match, the rivalry between me and Maya, and more. Many of them have racked up hundreds of thousands of views, which I can't even fathom.

'I guess people know that we're playing a match,' Maya says, looking from the videos to me.

I step back from her and take a deep breath, trying to clear my head from the heady scent of her.

'What are we going to do? Why do these papers even care about our match?' I ask. It was enough pressure before, but now I'm imagining my failures as a coach being broadcast everywhere and I'm not sure if I'm ready to deal with that. What had Jade been thinking?

'It's not a big deal, I'm sure they'll forget about it soon,' Maya says, but her breeziness only serves to annoy me. Maya has been used to being in the limelight, used to newspapers writing about her. Me and my team don't need that kind of attention. Especially when I'm sure that all it will do is magnify our failures and the fact that we aren't a 'proper' team. They've already been heartbroken when accused of that by Maya's team.

'I should get going,' I say, putting my phone away. 'Do you think they're gone?'

Maya looks like she might object to me leaving for a moment. I wonder if she's thinking about last night too, and the thought that she might makes my face warm. I need to get out of here before we fall into a conversation about yesterday. Then, in the cover of the night, everything had felt easier. Now, in the light of the morning sun, it feels more serious and I don't want to deal with that.

'Let me check,' Maya says. She shuffles to the sitting room and parts the curtains, peeking out. She turns back around and smiles. 'All clear.'

'Well, good. I'll just . . . Thanks for . . .' I drift off, not sure what to even say, or how to say it.

'Will your flatmates be home, to let you in?' Maya asks, tilting her head to the side as she takes me in. She acts like she doesn't even notice how flustered I am. She's probably trying to spare me the embarrassment of having to deal with the fact that I kissed her unprompted last night, and then told her that I missed her when she was away.

'They should be, yeah. So don't worry. I'll . . . I'll go. Bye.' I twist the doorknob and step outside. The sun is bright but feels like an intrusion. I half want Maya to call me back, but as I start making my way back towards home, she doesn't. And I don't know if I feel relieved or disappointed.

Chapter 28

Maya

Four days to the match

The posts from Dina's player – Jade – don't stop. If anything, they actually get more numerous with each day that passes. She posts videos of the team playing, hanging out and even a couple of Dina coaching, though I doubt she consented to that. And yes, I may have watched those a few more times than necessary, but all in the need of monitoring media activity.

I receive emails from various journalists, asking for a quote about the upcoming match. And despite my threat about the police, I spot a couple of them hanging about outside our house.

The kicker comes, though, when Amma approaches me with a newspaper in her hands while I'm having breakfast.

'Is this you, Maya?' she asks, eyebrows creased. She lays out the broadsheet on the table in front of us, to a picture that is – decidedly – of me, though it's old. It's a mid-game shot from a match that I played years ago. In it, I'm about to pass the ball to another player, my head ducked down low and my eyes slightly narrowed in concentration. The picture saw a lot of use when I was being called aggressive and a bitch. Somehow, the candid image of me where I'm not smiling meant that I'm some kind of bully. As if brown women should look approachable in every second of their lives.

This time, though, the picture is not accompanied by a headline about my supposed transgressions as a player.

Local Football Player Maya Alam's Compassion Shows In Upcoming Football Match!

Maya Alam may not be an A-lister, but that doesn't make her celebrity appeal any less, especially among our locals. You may know her because she attended Westbrook Secondary, where her stint on the football team led Westbrook to its first championship victory in decades. After joining the Dustreet Abbey Under-18s football league, she earned herself a spot in the US state team known as the Vikings, whom she helped lead to victory after victory. And even if you haven't followed her stellar career, she made headlines more recently when she declared an early retirement from the game.

But Maya certainly hasn't let her early retirement go to waste – instead, she has recently taken up a coaching position for the Westbrook football team – giving back at the place where she first found her success.

The principal of Westbrook only has praises to sing of the former student turned coach.

'We always knew Maya was going to be a star. She was one of the brightest students in the school, and now she's turned her talents to inspiring our current students!'

But that's not the end of the story. Recently, viral clips from social media influencer Jade Thornton have shown her football team – the Divas – preparing to play a match against the Westbrook team, with the Divas being led by none other than Maya's former school teammate, Dina Chowdhury. And rumour has it that the two have a terse history.

Will our local football hero manage to lead her team to a historic victory? Come and watch the match of the decade on Wednesday, 30 August!

I can only blink at the newspaper once I've finished reading the article. I guess the reporters got tired of asking me for a quote and decided to do whatever they could with what they had. Jade's videos definitely haven't helped, and I can't believe Ms Jacobs would succumb to these journalists.

'Why didn't you tell me about this match?' Amma asks.

'It's not a big deal,' I say. 'They shouldn't have published it in the newspaper.'

'It seems like a big deal,' Amma says, the frown still in place. She sits down on one of the empty chairs beside me and eyes me closely.

'This is Dina Chowdhury? From school? She's a football coach too?'

'Yes, and yes,' I say. I definitely don't want to talk about Dina to my mother, but seeing as she was my longest relationship, I have confided in Amma about her. Especially after Dina and I broke up. If anyone knew what kind of heartbreak I went through because of Dina, it was my mum. Now, she looks at me with concern etched all over her face.

'I didn't know you got in contact with her again,' she says.

'I didn't. It's . . . complicated,' I reply. I wonder what Amma would have said if she'd run into Dina the other day. If she knew that Dina had spent the night in my bedroom. I doubt she would have been jumping for joy, even though her life's objective lately has been seeing me in a romantic relationship. Or wanting to see me happy, as she likes to put it. It's just sometimes she equates those two things.

'You almost didn't go to America because of her,' Amma says.

I sigh. I don't need her to remind me of what I almost

gave up because of Dina, because she really made me believe that I was in the wrong for taking the opportunity that she believed was all hers.

Half my nerves during my first few games were about Dina. It was me wondering if I really belonged there or if Dina had been right that I had taken her rightful spot. It's not like South Asian women get a lot of opportunities in football.

'I remember. Dina and I aren't . . . Our teams are just playing a match against each other. And it isn't a big deal, Amma.' I speak slowly in the hope that it will hammer home my words. Then, I quickly get up from the table, taking my finished breakfast plate with me to the sink. I turn on the tap and start scrubbing, though I'm still thinking about the article, thinking about the match, thinking about Dina and everything that has happened in our past. The last words she said to me before I left still echo in my head sometimes, the vitriol with which she said them to me all the more. That was the reason why I almost cancelled taking the position for the Vikings – the hurt and anger in Dina's voice, in her eyes, before she turned and left. I had to live with the fact that I had caused that hurt and anger, I had to deal with it. I wasn't sure if it had been fair to me back then, and I wasn't sure if I had really reckoned with it now.

'Dina is bad news,' Amma says firmly, suddenly appearing behind me.

I'm so surprised that I nearly drop the plate in my hands, only managing to grab hold of it at the last minute.

'Amma,' I groan.

'And you haven't had any serious relationships since Dina. I told you I can set you up with someone if you want.

Then, when you see Dina for the match, you can tell her that you're already in a relationship,' Amma says.

I turn off the tap and wipe my hands on a kitchen towel with a sigh. 'Amma, I don't want to be set up. And nothing is going to happen between me and Dina. I remember everything that happened, and you have nothing to worry about.'

Amma studies me like she's trying to figure out if I'm lying. I don't even know if I am. She nods firmly a moment later. 'Your abba and I will come to the match to support you.'

'You don't have to do that,' I say quickly. I definitely don't want to have her glaring daggers at Dina across the football field.

'We want to come and support you,' Amma insists. 'We never missed watching any of your matches on the TV when they were on. Or any of your interviews. We're not going to miss this one – we get to watch it live, finally.'

Even though I don't want Amma and Abba there, I can't help but smile. There are some parents who wouldn't have wanted their daughter to ship off to America at the fresh, young age of eighteen. Who would have felt uncomfortable with the TV appearances, the celebrity-adjacent life. But Amma and Abba have been nothing but supportive of every single thing in my life. How can I tell them not to come to this match?

'OK, but you have to behave,' I say firmly.

'We always behave,' Amma says brightly.

'Maya!' Ms Jacobs is waiting by the football pitch when I arrive for training later that day. I have to stop myself from frowning at her. I may be annoyed at her for speaking to the reporters, but at the end of the day, she's still my current employer and I shouldn't get on her bad side.

'Hi, Ms Jacobs.' I force myself to smile. 'What can I do for you?'

'I heard about the match,' Ms Jacobs says. 'You should have told me that you were setting something like that up. It's a fantastic idea. I mean, what a great way to inspire and motivate the team.'

'It wasn't really my . . . Yes, it'll hopefully be a good match.' I sigh. The match is happening with much more pomp and circumstance than I had expected, and I have to get used to it.

'Well, I've sent out an email, inviting everyone to be in attendance,' Ms Jacobs says enthusiastically. 'The parents, teachers, supporters of the school. Hopefully we'll get a good turnout. I spoke to Jen and we agreed that it would be best if you used the school football pitch for it. We want it to be as professional as possible, especially with all the media attention. There was an article in the local paper the other day, I don't know if you saw that.'

'I did, my mum showed it to me,' I say. I can hardly believe that somehow even more people are going to be turning up to this match. I'm not sure if I want our team to win or lose. If we win, I wonder if that will be the nail in the coffin for me and Dina. I'm not sure if I would be OK with that. If I *should* be OK with that.

'Well, I just wanted to tell you how great a job I think you're doing.' Ms Jacobs practically beams at me as she says this. 'Maybe if everything goes well, we'll have a coaching position for you as we start the school year as well. I think the students would really like that. It seems they've really taken to you.'

As frustrated as I am by Ms Jacobs speaking to the reporters, and inviting so many people to our match, I can't help but feel touched at her support. After all, without her, I wouldn't even be here. I'd probably still be moping around the house with no reason to get out of bed in the morning. She's given me the motivation to actually move past what happened in my football career. She's given me the chance to look forward, to see that I have more to offer to the world even if my football career is over.

'Thanks, Ms Jacobs,' I say, giving her another smile. This time, one that's actually genuine.

Chapter 29

Dina

Three days to the match
I spot Maya through the glass doors of the cafe. She's sitting on one of the couches to the side, her black hair swept out of her face, a frown on her lips as she stares at her phone.

I have half a mind to turn around and just go back home. Despite what I said to Maya about the two of us starting something being a bad idea, I've spent the past few days doing little else but thinking about her.

Taking a deep breath, I push the door open and step inside. Maya must hear it, because she turns towards me as soon as I'm inside. A hint of a smile crosses her face, and I ignore the fact that it makes my heart skip a beat.

I march towards her as nonchalantly as I can.

'Hey,' Maya says.

'Hi.' I take the seat opposite her, trying not to show her just how much simply being in her presence these days rattles me. 'You wanted to talk?'

'Yes . . . did you want to get something?' She looks from the steaming cup of coffee in front of her to the menu on the wall on the other side of the room.

'No, I'm okay.' A cup of coffee would be good just to distract myself, but it would probably also make me even more jittery than I already am.

'OK, well . . . have you seen the newspaper lately? And your player Jade's Instagram?' Maya asks, her frown returning.

I wonder if that's what she was looking at before. I should have known this is what Maya wanted to talk about.

'Yes.' I sigh. The whole match has blown up more than I wanted it to. Clearly, more than Maya wanted it to either. I've even had a conversation with Jade, but she just shrugged and said that if they were going to show Westbrook that they were a real team, they might as well have an audience for it. I hadn't pointed out the fact that the Divas have yet to win a single match, not wanting to crush their spirits. And it's not like I can dictate Jade's social media.

'We have to do something about it. I spoke to Ms Jacobs, and she's invited people from school – parents, students, teachers,' Maya says, sounding a little distraught. 'Who knows how many people are going to show up? And Jade isn't slowing down with her posts.' She holds up her phone to show me Jade's latest viral post. She has started counting down the days to the match now, and the people in her comments are loving it.

'Jade is passionate about the match,' I say. 'All the players on my team are. That's why they're posting about it. I can't ask them to stop.' I don't mention that it has taken a lot to get them to care even a miniscule amount about football, and while I'm not a fan of what they are choosing to do now that they are invested, I'm proud of them too for how far they've come.

'You're their coach. You can tell them to stop,' Maya insists. 'Or Jen can. Maybe we should talk to her.'

I shake my head. 'No way. We're not dragging her into this. She didn't even want this match to happen. Besides,

Jade's not hurting anyone with her posts, she's just hyping people up.'

Maya's frown just deepens with every word I say. I try to meet her halfway.

'I'm not happy about the attention either,' I say. 'Clearly. But . . . it is what it is.'

Maya takes hold of her cup of coffee, lifting it to her lips and taking a long sip, before putting it down on the table between us with a little more oomph than necessary. Some of the coffee spills over from the cup, sliding down the edges and onto the saucer under the cup.

'I think we should call off the match,' Maya says. I have thought about calling off the match too, but I can't admit that to Maya. I don't think the Divas would take it very well, either.

'I don't know . . .'

'Do you really want your team's loss to be announced in the local papers, to be seen by everyone?' Maya asks.

It's my turn to frown as I turn over what she's said in my head.

Our loss.

Not hers.

'Are you serious?' I ask, settling her with a glare.

Her eyes flicker up to mine, and I can see the glint of realisation about what she's said dawn on her. She said it so inconsequentially – like there is no other outcome that she can even imagine.

'I didn't mean—'

'Clearly you did,' I huff. 'Look, we're *not* calling off the match, because your team are the ones who bullied mine, and my team deserve a chance to prove that they're good. I'm sorry if the great Maya Alam is afraid of losing face in front of an audience, because I'm *not*.'

Maya sighs again, and leans back in her seat, looking at me. She doesn't even try to defend herself.

'Are we going to talk about the other night, or just fall back into old patterns?' she asks coolly.

My stomach drops, but I try not to let it show that she's fazed me with the sudden subject change. 'I don't know what that has to do with anything.'

'Isn't it the whole reason why we're doing this? Our teams are caught up in our feud?'

'We don't have a feud,' I say firmly.

Maya just continues to stare me down, but I don't cave in. I'm definitely not going to admit that I've thought about her every day for the past nine years, that I've obsessed over her career and our past, and everything that we had and everything that we don't have anymore. I was already too vulnerable with her the other night, after working to build up my walls for years and years on end. I'm not ready for Maya to hurt me again. For anything to hurt me again.

After what feels like an eternity, Maya looks away from me and shakes her head, like she's disappointed in my response. 'You know, the other night, I was happy for a second,' she says. 'I thought that maybe things could be good between us again, but I should have known that it was just some kind of a blip. Things with you are always like that.'

I frown. 'What the hell is that supposed to mean?'

'It means that this is how it always is with you. As soon as things get complicated, that's the end for you. That's what it was like last time. You broke my heart, and I won't forget that.'

My eyes widen at her insinuations – that I'm somehow the problem, was ever the problem in our relationship.

'I broke *your* heart? What about you? You betrayed me, you took my spot, you took *my* dream. And then you just left. For nine years. You can't just . . . revise history.'

'I played a match, I was given an opportunity,' Maya says. 'And I took it. You could have still had your dream, we could have still been together. We could have had the life that we talked about. You were the one that gave up. You sabotaged yourself.'

Maya says all of this so calmly, like she's reciting some history book, instead of sharing a twisted version of what really happened. I can't believe that after so many years there's not a hint of remorse from Maya. A thread of anger makes its way through me, boiling in my blood and making my face burn up.

'I can't believe this is the bullshit you tell yourself to make yourself feel better,' I manage to spit out.

Maya holds my gaze for a moment, before swiftly standing up. 'I'll see you at the match, Dina.'

With that, she turns around and walks out of the door, disappearing from sight. I can only watch after her, my rage almost spilling out of me.

I stomp my way to the restaurant, my head still spinning with all of the things that Maya said. I have half a mind to storm after her, to say my piece. But I don't even know what I would say since my head has been a slew of angry gibberish.

'You're early,' Deen says, looking up from where he's sitting on the floor, surrounded by a pile of stuff that I've never seen before.

'What's all this?' I ask, picking up a decorated red clay pot from the pile.

Deen clambers up to standing with a triumphant grin. 'I went to a couple of charity shops, hoping that I could find some decor items to spruce up the place.'

'And you found all of this?' I ask, studying some of the items. They certainly don't look like things from a London charity shop – more like knick-knacks you might find in Bangladesh: a slightly beaten-down rickshaw figurine, a hand-painted spinning top, a gaudy beaded wall hanging.

'No!' Deen exclaims. 'Well, a couple of the things. But I had a brilliant idea when I was there, and I got in touch with some of the aunties and uncles around the neighbourhood. I scrounged some of *their* stuff. They weren't doing anything with it, and everyone had things. Stuff they bought from Bangladesh, stuff from weddings and holuds . . . they were probably just going to toss it all at some point, but now I get to give it all a second life here!'

It's a good idea, I have to give him that. Bengali weddings are usually a whole affair, and while the decor sometimes gets passed around from one wedding to the other, there's so much stuff that's thrown out too.

'I like it,' I say with a conclusive nod. 'So, you want to tell me where you want all of this?'

'I'm still figuring it all out,' Deen says, looking around the restaurant. 'Still developing my vision.'

'Well, while you're getting your vision,' I say, 'do you have any food lying around? I'm starving.' The conversation with Maya has left me with a strange sort of emptiness. I might as well try to fill it with some of Deen's cooking.

'Sure, there should be some leftover korma in the fridge . . .' Deen tilts his head towards me. 'Are you OK?'

'I'm fine.' I wave my hand dismissively, making my way to the kitchen and grabbing some korma and polau. Sticking it in the microwave, I heat up the food, and head back to the main restaurant area, taking a seat at one of the tables. Deen is now holding a dhol in one hand, and a painted pakha in the other, frowning at both in consideration.

'What do you think about putting the pakha on one of the walls, and maybe the dhol on the windowsill?' Deen asks, looking over at me.

'Let's try it,' I say.

Deen goes over to one side of the restaurant, holding the painted hand fan up to the wall. I nod in approval, and Deen puts it aside, trying the replica Bengali drum on the windowsill next.

He turns to me again as I chew on my food quietly.

'You really aren't going to tell me what's wrong?'

'Who said something was wrong?' I ask.

'Well, you're usually way more opinionated about things,' Deen points out.

'I just gave my opinion,' I insist.

'Yeah, no . . . you agreed with my opinions. Different things,' Deen says. He marches towards me and sits down right next to me. 'Once you tell me what's wrong, I might stop pestering you about it, and we can get back to the real work.'

I sigh. I know that Deen won't leave me alone until I spill, so I start to speak. At first, I think I'll only tell him about the conversation with Maya, but before I know it, I'm telling him everything. Her team bullying mine, how we came to agree to the match in the first place. The other night at Maya's house, the kiss. And, finally, the conversation we just had, which left me boiling with rage. As I get to the end, I'm practically crushing the food on my plate with my hands and glowering down at it.

'I just can't believe she has the gall to say all of that to me. I feel like she only wanted to speak so she could . . . act like she was better than me, and act like I was the problem, when it's clearly her,' I finish off.

Deen is contemplative for a moment, and silence washes over us. Speaking everything aloud does make me feel at least a little bit better.

'I'm not saying that I agree with Maya . . .' Deen starts.

I turn my head towards him so fast that I almost get whiplash. 'You're *agreeing* with Maya?'

'I said I wasn't!' Deen replies, holding his hands up as if in surrender. 'But I always wondered why you took it so hard that she got offered that spot in the US. And why you decided to give up football right then and there.'

'Because . . . because it was tainted. Forever. After what Maya did. She . . . she *knew* how much that match, and that opportunity, meant to me. And she still took it.'

'But it wasn't yours,' Deen says. 'I mean, you were injured. You were never going to get that opportunity. And Maya is right, you could have still had a career. I mean, Jen was clearly obsessed with you – she *still* is. She would have done everything in her power to make sure you got more opportunities. You could have played in university; you could have tried out for teams. You could have gone down a million paths, but you didn't.'

'Because Maya ruined it for me,' I say firmly, but my confidence in that statement is quickly dwindling. I'd been so angry at Maya that day, but I'd been angry at more than that. I'd been angry at the scouts for thinking of me as so disposable, angry at Jen for letting Maya be given that opportunity over me, angry at myself for getting hurt. Angry at the world for all of it.

And maybe I'd let the anger get the better of me. It was easier to blame Maya than to accept that I'd lost out on something I'd dreamed about for years. It was easier to blame her than to risk failing again. Easier to blame her than to go after my dreams.

'I just think it was more complicated than that.' Deen shrugs, as if reading my thoughts. 'And maybe you should think about what Maya said, and not just jump to anger like you usually do.'

'I don't—' I start to say angrily, before cutting myself off and taking a deep breath. 'Yeah, maybe.'

Deen raises an eyebrow, clearly surprised that something he's said has actually got through to me.

Chapter 30

Dina

One day to the match

I run through Maya's words in my head over and over again. Even when I don't want to. Her words, our entire conversation, are like a broken record in my mind. Even as I put in twice the hours at training with the team, I can't help get her words out of my head.

The day of the match draws nearer and nearer, until there's only one day left.

When I arrive at our final practice session, the girls are already kicking a ball around between them. I stand there for a moment, watching the intensity on their faces, the concentration. It's strange to think that I had a hand in getting them here. A bloom of pride rises in my chest. A feeling I haven't felt in years, maybe since I decided to quit football.

Then, Sophie stumbles on the ball and falls face first on the grass, breaking my reverie. I hurry towards her.

'You OK?'

'Fine.' Sophie is already standing up, a blush rising up her cheeks as she brushes off bits of grass from her clothes. I spot the scrape on her knees, though, and it doesn't look good.

'Come on, let's put a plaster on that,' I say. 'The rest of you, keep it up.'

Sophie and I sit down on one of the benches nearby and I take out the first-aid kit, pulling out a stack of plasters.

'I wish I was as good at football as Jess and Jules,' Sophie mumbles.

'You know that was just a movie, right?' I ask, with a chuckle. 'Besides, the more you practise, the better you'll get. You're already heaps better than you were at the start of summer.'

'Yeah, but if we don't win tomorrow, those girls would be right about us,' Sophie says. 'We *have* to win. Otherwise, we wasted all our time practising for nothing.'

I frown as I carefully place the plaster on Sophie's knee. 'Winning isn't everything,' I say. 'And besides, you had a good time this summer, right? You made friends, and you and Sara aren't always at each other's throats anymore.'

Sophie nods sheepishly. 'Yeah, I actually play better when I play with her. We practise together sometimes.'

'So, you shouldn't think of all the time you've dedicated to football this summer as a waste, win or lose.'

Sophie doesn't look convinced. I guess I shouldn't exactly be surprised. I've been pushing them so hard because we have this match with Westbrook, because I wanted to beat Maya. They've learned my competitiveness, inherited my frustrations.

Sophie reminds me so much of me when I was younger, and I don't want her to take away what I did from football. I want her to love it and enjoy it, even if nothing ever comes out of it.

'You know, when I was around your age, I loved football. So much. It was everything to me, and I had so many dreams. I thought that I would go on to become some kind of football legend. It didn't happen.' I shrug nonchalantly, but I can feel the pinprick of tears behind my eyes. I try to blink them away. 'And I was angry about that, for a long time. I blamed other people for it. I blamed the wrong people, and it cost me . . . what I loved. But you and the rest of the team helped me find my love of football again. So, whatever happens tomorrow, I just think you should have fun and enjoy the game. Win or lose, I'll always be proud of you, and you should be proud of you too.'

'Even if we're terrible?' Sophie asks, like it's a real concern for her.

'Yes, no matter what,' I reassure her. 'And I know Jen feels the same way.'

Sophie offers me a small smile, and I return it. I don't know if she's really taken in what I've said, but I know that this is the best advice I can offer her.

After training is over, I tell the girls to go home and rest up, before gathering up my things. I'm wishing that I could go home and rest up for tomorrow too, but Jana has texted me about another catering job. Which means that I have to get on a tube to central London, change into my server's uniform, and put on a fake smile for the rest of the evening. I'm not looking forward to it.

A woman approaches me while I'm at the park gate, smiling as if we're old friends. I smile back, only because I'm afraid that she's someone I know from university, or work, or school, that I've forgotten. I've never been great with faces.

'Hey. Dina, right?' the woman asks.

'Um, yeah.'

'I'm Rosemary Clarke, and I write for the *Daily Standard*.'

My smile immediately dissipates, but that doesn't deter Rosemary.

'I've seen all the viral posts on Instagram and I'll be covering the match. I wanted to reach out and see if you had a comment about Maya Alam, since you must be keyed into her history.'

I'm straight-up scowling at Rosemary now. 'I don't. Excuse me, I have to get going.'

I push past her, but Rosemary follows me into the streets. 'I'll be writing about Maya, whether you want to share a quote or not!'

That manages to stop me in my tracks. I turn around to face Rosemary. 'What do you want to know?'

'Well, from my research, you and Maya went to school together, you were on the same football team. *You* were the star player of the team, not Maya. So, how exactly did she make it all the way into a professional team, while you're coaching a council team that can't even afford kits?' Rosemary asks.

If Rosemary had asked me this question even a few days ago, I know what kind of answer I would have for her. But after my conversation with Deen, my pep talk to Sophie, my anger seems to have dissolved into a soft pang of regret.

'She was a great player,' I reply. 'And she's always been hard-working and dedicated. The Vikings were lucky to have her.'

This is clearly not the kind of scoop that Rosemary was hoping for, because she looks far from impressed. 'So, all the rumours about her being terrible to work with, bullying other players . . . they don't ring true with the person she was in school? She didn't sabotage your chances to get her shot?'

'She's not that kind of person. She never has been. I wouldn't let my team play against hers if she was. Now I really have to get going.' I turn around, leaving Rosemary behind. This time, she doesn't follow me and I let out a breath, suddenly feeling a thousand times lighter.

Chapter 31

Maya

Match day

I barely sleep the night before the match. Instead, I find myself staring up at the ceiling, running through all of the possibilities of tomorrow. I imagine arriving at the park and Dina marching up to me, angry about the conversation we had at the coffee shop the other day. I imagine how she might react if she loses the match – her disappointment, her heartbreak. I'm sure she'll blame me for that too.

I close my eyes and try to sleep, but I can't get Dina's face out of my mind.

By the time it's morning, I'm already exhausted, but I scramble out of bed, shower and get dressed.

Amma and Abba share excited chatter about attending the match over the breakfast table, but I can only smile and nod.

'If the match goes well, I bet the school will give you a permanent position,' Amma says as she starts clearing the dishes. 'I mean, they would have no reason not to. Wouldn't that be amazing?'

'Yeah, Ms Jacobs mentioned that it might be a possibility the other day,' I confess.

Amma is right – it's the exact kind of opportunity that I need. No matter what has been happening with Dina, coaching this team has been amazing. When I retired from football a few months ago, I felt like my life was over and like I would never have another opportunity again. I listlessly thought about other jobs I could do, I even briefly thought about going to university, though the idea of that wasn't attractive. And then this job happened out of the blue.

'That sounds like the perfect job for you,' Amma says encouragingly.

Abba gives me a hesitant look. 'I know it's not the career that you dreamed about.' This is the first time that either of my parents has mentioned my impromptu retirement from football. I've barely explained the ins and outs of everything to them, feeling too embarrassed of my failures. And seeing how touchy I've been about the subject since I got back, they've always skirted around it.

'I know, but . . . I like it,' I say, realising that I mean it. I didn't think I would enjoy it the way that I have. The ability to pass on everything that I have learned over the past few years, to not let my knowledge and skills fall to the wayside, like I thought I would have to once I quit football. It feels good – it feels like what I was meant to do in the same way I felt like I was meant to play football.

Abba smiles. 'Sometimes, life takes you down unexpected avenues. When your amma and I got married in Bangladesh, we never expected that we would build our family here in London, but now we can't imagine a different life for us.'

It's strange to think about, but Abba is right. What had felt like the end of the world just months ago doesn't feel like that anymore. I tried to live my dream life, and it had been less of a dream than I'd imagined. Now I'm here, back in my parents' home, working a job at my old school, still confused about my ex-girlfriend, but I don't hate this life. I like the way I fit into it. It's an unexpected realisation, but it's what I need going into this match.

Because no matter what happens, no matter how Dina reacts, I will be OK.

Chapter 32

Dina

Being back at this football pitch after all these years feels like taking a step back into the past. The place is crawling with people when I arrive. It's more packed than it ever was for any of our matches. A lump forms in my throat as I glance around the crowd, looking for a familiar face. But everyone starts to blur together. My heart goes into overdrive when I spot a camera crew and reporter by the touchline, already filming the crowd of people.

'Hey, you OK?' Deen's voice brings me back to reality, though the rush of blood in my ears is still a little loud.

'Why are there so many people here?' I ask. Maya had said that there would be more people than anticipated, but I didn't think the local paper would get this much attention. And I had no idea that people on the internet would actually be motivated to leave their house and come to watch this match. I just hope that the girls on the team can handle it.

'Your team is a viral sensation,' Deen says enthusiastically. He rubs my back, like he knows I need the reassurance. 'You going to be OK? You don't have to talk to the reporters.'

'Yeah, I know. I won't.' I spot Jen, leading the Divas towards the pitch, a frown on her face. She's clearly as unhappy about the turnout as me. But seeing her, and seeing the team, actually helps put my mind at ease. It reminds me of the real reason why we're here and why we're playing this match.

'I should go and talk to Jen,' I say, turning to Deen. It's only then that I see the large cardboard sign that he has tucked under his arm. 'What's that?'

'Oh, this?' Deen asks, innocently. He grins as he untucks it and flashes it in front of my face. *The Divas are number one – they'll score a home run!* it reads in glittery gold bubble letters.

'You know that a home run is . . . baseball, right?'

Deen just shrugs, looking at his sign with a proud smile. 'It gets the job done. I was initially trying to find a rhyme for the Divas, but the best I could come up with was "Go, go the Divas, give them amnesia," which seemed a bit aggressive.'

I roll my eyes, glad that Deen didn't go with his first instinct. I would take the baseball reference over *amnesia* – which doesn't even rhyme with the Divas, but I don't have the heart to tell Deen that.

'I'll see you after the match, OK?' I say.

Deen nods, giving me an encouraging pat on my shoulder. 'I brought some snacks from the restaurant, and I'll be handing them out to the crowd with your friends and Ma.' He nods to a corner of the field, where my friends are talking to Ma, each with multiple tote bags bursting with snacks slung around their arms.

'Ma came?' I ask, astonished. We haven't really talked about football or my coaching since she helped me source t-shirts for the team. Every time I've had dinner at hers, we've skirted around the topic, even though it has taken over my life. Instead, we reminisced about Baba and talked about her thriving garden.

'Not only did she come, she invited a bunch of Bengali aunties and uncles,' Deen says. He points to the crowd, where I can see a small gathering of familiar faces. I even spot a smiling Zulaykha with her fiancé, and they wave at me enthusiastically when they spot me.

Deen doesn't seem as fazed by Ma's sudden support as me. Maybe because Deen has always been able to read her, in a way that I haven't.

'Did she . . . say anything?'

Deen shakes his head. 'No. She must have seen it in the papers or something . . . She just told me that she wanted to come with me, and she asked if your friends were going and when I said I didn't know, she made us drive to your place to pick them up.' Deen must see the worry creasing my brow because he gives me a reassuring smile. 'It's good that she's here, I promise. Now go, and stop worrying so much.'

I take a deep breath and nod. 'Thanks. I'll see you soon.' I turn away from him and walk towards Jen and the team.

'Wow, what a turnout, right?' Jen says, feigning a smile as I approach. She's clearly just as nervous about all the attention as I am. 'Who could have predicted this?'

Apparently, Maya, but I don't say that.

At least the girls seem enthused about the crowd.

'Do you think they'll interview us for the news?' Sara asks, trying to fix her messy ponytail into something more presentable.

'You can borrow some of my make-up if you want!' Jade offers enthusiastically, offering her a clear plastic make-up bag that's full to burst. I intercept it from Jade, frowning at the girls.

'You know you can't wear that much make-up while playing football. What you have on already is fine,' I say firmly. 'And . . . you shouldn't talk to the reporters. It's not a good idea.'

Sara frowns, deflating a little, but when Jen nods in agreement with me, the girls seem to remember the real reason why they're here. I hand Jade back her make-up bag and pass around some hair ties for the girls who need them.

I see Maya, leading her team onto the pitch. She gives Jen an enthusiastic smile and greeting, before turning to me with only half the enthusiasm she had for Jen. There's so much I want to say to Maya but now is not the right time. And I'm not brave enough anyway.

'Should we get started?' Maya asks.

'Yes, we're ready to go,' Jen says. She waves to the referee, who starts to get everyone organised.

Westbrook win the toss for kick-off, and Jen, Maya and I move off to the touchline, letting the teams take their positions. With a blow of the referee's whistle, the match begins.

Despite Westbrook kicking off, Sophie manages to get the ball from them quickly. She weaves it around a few players from the other team, but just as she's about to pass it to Sara, she's tackled. But Sophie doesn't just lose the ball, she falls to the floor, and a loud crack reverberates around the entire park.

The whole thing seems to happen in slow motion, and I can see Sophie's face contort in pain. For a moment, I'm stood frozen. My mind floods with the memory of the practice where I injured myself. How it had ruined everything for me.

'Dina?' Maya's voice pulls me out of my head. She's suddenly right beside me, studying me. 'Jen's calling you.' She points to the centre of the pitch, where Jen is already standing over Sophie, studying her foot, which definitely looks like it's sprained.

'Right, thanks, sorry,' I mumble, before jogging towards

THE PERFECT MATCH

Jen, and trying my best to rid myself of the thoughts of my past.

Sophie looks to be in a lot of pain, but she's trying to power through it.

'You OK?' I ask sympathetically, crouching over her.

'Yeah, I'm . . . fine. Maybe I can still play?' Sophie asks hopefully.

As much as I wish she could, I shake my head. 'No way, you need to see a doctor,' I say.

'I don't want to miss the match. Can I at least stay and watch?' Sophie asks. The rest of the team, who have gathered around us too, chime in to allow Sophie to stay.

Jen looks hesitantly from me to Sophie. 'We really should get you checked out.'

'I can get checked out after the match. I'll be OK, promise,' Sophie says. 'I can't just abandon the team, especially since I can't play. It's the least I can do.'

I know that if it had been me in Sophie's place, I would have been making the exact same arguments, so I can't fault her.

'OK, fine, but as soon as the match is over, I'm taking you to see a doctor,' Jen says with a warning in her voice.

Sara and Jade give Sophie encouraging pats on the back, while Jen and I help her over to the touchline, where we sit her down on a bench and make sure that she's OK before telling our sub to join the game in Sophie's stead.

The match begins again, but with Sophie's injury, it seems like all the players have deflated a little. Sophie was by far our best player, and it feels like we've lost our only advantage in the game just a few minutes in.

'They'll be fine,' Jen says, obviously noticing the nerves clear as day on my face.

'Yeah . . . yeah, they will be,' I say, though I'm not feeling so sure about that.

I glance over to the reporters, who are still here, taking video footage of the match. Then my eyes drift across to where Aisha, Thea and Ma are still handing out snacks, while Deen is holding his terrible sign up high. If Baba were here, he would be there, right beside Deen, cheering on the loudest out of everyone.

When Deen notices me looking, he pastes on a grin and gives me a thumbs-up.

I roll my eyes, a smile finding its way to my lips. But a burst of applause goes through the crowd, snapping me back to the pitch. Westbrook have already scored their first goal. Cheers ring out from the other side of the pitch, with Maya leading the charge, though her heart doesn't quite seem to be in it. Her shoulders are tense, and she chews on her lips.

Almost as if she can feel my eyes on her, Maya's eyes meet mine, sending a bolt of lightning through me. She ducks her head before I can look away. She clearly doesn't want anything to do with me – not after the last conversation that we had.

The game continues, and after a few more minutes, Westbrook score again. I can see the faces of the girls on my team getting more and more dejected. They didn't play this badly in their last few matches, where they had been enthusiastic, even when the other team were winning. They're really taking a beating here, and it's making dread crawl through my entire body. This is what I didn't want to happen, but I have walked them into this situation. I set up this match because I wanted to beat Maya.

I have let them down, and there's nothing I can do about

it now. I just have to support them and be the coach that I should have been from the start.

'Come on, Divas, you can do this!' I cheer, clapping my hands together.

The girls don't seem particularly enthused by this display, until a chant breaks out through the crowd on our side of the pitch. I look around to find Ma and my friends enthusiastically leading the cheering for the Divas over and over again.

Some of the girls on the pitch start to grin. I notice the cameras zeroing in on the cheering crowd.

On the pitch, Sara gets hold of the ball. She dribbles it forward and towards the goal. There are no players standing in her way, and it seems like we might finally score a goal. But just then, the referee blows the whistle for half-time. Sara's face falls and I let out a frustrated breath.

The girls jog off the pitch, their breathing fast and heavy, their clothes soaked with sweat, and their faces downcast.

'They're so going to rub our faces in this after the match is over,' Sara says as she sits down on one of the benches, trying to catch her breath.

'What am I going to tell my Instagram followers?' Jade asks, frowning. 'I bet I'll lose a bunch after this. I should never have told them about the match.'

'Hey!' I interrupt them, having to almost shout to be heard over all of their complaining. 'I told you guys, winning isn't the only important thing.'

'Yeah, but that's just something people say; they don't actually mean it,' Jade argues, crossing her arms over her chest and frowning at me. 'I mean, of course, everybody wants to win. We want to *win*.'

'I don't even care if we win,' Sara says. Considering she's one of the most competitive girls on the team, it's a pretty shocking confession. 'I just don't want to suck out there.'

The other girls mumble dejected agreements.

'I'm sorry I got hurt and can't play,' Sophie says, looking every bit as downcast as the rest of the team. Almost like she blames herself for how the match is going.

'Look, guys,' I say. 'I know you have it in you to play well. Remember the match you played against the Greens? You guys were tied until almost the end of the game, and you played a great match. Don't let Sophie's injury get you down. Take this half-time and then go out there and play your hearts out. That's all you can do at the end of the day, win or lose.'

'But if we lose, it will be in front of so many people,' Jade complains.

'And you'll pick yourselves up and live to play another match, and hopefully you'll win that one,' I say. It's the advice I wish someone had given me when I was younger – when the loss of one opportunity felt like the end of the world. *Was* the end of the world for me. But now I'm realising that I let a single loss keep me down, instead of trying again. I let myself get defeated.

The team don't look enthused by my speech, though they don't look as depressed as they did when they came off the pitch.

By the time the second half gets underway, the girls seem to have at least regained some of their excitement. As the Divas kick off, Sara receives the ball. She dribbles it around a few players, before passing it to Jade, who is clear in the box. I watch her eyes flicker between the ball, the goalpost, the goalie. My heart clenches tightly as I look on.

'Please, please, please, come on . . .' I mumble under my breath.

Jade goes to kick the ball, and the goalie dives. But just at the last minute, Jade changes direction. Realising this, the goalie tries to reach out her hand. But she's too late – the ball goes sailing past her and bounces into the net.

The crowd erupts into cheers, and I realise that I've joined them, that my arms are up, pumping the air with all my excitement.

Beside me, Jen is grinning from ear to ear. Jade beams at us from the pitch – all her worries from before, seemingly gone now.

We're still one goal down, but maybe we have a shot at this match after all.

The rest of the match seems to pass by in the blink of an eye. There are a few more times when the Divas almost score, but the Westbrook goalie intercepts the ball each time. It doesn't get the team down, though. In fact, it feels like every single time they're thwarted in their efforts, they come back even stronger.

The girls in defence put up an even bigger fight. For most of the second half, Westbrook don't even get close to the goal. When they finally do with five minutes to spare, one of the girls manages to block the shot. The frustration from Westbrook feels palpable, though on the other side of the pitch, Maya seems pretty unbothered. I guess she shouldn't be, considering they're still one goal up.

With only a few minutes left of the game, Westbrook make a sub. The girls take the opportunity to jog back towards us, taking swigs of their water bottles. Unlike half-time, their faces are bright with excitement.

'You guys are killing it,' I say, beaming at them.

'We still have a few minutes. Maybe we can score one final goal!' Jade says enthusiastically.

'You guys can do it,' Sophie agrees.

'Just go out there and do your best,' I say.

There's only eight minutes left, but as soon as the referee blows the whistle this time, the Divas are on the go. Sara gets the ball and immediately guns for the goal, but one of the Westbrook defenders tackles the ball away from her. It's like that for the next five minutes; back and forth, with neither team taking any clear-cut chances.

Finally, with just a minute to go, Jade gets the ball and the pitch is fairly open in front of her. I chew on my lip as I watch her dribble the ball for a little bit, before playing it through to Sara in front of her. One of the Westbrook midfielders almost manages to intercept, but Sara keeps hold of the ball, quickly running towards the goal in front of her. My chest squeezes as I watch. The seconds are ticking down, I can feel it. Any minute now, the referee will blow her whistle, and the match will be over.

This is our last chance to score – our last chance to snatch a draw, which would lead to a penalty shoot-out, where maybe we could actually win.

As if in slow motion, Sara pulls her foot back and strikes the ball. It goes flying through the air, and the Westbrook goalie dives for it. Her fingertips reach out, grabbing for the ball. For a moment, it looks like she'll miss it, but somehow she manages to get hold of the ball.

I let out a breath as the referee blows her final whistle. We were so close. So damn close.

The girls seem anything but deflated, though. Even Sophie, sitting beside me and Jen, is smiling as she cheers the girls on as they go across the pitch, to shake hands with the girls from the other team – the winning team. Even after everything they said to the Divas. I feel my heart fill with pride at the sight – at the fact that we played this game at all, that the girls went out there and did their best, even if they didn't end up winning.

This is the best match that the Divas have ever played after all, and I know that it won't be long until they finally start winning. But if they had given up because of how bad the first half went – if they had let themselves get dejected – then they would never have played that amazing second half.

'Not a win, but still pretty good, I think,' Jen says.

'Yeah, really good.' I nod in agreement.

I spot Maya smiling encouragingly at her team as they meet the Divas on the pitch, talking and laughing, instead of at each other's throats for once, and I know that there's still one thing left for me to do. Taking a deep breath and trying to swallow my pride, I make my way over there.

Maya's gaze snaps to me as I approach her. There's something behind her eyes that I can't quite read.

'That was a good game,' I say, the words a little harder to get out than I thought they would be. 'Your team played really well.' I hold out my hand for Maya to shake.

She looks down at it, inspecting it like there might be something poisonous in my hands. She looks up at me again, studying my expression, before reaching her hand forward.

The touch of her warm skin makes a shiver run through me.

'Thanks.' Maya's voice is barely a whisper. She clears her throat and says a little more loudly now, 'Your team did a really good job as well. They're good players.'

'Thanks, and seriously, congrats.' I withdraw my hands from hers, already missing her touch. There's more I want to say to her – more I should say to her – but the words feel trapped inside my throat.

'Dina, I know that things have been—'

'It's OK.' I cut Maya off before she can start delving into it. This is supposed to be Maya's moment – her win. All around her, her team is celebrating, while Maya is here with me, feeling like we still need to hash out the past. Maybe this is what Maya has been feeling like for a long time, for the past nine years. We've been holding each other back, and I don't want to do that anymore. We both deserve better than that. 'We don't have to talk about any of that. We were both . . . It doesn't matter.'

'Really?' Maya seems surprised, and I can't exactly blame her. The last time I lost out on something, I broke up with her and gave up on football. This was definitely a far less dramatic reaction.

'Yeah. You should go and celebrate with your team.'

'Oh . . . yeah, I probably should.' She glances behind her at the team for a moment, like she'd forgotten that they were even there, before turning back to me. I wouldn't blame her if she held the past over me, but there's some part of me that aches for her to forgive and forget. That wants us to move on and go back to what we were. But I know that I've probably broken that too badly to even repair it. 'I'll see you around, I guess.'

'See you.'

Then we're both turning around, going our separate ways. And even though I feel my heart constrict at the idea of the match being over, about the fact that I have no reason to see Maya again, I keep going, and the distance between us grows with every step.

Chapter 33

Maya

Two weeks later

The lights around me prickle my skin, making me flushed. Beside me, Erica Hadley and Karl Griffin shift in their seats, engaged in a whispered conversation. Finally, Erica turns to me with a reassuring smile.

'This will be great, Maya. Don't worry.'

'I'm not worried,' I say, although I clearly am. If I wasn't nervous about being interviewed on live TV, I would be nervous about finally getting the chance to say my piece. But I'm doing both at once, so my anxiety is through the roof.

Before I know it, the cameras are on us and we're live.

'We're so excited to welcome Maya Alam to *The Warm Up*. I know all of you have heard the speculation about Maya in the news cycle over the past few months, and we're lucky to have her here with us today, finally ready to share her side of the story,' Erica says, turning her thousand-megawatt smile on me.

'Thanks for having me, Erica and Karl,' I say as graciously as I can, picking at the skin around my fingers where the camera can't see it.

'So, Maya. You were having the kind of career that footballers can only dream of. The Vikings were on the rise, winning matches, winning championships. And then suddenly, it all came to a halt because you decided to retire. Why did you do it?' Karl asks.

I take a deep breath. I've practised what I planned to say, gone over it again and again with Isabel on video calls. If I'm going to tell the world my side of the story, I can't mess it up.

'Honestly? For my own mental health.'

Karl nods, his eyebrows drawn together.

'A lot of people don't understand how much pressure it can be. I mean, for *anyone.* You have a pretty brutal schedule, you never see your family and friends, so your entire world becomes football. But there was a lot more on top of that for me. I felt like the more attention I received, the more vitriol there was. I would score a winning goal, but the story would be rumours about how I was a bitch behind the scenes.'

I take a deep breath and look at the camera instead of at Karl and Erica. I might be doing an interview with them, but it's really the people watching who need to hear this. Who need to understand.

'There are very few women of colour in football. Even fewer South Asian women. And Bangladeshis? Practically unheard of. When I was facing all of this, I didn't even have anyone that I could speak to about any of it. Nobody who would truly understand or sympathise. My coaches and teammates told me that everything would blow over, that it was just part of football and I had to learn to deal with it. But the thing was, they were dealing with so much less. On top of that, they were getting opportunities left, right and centre. A couple of my teammates went on to play in world cups for their country, or they transferred to different teams because they were wanted by them. The English football team didn't want me, the clubs here didn't care about me. I was passed over continuously, no matter how well I played, how many championships I helped win. It just felt like I could never succeed.'

Karl and Erica nod sympathetically.

'We were surprised that you weren't on the World Cup team. We talked about it on the show, didn't we, Karl?' Erica remarks.

'We did. We speculated about who would be on the team, and you were one of the first players we thought about,' Karl agrees.

'That's why I felt like I had no choice but to retire.' I sigh. 'I joined the Vikings when I was eighteen years old. So many of my teammates went on to do amazing things. I was still stuck in the same place and I was getting abused in the media and online spaces. At a certain point, I just felt like I couldn't do it anymore.'

'And now that you're retired, you're back home. What have you been doing?' Erica asks.

'Do you have plans to go back into football?' Karl presses.

'I've been coaching a football team. My old school's team,' I say. 'I think that's as much football as I can take these days.'

'And you had a phenomenal match just the other day!' Erica exclaims. She picks up a notecard in her hand and reads off it. 'Westbrook vs the Divas. And Westbrook – that's your team, I believe – won. Blew the competition out of the water.'

I smile wryly. 'Yeah, Westbrook won. But it was a close match; the Divas played a really good game. Those teams are really the future of football.'

'Yes, youth football clubs for women are definitely *very* important. It's how we nurture our young talent. And we're glad to see you at the forefront of that, Maya. Especially with all of your experiences.' Erica smiles.

The show cuts to an ad break, and Erica and Karl visibly relax as soon as the cameras are off them. I feel a little looser as well. I've done it: I've said my piece and it doesn't feel like it was a disaster.

'Thanks for sharing all of that, Maya. I know it couldn't have been easy,' Erica says, standing up and extending her hand towards me.

I stand up too and shake her hand, and then Karl's.

'I know that we shared some of those rumours about you too, but I hope that there's no hard feelings.' Karl chuckles. 'You have to understand, it's just our job as journalists.'

I raise an eyebrow. 'Sharing unfounded rumours?'

'Well, no. But sharing what people are saying. What's in the current news cycle,' Karl says.

'Without doing any due diligence to check facts?' I press.

'It is a *talk show*, Maya. Not exactly hard-hitting journalism,' Erica says. 'It was nice to see you again. Good luck with your coaching.'

With that, I'm officially dismissed. I walk out of the studio and I don't feel angry at Erica or Karl or *The Warm Up*. I actually feel like a weight has been lifted off my shoulders. Sure, it would have been nice if the journalists who peddled these rumours understood their impact, but I've done my part. That is really all that I can do.

With the summer almost at an end, and our match against the Divas over and done with, coaching sessions have slowly dwindled down to nothing. There's a little bit of a respite for the girls over the last weeks of summer, and then school will start up again.

All of this means that I've had too much free time on my hands – free time that I've spent spiralling and thinking too much. Despite beating the Divas and finally getting to share my side of the story with the world, it has been hard to feel happy, knowing that Dina and I will probably not have many reasons to see each other again. And from the last conversation we had, it's clear that Dina is ready to put the past behind us – but that means putting me behind her too.

I shouldn't be surprised. After all, Dina was always one of those people who was good at holding grudges, and she was also good at curating the people that she wanted to know and spend time with. Back in school, it was the reason she barely had any friends or acquaintances. She needed to trust someone to be vulnerable with them, and it had taken a long time for her to trust me. And I broke it, even if I didn't mean to. Dina isn't the kind of person to give people second chances.

Having all of this time to do nothing means that I've fallen into bad habits. With no more coaching to give me a routine, I'm all too happy to languish in bed until mid-morning, thinking about Dina and our past and feeling a little sorry for myself.

If Amma and Abba think it's weird that my team's win hasn't spurred much excitement for me, they don't bring it up. Most likely, they think I've burnt myself out with all my coaching and I'm taking time to refresh before Ms Jacobs offers me a full-time job – *if* she offers me a full-time job.

It's on one of those mornings that my Google alert goes off. I know I should have deleted the alert a long time ago, and I'm about to swipe it straight into my email's trash, when I see Dina's name. A lump forms in my throat as I click into the article. It's from the *Daily Standard* about the match between Westbrook and the Divas, and about me.

Maya Alam has been in the news a lot recently. When it wasn't the rumours about her behaviour behind the scenes, it was her explosive interview on *The Warm Up*, where she demanded the football community consider their own biases. It's difficult to know who Maya *really* is. Are the stories about her true, or is she the do-gooder coach who has been caught up in undeserved backlash?

Her rival coach, and former classmate Dina Chowdhury shed some light on the controversial player.

'She's always been hard-working and dedicated,' Chowdhury says, when asked about how Alam made a career playing professionally when Chowdhury was considered the star player in their school team. Chowdhury also dismisses the rumours about Alam: 'She's not that kind of person. She never has been.'

The article goes on, but I've stopped reading. The words have started to blur together. Dina had the chance to tell people *her* side of the story too. The side that she's believed all these years – that I sabotaged her, took her spot. That she was the one who deserved my career. But she didn't say any of those things. I'm not sure what that means.

I find myself on her Instagram again, and realise that there are several new posts on her account, but they're all about her dad's restaurant. There are no photos of her or her friends, or family. It's pictures of the food, each announcing a grand relaunch happening in just a few days.

I try to remember if Dina ever had an interest in cooking. I wonder if she's given up coaching now to take up the helm of her father's restaurant. But then I remember her brother,

Deen – who would keep stocking a supply of freshly baked goods in Dina's house whenever I visited. Who gave me knowing looks when Dina and I were still dating in secret, refusing to tell anyone about what we really meant to each other. Who had been passing out food to the crowd at the football match two weeks ago. It would make sense if he was the one who was responsible for the relaunch.

I still remember how important that place had been to Dina's father, and how often he served me dinner there when I had clearly overstayed my welcome. Dina's parents never minded me hanging around. Even then, the restaurant wasn't booming with business; I can't even imagine how it survived after Dina's father passed away.

Mentally, I start taking note of the time and date of the relaunch, but then I stop myself. I can't just show up to Dina's father's restaurant to celebrate a relaunch. Just because Dina said something nice about me to a reporter doesn't mean she wants to see me.

I try to go about my day as usual, but try as I might, I can't stop thinking about Dina or the restaurant relaunch. By the time the afternoon rolls around, I'm looking at the restaurant's new website on my laptop, scrolling through the menu chock-full of Bangladeshi dishes. I wonder if there's something I can do for this place that means so much to Dina and her family.

Before I know it, I'm going through my phone and emails, trying to find old media contacts. Surely, they must know people who they can send to the restaurant for the relaunch – reviewers, influencers and journalists – who can talk up the place. The least I can do is try to help Dina and Deen make sure the launch is a success.

'What's this?' Amma asks just as I'm finishing up a call

to an old reporter friend of mine, who has promised to try to get someone to the restaurant. Amma is looking at the restaurant website open on my laptop, a crease between her eyebrows.

'Just . . . a new place that's opening up. I thought maybe we could go,' I lie.

Amma looks up to me, her frown still intact. 'Wasn't Ekushey Dina's family's restaurant?'

I should have known Amma would remember. She has the memory of a goldfish half the time, but when it comes to remembering anything Bengali, she's sharp as a tack. It's a weird superpower.

'Yes,' I admit. 'They've renovated, and they're opening it up again. I thought maybe I could help them out. See if I could convince some reviewers or journalists to go to the launch.'

I expect Amma to be mad. She made it pretty clear last time Dina was brought up that she's not her biggest fan. To my surprise, though, Amma's face softens. She sits down in one of the chairs and indicates for me to sit down beside her too. When I do, she gives me a serious look. It feels like she's looking right through me, reading all of the thoughts in my head.

'You still care about Dina,' she finally says. It's not a question, it's a statement.

I can't even refute it. I do care about Dina – of course I still care about Dina.

I nod. 'Yeah, I guess I do. I know it's stupid to, but . . . I can't help it.'

'You two talked at the match. I saw her come up to you afterwards,' Amma says. I didn't know that she had been watching.

'Yes. She just . . . wanted to say congrats for winning.'

Amma frowns. 'It didn't seem like that was all she said. You were quiet afterwards. You've been quiet since the match – different. Is it because of her?'

I'm surprised that she noticed all of that. I guess I shouldn't be. Amma has always been scarily attuned to how I am, and how I'm feeling. I guess it must come with the territory of being a mother.

'No . . . and yes. It's not her fault. She didn't do anything wrong. We're on better terms.' I shrug. 'But I guess I hoped that we could go back to where we were before. Before everything happened. That we could be . . .' My voice wobbles a little and I feel the pinprick of tears behind my eyes. Which is ridiculous, of course, because it's ridiculous to miss my teenage relationship. It's ridiculous to still be hung up on my high-school sweetheart. It's ridiculous to still be in love with a girl who broke my heart and never even looked back.

Amma takes my hands in hers, peering at me with kind eyes. 'I don't want you to get hurt, Maya.'

'I know,' I say. 'Which is why I'm trying to put her out of my mind.'

'No . . .' Amma shakes her head. '*This* is hurting you. Trying to forget about her.'

I'm taken aback by her words. Of all people, I would have thought Amma would be against me and Dina being together again.

'But you said that she was bad news,' I point out.

'I'm not convinced that she's good news, but if she's important to you, if you still care about her in this way, there must be something about her. And you shouldn't try to forget about her, if it hurts you. Maybe you should try to talk to her.'

Amma's about-face is definitely encouraging, but I don't know how to tell her that it's too late. That I might not be able to forget about Dina, but it's clear Dina has never had a problem with forgetting me. I've thought about her every day since we broke up, and while Dina may have said she missed me, I doubt she thought of me much after she left me on my doorstep, heartbroken.

'I don't know if I can,' I say.

Amma gives me a sympathetic smile. 'You can. You can do anything.'

I let out a chuckle, because Amma has been telling me that since I was a kid. It's what has spurred me on to do all of the things that I've done, it's what gave me the confidence to take on all of the opportunities that I've had. I'm not sure if I would have had the bravery to travel across the world to join a professional football team if it wasn't for Amma and her ever-present encouragement. But this isn't the same thing as any of that. It requires a different kind of bravery. It needs me to brush off my old wounds, sew up my broken heart and put myself out there again – ready to be wounded and heartbroken anew.

I'm not sure if I have that in me.

Chapter 34
Dina

'. . . Practically unheard of. When I was facing all of this, I didn't even have anyone that I could speak to about any of—'

'Does this look crooked to you?' Deen's question interrupts me rewatching Maya's interview on *The Warm Up*.

I lock my phone, slip it into my pocket and look up to see Deen eyeing the peacock painting that we salvaged from one of the charity shops. He tilts his head this way and that, frowning at the painting as if this is the crowning achievement of the restaurant, even though it's a small painting off to one side. He has been up since the crack of dawn, working on finishing touches, even though everything was already finished and ready days ago. Still, even as we wait to open up the restaurant, he adjusts things.

'It looks fine,' I insist.

'I'm just not sure. Maybe this is the wrong painting to have here. Maybe there shouldn't even be a painting. I mean, do peacocks even fit into the aesthetic of the rest of the restaurant?'

I can recognise a spiral when I see one, so I march towards Deen and grab him by his shoulders – which is a little difficult considering he is significantly taller than me, and he's craning his neck to look up at the painting. I still manage somehow.

'Deen. The restaurant looks great. Stop freaking out.'

He looks down at me before taking a deep breath. 'Yeah, you're right. I need to stop freaking out. I mean, if this doesn't work, all it means is that my dreams are over, and so are Baba's, and Ma will be disappointed, and you will be disappointed, and—'

'I won't be disappointed,' I interrupt before he can list a string of other relatives who probably don't give Deen a second thought most of the time, but Deen will somehow convince himself that he and this restaurant are the centre of their universe. 'Ma won't be disappointed. And if Baba were here right now, he would be proud of you. For taking a risk. That's what he was doing when he started up this restaurant in the first place.'

Deen nods, though I'm not sure if I've really got through to him.

'Come on, sit down and take a deep breath.'

I drag him by his hands to the seat that I have just been occupying and he plops himself down on it. Closing his eyes, he takes another deep breath, and when he blinks his eyes open again, he seems at least a little bit calmer.

'You would tell me if the restaurant looked terrible, right?' Deen asks, looking around at the place.

'Yes, I would. It looks good.' I look around too, trying to see things from Deen's point of view. The place is a mishmash of things; it's difficult to even focus on one specific thing because there's so much to look at. There are colourful lanterns strung up corner to corner; they cast a dim, romantic light over the tables. The walls have been repainted to a dark, sophisticated shade of green, and a variety of paintings line the walls, each somehow evocative of Bangladesh. Then, there's the mural on the centre wall, which is visible as soon as you walk into the place. Against the green wall, in dark red paint, it reads *Ekushey* in both Bengali and English, each language shadowing the other, as if they're caught up in some kind of dance.

It's nothing like the different iterations of the restaurant that Deen and I have discussed over the years, but it's a beautiful combination of all of those things. Only Deen could have done this; it feels like his vision.

Deen takes another breath and nods. His shoulders relax a little, almost like he's making a conscious decision to let go of the rest of his worries. 'OK . . . I guess we're ready to open then.'

I give an encouraging smile as he stands up and walks over to the front door. He flips the sign from closed to open, and peers outside for a second, as if he's hoping for a queue of people. Clearly, he doesn't find one, because he returns from the entrance, looking nervous.

'People will come soon,' I say.

Just then, the door whooshing open sounds. Both Deen and I eagerly turn towards the entrance, but only Thea and Aisha walk in, waving at us hesitantly.

'Hey, are we early?' Thea asks.

'No, you're right on time, actually,' I say, glancing at Deen, who looks a little crestfallen that it's just my friends. 'You guys want some free samples?'

'Yes, obviously!' Aisha says enthusiastically.

I walk them over to the table Deen has set up with samples of a selection of his dishes, offering each of them a plate.

'How's your brother doing?' Thea asks as she piles a variety of foods onto her plate – creamy chingri malaikari, tangy shatkora mangsho and murighonto. I'm not sure she has any idea what she's actually taking, but she's always been a fan of Deen's cooking from the leftovers I've supplied.

'He's pretty nervous,' I say.

'I can just imagine,' Aisha mumbles, though she's too busy eyeing all the different types of bhortas that Deen has laid out to really pay much attention to the conversation. Bhortas aren't fine dining, but considering they're such a signature Bengali dish, Deen thought he'd go all out. He basically tried to make bhortas of everything that felt right – aloo bhorta, daal bhorta, begun bhorta, even chingri bhorta.

'This food is so good,' Thea says, taking a massive bite of a mix of things. 'Somehow, way better than the leftovers you always have in the fridge.'

'You mean to tell me freshly made food tastes better than days-old leftovers that smell like the back of our fridge?' I ask.

'Good point.'

Thea and Aisha grab a table and tuck into their food, and I leave them alone to go and sit by Deen again. His legs are going up and down, up and down, and his jaw is clenched tight. He doesn't tear his eyes away from the door for even a second.

'Thea said the food was really good,' I say, in the hope that it will help with his tension.

'That's nice of her to say.' Deen's voice is tight, and he doesn't look away from the door.

'You know what they say, Deen, a watched pot never boils,' I joke.

Deen finally turns to me and almost cracks a smile. 'I know, I know. It's only been a couple of minutes. OK . . .

distract me. You've watched that video of Maya like a billion times.' He turns to me with a raised eyebrow.

Now I wish he *was* freaking out about the restaurant because I really don't want to talk about Maya.

'It's a good interview.' I shrug.

'Uh-huh, sure. And you're not watching it because you miss Maya. You know, she doesn't live far away, you could go and see her at any point.'

'I can't, we left things . . . complicated. I just . . . I'm watching the interview because it reminds me of how wrong I was about so many things.'

Deen smiles – his first proper one in weeks. 'You often are wrong about many things.'

I roll my eyes and poke him in the ribs. 'You know the comments on that video are all deriding Maya for saying what she said. I mean, there are comments saying that maybe Bangladeshi women don't belong in football. How messed up is that?'

'Pretty messed up.'

'And then you think about the fact that Maya has been dealing with that for the past nine years. I thought she was living the dream – living *my* dream.' I shake my head.

'Dreams can be complicated. I mean, look at me,' Deen says, extending his arms to the empty restaurant.

'They can be,' I agree. 'But . . . Maya turned things around. I mean, despite everything, she went on national TV and told everyone her side of the story. So, if she can do *that*, *we* can make this place a success.'

It's easy to say that, but much more difficult to achieve. Because a full half-hour later, not a single other person has shown up. I know that Jen said she would stop by at some point, and I'm itching to text her or call her and demand when.

If only to help assuage some of Deen's worries.

'Maybe this whole thing was a huge mistake,' Deen says. He buries his face in his hands. 'I mean, I took money out of my savings, I spent weeks doing all of this – maybe Ma was right. She has way more life experience than us and she knows—'

But he's cut off by the sound of the door opening. Deen and I both look up at the same time and see a woman at the door that neither of us recognise. She looks around with scrunched eyebrows, before she spots the two of us and a small smile appears on her lips.

'Hello! I'm here for the . . . restaurant launch?'

'Yes!' I say, standing up quickly and dragging Deen up with me. 'I'm Dina, this is Deen. It's his restaurant actually.'

'Hi,' Deen says. 'Thank you for coming. There are free samples over there.' He points to the table with the samples. 'But if you'd like a table so you can peruse the menu and order, we can arrange that for you.'

'Oh, I'll definitely need a table,' the woman says with a smile. 'Can you do a table for six?'

'Six?' As Deen asks this, a flood of people appear behind the woman. Not just the five other people that will apparently be joining her for dinner, but even more people that she doesn't seem to know. Each of them scrambles for our attention, looking for a table. My eyes nearly bulge out of my head at the sight, but I don't have the time to be shocked.

Deen and I quickly get to work, trying to get everyone seated and served. It's not long before the whole restaurant is full; every table is occupied, and the free samples are almost completely gone. And there's a queue of people waiting for tables to free up.

'I don't have any more free samples,' Deen whispers to me.

'Don't worry, people will pay full price for your food, clearly,' I say, just as the first group of people that had come into the restaurant take their leave.

'The food was wonderful, we'll definitely be back,' the woman we'd spoken to earlier says with a smile directed at Deen. She digs into her bag and takes out her phone. 'I'm actually a food influencer; I talk about new and up-and-coming restaurants around the area. Ekushey wasn't on my radar before, but it definitely is now, and I've taken a bunch of photos and videos to post. Do you guys have an Instagram account that we can tag you on?' She's already typing on her phone, looking up at us expectantly.

'Yes. It's @ekusheyrestaurant,' Deen quickly pipes up.

'Great.' The woman grins. 'Thanks for everything.' She waves goodbye, and I turn to Deen with raised eyebrows.

'We should have got her information so we can look up her account,' I say. 'I wonder how many followers she has.'

That's not the end, though, as more and more people flit into the restaurant, I realise that she isn't the only influencer who has been alerted to our relaunch. A couple more let us know who they are, and Deen makes sure to provide each of them with at least one free item off the menu.

I can't help but wonder, though, how they found out about the launch. I guess that it must have been Jade – she does have a habit of posting about anything and everything on her Instagram account, and considering the amount of buzz she generated about the football game, I wouldn't be surprised if she went all out to generate buzz about the restaurant's launch too. I would have to thank her.

Then, Jen shows up with half the team, big grins on their

faces. It's good to see them again. The past two weeks have been such a rush of preparation for the relaunch that we paused training. As I sit them down, I take Jade aside for a second.

'Hey, you haven't been posting about this relaunch on your account, have you?' I ask.

Jade gives me a confused look. 'Maybe once or twice, but, honestly, it wasn't getting a lot of traction. I mean, my followers care about *me*, and now about football, I guess. I don't think they really care about a random restaurant opening, unfortunately,' Jade says matter-of-factly.

'So . . . you aren't the reason a bunch of food influencers have been showing up here tonight?' I ask.

Jade just shrugs. 'I don't think any food influencers even follow me. I'm not into the whole food scene. I'm a lifestyle influencer, which is *very* different from food influencing.'

'Got it,' I say, even though I really don't get it.

Jade goes back to the team, while I continue to be confused about how all of these influencers heard about our relaunch. My confusion ends, though, when I notice Jen deep in conversation with one of the guests. She calls me over when she spots me watching them, and makes introductions.

'Dina, this is Sallie Fischer. She used to play for a women's football league in Liverpool. This is Dina, she's assistant coach to the football team I'm helping to run for the council, and her family owns this place.'

I extend my hand to Sallie with a smile.

'This is a great place you have here,' she says. 'When one of my colleagues reached out to tell me I had to check it out, I wasn't sure what to think, but the food is top-notch, and I love the decor. Really different from any other Indian restaurants that I've been to.'

'Well, it's a Bangladeshi restaurant,' I explain. 'Everything here is inspired by Bangladeshi culture.'

Sallie nods. 'Well, it's amazing. And it's your place? You run a restaurant and coach football?'

I chuckle, and shake my head. 'No. It's mostly my brother's place, but it used to be my dad's. I just helped him out a little with the relaunch.'

'Well, ever since I retired from football, I've been dabbling in a few different things, and one of them is helping out up-and-coming restaurants. I know how difficult it can be – my family used to own one too, back in the day.' Sallie takes out a business card from her bag and hands it to me. 'Give this to your brother – maybe the two of us can get in touch and discuss a few things. Though, he's already got a pretty good thing going. Maybe he doesn't even need my help.'

I stare at the business card in awe, already knowing that Deen will be over the moon when I show it to him. 'Thank you. You said . . . you heard about the launch from a colleague?'

'Oh, yes. Kind of. I guess we're not really colleagues anymore. She played for the Vikings, and I mentored her for a little bit a couple of years ago. We still keep in touch.'

The Vikings – that was Maya's team. Slowly, everything clicks into place. Of course, Maya would be the one to get all of these people here – people with connections. She has been in the public eye, she knows how these things work. She has somehow got people to come here, to try Deen's food. I'm not sure what that means, but it fills me with a sense of elation that I can't even begin to describe.

Chapter 35

Dina

The restaurant is so busy that it feels like it might never empty out, but as it gets dark, customers begin to trickle away, until there are only a handful left near closing time. Deen and I have been so busy serving everyone, and talking to people, that we have barely had any downtime.

Now, I go up to Deen, who is waiting by the register. I expected that he would be smiling from ear to ear, but he looks a little downtrodden.

'Hey, what's wrong?' I ask.

Deen looks up at me and a smile appears on his lips, though it doesn't quite reach his eyes. 'Nothing. This has been great. I could never have expected this kind of turnout.'

'Yeah, it's been so amazing. And so many reviewers and influencers – hopefully they'll just drive more people to come here.'

'Yeah.' Deen nods. 'How did so many of them even know to come here? Did you tip them off?'

I shake my head. I've been too busy to really think about Maya and what she's done. Now that I am thinking about it, I don't know how I'm supposed to feel.

'I think it was Maya,' I admit.

Deen raises an eyebrow. 'Really?'

I shrug. 'She has connections, I guess. There were a few people here that she would know, so it would make sense.'

'Wow. I didn't know Maya was such a big fan of me,' Deen says haughtily.

I roll my eyes and elbow him in the ribs.

He smiles. 'You should talk to her.'

'I don't know. I mean, why would she want anything to do with me, after everything?' I ask.

'You're joking, right? If she didn't want anything to do with you, she wouldn't send influencers to this launch. She wouldn't even know about it, because she wouldn't be keeping tabs. Dina, Maya did this for you, not for me. Because she obviously still cares about you.'

I have a hard time believing Deen's words, even though I want to. Because Maya isn't here. If she really cared about me, if she still wanted something to happen between the two of us, wouldn't she be here? Wouldn't I be having this conversation with her instead of my brother?

'I don't know. It felt like last time we talked it was over between us. For good. I mean, she could have come here. That would have been a reason to see me, to hash things out, but she hasn't. She's never tried to see me since she came back, since we broke up.'

'Well, she was in America after you broke up,' Deen says. 'And after she got back here, she was probably just reeling from everything. Besides, didn't you say she told you that you broke her heart?'

'Well, she broke mine too!' I say.

'I just think that it must be hard for her – to put herself out there with you again.'

I can't believe Deen is taking her side over mine. And

almost as if Deen can read my mind, he puts up his hands as if in surrender.

'And it's hard for you too, I know it is. But *this* was Maya putting herself out there. Maybe it's your turn now.'

I swallow thickly, thinking about the last time I put myself out there with Maya. The night that we kissed. It hadn't fixed anything. It had only made things a million times worse. But maybe I wasn't in the right state of mind then – I was drunk and sad, still blaming Maya for my failures. I'm not sure if I blame her for those things anymore.

'I guess . . . maybe I'll try,' I say. 'I'll think about it.'

Deen rolls his eyes, but nods, like he knows it's the most he'll get out of me for now.

'So, why don't you look happy about the restaurant?'

Deen blinks at me, clearly not expecting the question. 'I'm happy,' he says defensively. Then, he sighs and leans back against the counter, his eyebrows creasing. 'It's just . . . Ma never showed up. I told her about it, and I thought that she would but . . .' He shrugs, like he doesn't even care, but he clearly does. Ma showed up for my football match, even though I know that she probably didn't want to. But maybe that was different – it's not like Baba was tied up in football the way he was tied to this place.

'Maybe it's hard for her, the idea of coming here and seeing it so different to what it was when Baba was alive,' I suggest.

'Yeah, maybe,' Deen says. 'I just would have thought . . . I don't know, I tried to honour him and his memory, you know? I tried to do things the way I thought he would want them to be done. I mean, this place is me and my vision, but it's also his. It always will be. It wouldn't exist without him. I thought . . . Ma would want to see that.'

'I know.' I put a hand on his shoulder, but there really isn't much else that I can say to him. 'She'll come around, I'm sure of it.'

'Yeah, maybe.'

Only a few minutes go by before the door to the restaurant opens again. With it being as late as it is, I go to turn the customer away, only to notice that it's Ma.

'What are you doing here?' I ask, surprised that she made it here after all. Surprised that she made it here *so* late. That's not really like her.

'Deen asked me to come,' she says. She walks past me and towards Deen, and I notice that she's carrying a cardboard box in her hands, which she sets down on the counter in front of Deen.

'Ma, you came.' Deen is clearly as surprised to see her as I am, having given up hope.

'I would have been here earlier. Actually, I *was* here earlier,' Ma says. 'But I had to get something.'

'You were here?' Deen asks, while I peer at the cardboard box and ask, 'What did you have to get?'

Ma frowns at me before turning to answer Deen. 'I came here, and I saw the place. And then I left to get this.'

Deen looks to me, worry visible in his eyes. Nothing about Ma's expression or her words are giving away whether she hates the place or likes it. Maybe she was so offended by what Deen has done with the restaurant that she had to leave and come back with all of the old decor, which Deen had stuffed away in the attic. Maybe she's going to demand that Deen put it all back. From the look on Deen's face, he definitely fears something like that.

Ma doesn't say any more, she just opens up the cardboard box and takes something out, brandishing it towards Deen.

It looks like a piece of paper – no, a poster. I lean forward, trying to catch a glance at it, and when I do, I don't know what to think.

It's an old poster – a little worn around the edges – but I know what it is immediately. It's a poster of a Bengali movie. From the looks of it, a fairly old one too. There are bold red Bangla words brandished on the front, with a girl with her black hair in a floral bun standing back to back with a guy wearing a biker jacket.

'What is this?' Deen asks.

Ma's face seems to soften at the question, and she sighs. 'I used to collect these movie posters, back when I had dreams of becoming an actress. All of these Bangladeshi movies that I went to watch, or even the Indian ones. I would squirrel away the posters. It was my prized collection because I imagined one day adding my own movie poster to it.' Ma has a faraway look in her eyes, like she's imagining that scenario, like she can see it even if it's not real. 'But . . . it never happened, and so I put them away in this box, and never looked at them again. Your baba always wanted me to go after my dream. Even when we were struggling, and I was working night shifts all the time. Even when we were barely able to make ends meet – your baba never gave up on his dreams, and he didn't want me to give up on mine either.'

Ma pauses, looking around at the restaurant, her face softening even more. I can almost see the younger version of her; the one who still had bright dreams and hope in her eyes.

'He had so many dreams for this place and he did so much to make those dreams come true. But he couldn't. Yet when I walked in here, I thought, this was it. This was his dream. For this place to be full of people and love and laughter. He may not be here to see it, but I know he would be proud. And you made it happen, Deen.' She pauses to look between me and Deen, wearing a smile that I don't think I've ever seen on her before. 'You both went after your dreams, went after what makes you happy. Your baba would have been so happy.'

She looks from Deen to me, pride sparkling in her eyes.

She reaches forward, cupping Deen's cheeks in her hands. 'When I came in here, and saw this place, I thought about these posters, and my dreams. I want you to have them, for the restaurant. I know you asked all of your aunties and uncles for things, I know you went around the charity shops—'

'How did you—' Deen begins to ask.

'I see a lot more than you think I do,' Ma says, and it's true. It does sometimes feel like she has some kind of sixth sense about everything and anything going on with the two of us. 'But you never asked me, and if you had, I would never have offered these or anything at all. But seeing this place so lively and full of people made me realise that they deserve to do more than collect dust under my bed. They should be here, on the walls.'

Deen nods, looking at the poster again. I can see it in his eyes – he can already envision these posters lining the walls. I can too.

'I think this is what's been missing,' he says. 'Because this place has Baba, me, Dina.' Deen looks to me with a smile. 'And now it'll have you.'

Chapter 36

Maya

I hold up my old football shirt in front of me. In the bright light of the sun flooding in from the window, the blue of it looks a little washed out. Or maybe it's just been through so many wash cycles over the years that it *is* washed out.

With the summer almost over, I've finally decided to close the chapter on my professional football career. Especially now that I've realised that being back home is actually making me happier than I have been in a long time. Even after retiring from the team, it felt like a part of me was back there. Longing for everything that came with my career. But I know that it's time to officially say goodbye. To make my peace with it.

I turn the shirt around, to the back with my name printed on it. *Alam* in stark white letters, which stand out against the blue. All around it, my teammates have signed their names. Before, this would have led me down a spiral, but today, looking at their names, I only feel a warm sense of nostalgia. Like the past is a fond memory that I'm happy to remember but don't quite want to relive.

Amma suggested that we frame my jersey, and hang it up in the sitting room, so that everybody who comes to the house can see it. I know her heart is in the right place – she wants to show off the fact that her daughter was a professional footballer. But the idea of looking at it every day doesn't feel right. It would be holding on to the past, glorifying and whitewashing it. Pretending that it didn't hurt me. So, I decide to put it away instead. Not throw it away, but keep it somewhere in my wardrobe, as a reminder of my time playing with the Vikings.

As I'm about to put it into my wardrobe, the bell rings. A sharp, loud trill reverberates through the house.

I put the shirt on my bed and walk down the stairs. Amma and Abba are out for the day so there's nobody else to answer the door.

The doorbell rings a second time, and I frown, wondering if it's a door-to-door salesman that I'll have to find some polite way of turning away quickly. I'm already trying to come up with an excuse for why I'm extremely busy and can't entertain whatever they're trying to sell, when I swing the door open and realise that it's not a door-to-door salesman on the other side at all. It's Dina.

'Dina . . . you're here.'

'Hi.' she smiles at me hesitantly.

'Hi,' I say, not sure of what else to say. 'Um . . . do you . . . did you want to come inside?'

'Yeah, OK.'

I hold the door open wider, and Dina steps in, past me. I lead her through the hallway to the sitting room, where Dina perches on the couch, looking around with curious eyes. I sit down next to her, and for a few minutes silence washes over us. I'm running through a list of questions that I could ask her to break the silence: 'How are you?' and 'How was the launch of the restaurant?' all the way to 'Do you hate me?'

But then Dina takes a deep breath and says, 'I'm sorry.'

I blink at her. Of all the things I thought she was about to say, it wasn't this. 'You're sorry? For . . . what?'

She looks at me, holding my gaze, and I can see so much emotion wading in there that I can't even decipher. 'For . . . everything. I'm sorry for how I reacted when you got an opportunity at your dream career. I'm sorry for how I broke up with you. I'm sorry for never, ever trying to make things better between us. I'm sorry for how things have been between us since you got back. I'm sorry about all of it.'

'Dina, you don't—'

But clearly, Dina isn't done speaking because she continues. 'All these years, I thought that I hated you for what you did, but, honestly, I never hated you. I missed you every day that you were gone. I've missed you since the second that Jen told me that you were offered the position in America, because I knew you would go. It was easier to blame you for things that were out of your control, and it was easier to tell myself and everyone around me that I hated you than to admit how much I missed you.'

There are tears swimming in her eyes now, and she blinks them away. I feel the pinprick of tears behind my eyes too, because in the past nine years, this conversation is all I've ever wanted to have with Dina. A conversation that explained why she broke my heart in the way that she did. One where she said that she missed me, and meant it. And I can tell that she means it.

'I missed you too,' I say, though my throat feels thick with tears. 'I missed you every day that I was gone. I wanted to call you so many times. The first time I met my coach, first time I went to practice, first time I played a match, the only person I wanted to talk to was you, but then . . . I remembered. We weren't together anymore.'

Dina reaches her hand out, linking our fingers together. The warmth of her sends a tingle all through me. I've missed her touch, her scent, her everything. I don't always admit that to myself, but now how much I've missed her overwhelms me, floods me.

'You were right, all the things you said about me. I blamed you because it was easier. And I missed out on so much because of that,' Dina says.

'You could still . . . I mean, you could still try for a career in football if you wanted. It's not too late,' I say.

But Dina just shakes her head. 'No, what I mean is, I missed out on us.'

In all the time that I've known Dina, I don't think I've ever seen her emanate this kind of sincerity. I certainly have never seen her put anything over her love of football. I almost wouldn't believe it, if she wasn't looking at me like that; as if I am the only person in her world. And I wish that I was.

'I know it's not as easy as saying sorry and pretending that everything that happened didn't happen. I know I broke your heart. And if you never forgave me, or trusted me, I would understand that. But . . .' And here Dina takes a deep breath, and I can feel her hands trembling. I squeeze them, and she cracks a small smile; one that brightens her entire face. 'Can you give me another chance? Can we reset the score between us?'

For a moment, I flash back to nine years ago. The last time Dina showed up at my house unprompted. I still remember the look in her eyes then, the venom in them. The last words that she said to me. But I look at Dina now, and there's nothing of that here. In nine years, the two of us have changed in infinite ways. And I'm ready to know this Dina. Now.

'Yes,' I say, my voice coming out breathless. 'Yes, I can give you another chance. Yes, we can—'

But I don't even get to finish my sentence before Dina is leaning forward and closing the gap between us. Her lips are on mine, her fingers in my hair, caressing my cheeks. I lean into her too, encircling her waist with my hands and pulling her closer. The scent of her fills me up; the feel of her hands on my skin sends goosebumps up my entire body.

When we pull apart from the kiss, there's still little space left between us. Dina rests her forehead against me, her skin warm on mine.

'Please tell me your parents aren't home,' she says.

'They aren't,' I say, and Dina kisses me again, her lips quirking up into a smile against my mouth. I feel like we're teenagers again, sneaking around behind our parents' backs. In those days, we were so scared of how we felt. Our every touch, every kiss, felt tentative yet filled with possibility. But here, right now, with Dina and I together, it feels like those possibilities have finally been realised. Like all our time apart, our heartbreak, everything, has led up to this moment.

I stand up, linking my hands with Dina's and pulling her up with me. We're still tangled in each other as I lead her up the stairs, all the way into my bedroom. This time, there will be no interruptions.

Chapter 37
Dina

One Year Later
'Come on, Sophie, you got this!' I shout, clapping my hands together encouragingly as she races towards the goal. Her face is serious, sweat dripping down her forehead. She kicks the ball, nearly falling in the process. But it's worth it because the ball hits the net, missing Julia in goal by a couple of inches.

I let out a loud cheer and clap my hands together as Sophie pumps her fists happily.

Glancing at my watch, I realise that we're already almost ten minutes over our practice time.

'OK, let's wrap up for today,' I say. 'And please, get plenty of sleep before the match next week.'

Jade rolls her eyes as she moves past me. 'You don't have to remind us of that before every single match.'

'But this is a special one,' I say.

'Don't worry, we are definitely going to beat Westbrook this time,' Sara says a little too confidently. The Divas have won quite a few games since our loss last year, but Westbrook still have a better track record than us and a pretty great coach.

'Just don't get too hung up on winning. Remember, it's just as important—'

'To have fun, we *know*,' Jade groans to the rest of the team. They make fun of me, but I know they do it with fondness. 'Can we go now?'

'Go ahead.'

Mumbling their goodbyes, they start making their way to the park gates, and I watch them go. Seeing them in their new kits with 'The Divas' emblazoned across them fills me with a strange sense of pride. Ever since the match against Westbrook, which ended up across several social media platforms, and a local newspaper report, a few organisations banded together to give the Divas some much-needed funding. We've finally been able to do away with makeshift kits and get real ones. Plus, I bought proper football boots for all of the girls. I even let Jade set up an official Instagram account for the Divas, which is half the reason she shows up to practice sometimes, I think. The other half might be because of some genuine love of the game.

I start gathering up my things, and just as I'm heading out of the park, my phone buzzes. The caller ID flashes Jen's name. I pick up immediately.

'Hey, Jen!' I say.

'Hey, Dina!' Jen says. 'How have you been? How's the team?'

'Good, and they're good. They still annoy me sometimes, but you know how they are.'

Jen laughs good-naturedly. 'Yeah, I know they can be a handful.' She pauses for a moment. 'Listen, I'm calling because I know you have the match coming up.'

'Right . . . you don't have to worry about it. The girls are excited about finally having a chance to play Westbrook again and show them what they're made of.'

'I'm not worried.' Jen chuckles. 'I know that you've got

them well trained. I wouldn't have given you the reins if I didn't trust you. I actually . . . heard from a scout who saw some of the social media hype surrounding the last match.'

I stop in my tracks. 'Seriously?'

'Yeah, seriously,' Jen says. 'She wanted to come and check out the match. I told her about a few of the girls, especially Sophie. And I also told her a little about you.'

'Me?'

'Yes, you. About your trajectory, and she was interested in talking to you. She seemed to think she might have an opportunity for you to be assistant coach to a professional team.'

'Wait . . . really?' I've been full-time coaching for the past few months, taking over for Jen, while she's taken a more hands-off position at the council. But coaching a professional football team?

'Really!' Jen says. 'This could be a great opportunity for you, Dina. The team play all around the country. You would get the chance to travel with them, train them, go to all their matches.' When I started coaching, I never thought it would lead me anywhere near professional football. Now, my players are getting scouted and somebody actually thinks I could be an assistant coach for a professional team. It isn't exactly the life I envisioned for myself when I was younger, but it feels close to it. Close to those dreams I had about being a real football player. But, for some reason, it doesn't bring me the sense of joy that I had hoped. My image of my dream life seems to clash with my real life: the girls from the football team, Deen and the restaurant, Ma, Maya.

'I just wanted to give you a heads-up. I'll send you her details, and I'll be at the match to make the introductions. How does that sound?' Jen asks.

'Yeah, that sounds good. I can't wait to see you soon.'
'Me neither.'

I hang up the phone and make my way back to the apartment, still thinking about the scout and the opportunity. I quickly take a shower and get changed, before heading out again.

When I arrive at Deen's restaurant, the place is buzzing with people, as it often is these days. Ever since the relaunch, business has been booming. Deen's had to hire a lot of help to keep things running smoothly, and of course I help him out during any downtime that I have. Even Ma chips in every once in a while, though Deen usually insists that she shouldn't. He says that Ma has earned her retirement after years of hard work to keep food on the table, and that now it is our turn to take care of her. I don't disagree with him.

I step inside the restaurant, and one of the waiters that Deen has recently hired recognises me almost instantly, though it takes me a second to remember her name.

'Dina, everyone's already at the table,' Sage says, pointing me towards the table in the corner.

'Right, of course I'm late,' I mumble.

Sage just gives me a smile as I move past her and reach our table. Ma and Deen are on one side, while Maya and her parents are on the other. They've saved me a seat opposite Maya.

'Hey, sorry I'm late,' I say, quickly slipping into my chair. Maya catches my eye and gives me a smile, and I smile back. Seeing her is definitely the highlight of my day – of any day.

'Not like we didn't expect it,' Deen mumbles under his breath, and I elbow him in the ribs. 'We've already ordered, because we knew you'd be ages and we're starving.' Deen has been so busy at the restaurant since the relaunch that it's a wonder he ever takes a night off.

'I said sorry,' I say defensively. 'Practice ran late, and then I had to go home and get changed. And I got a call from Jen, who had some news.'

Maya perks up at Jen's name. 'What news?'

'It's nothing too important. She's ... coming to the match next week.'

'Oh,' Maya brightens at that. 'It'll be good to see her again.'

Maya's parents nod enthusiastically.

'I always liked her,' Maya's mum says. 'She's so inspiring.'

'She inspired me,' Maya agrees.

'Me too.'

I catch her eye again across the table, reaching out beyond the edge to take her hands in mine. We saw each other just last night, but it already feels like too long has passed. To be fair, we have nine years of lost time to make up for.

'So, is this match also going to be on the news?' Maya's dad asks, peering between me and Maya. 'Maybe this time, you two can get interviewed.'

'We would rather it be about the kids,' Maya says. We've both agreed that we definitely don't want to be social media stars – or any kind of stars – in relation to this match, and the rivalry between us that people have played into. But now I wonder if that would change if I took the job as a coach. I wonder what else might change. If we would still have these dinners with my and Maya's families, which we try to schedule every other month. Or if I'd be travelling, or if I'd have to move away. What would that even look like?

'You OK?' Maya asks, leaning forward to whisper it so that only I hear the question.

'Yeah, fine,' I say. I'm going to tell Maya about Jen's call – the real news that she shared. But I don't want to do it in front of everyone.

'Well, I have some news,' Ma declares all of a sudden. We all turn to her with a questioning look. I can't even fathom what news she might have. 'We were talking about inspiration before and I've been inspired too.'

'By Jen?' Deen asks with a frown.

'No, of course not,' Ma scoffs. 'By the two of you.' Her face softens as she looks between us. 'You did what I thought was impossible. You continued pursuing the things that you love, and you made it happen. You achieved your dreams. And I want to do that too.'

Deen's eyes widen, while I try to soak up her words. Try to understand what she's really saying.

'You're going to go back to acting?' I ask.

Ma nods. 'Well, I'll try. I'll see what I can do. Even a few small roles would be good. I want to do something that brings me joy. I know I might be too old now to be some kind of film star, but maybe there's still something for me out there. I gave up so quickly when I was younger.' She gives all of us at the table a cautious look. 'You don't think it's a bad idea, do you?'

'No!' Deen says quickly. 'It's an amazing idea. I think you should do it, Ma.'

'I agree.' I nod.

Maya and her parents offer their agreement too.

'I actually know a few people who might be able to help you get your foot in the door,' Maya's dad chimes in. 'There's Bimi Bhabi's daughter, right? Didn't she study acting, and didn't she do a bunch of theatre shows on the West End?'

'Yes!' Maya's mum says, her eyes flashing with recognition. 'You should definitely reach out to her. I bet she can set you on the right path.'

Ma smiles at us, her eyes full of hope and promise – something that it seemed my mother had lost before I was even born. It's nice to see her like this.

'So, what's up with you tonight?' Maya asks later on, after her parents and Ma have gone home and we've left Deen at the restaurant to close up. We're walking hand in hand back to my apartment, the chilly air nipping at us.

'I've just been thinking,' I say.

'About . . .?'

'Jen's call.'

'I knew there was more you weren't telling me about the call!' She squeezes my hands and leans into me until her body is pressed flushed against me. 'Tell me what she said.'

'There's a scout coming to the match next week.'

'Oh, yeah. Ms Jacobs mentioned that might be a possibility at some point,' Maya says. 'She didn't say which match they'd be coming to, though. They're really coming to the one between us?'

'Yes, that's what Jen said.'

'And it's bringing up some bad memories for you?' Maya asks, peering at me closely.

'No, of course not,' I say, though I can't blame her for asking. I was caught up in the past for a long time and it kept me from moving forward into the future. 'She said that the scout was also interested in me. She thinks she has a position for me as an assistant coach for a professional team. She wants to talk to me about it apparently.'

Maya stops in her tracks, and since we're arm in arm, I

almost fall over when she does. I pull my arm away from Maya's and turn to face her. She looks shocked by my news – I guess as shocked as I was when I first heard it.

'This isn't bringing up bad memories for you, is it?' I ask.

Maya shakes her head. 'No, it isn't. I just . . . That's amazing, Dina.' And Maya sounds like she genuinely means it.

'Yeah, I guess it is,' I say.

'So, why aren't you more excited? Why didn't you tell us about it literally as soon as you got to dinner?' Maya inquires.

'I guess I don't know if I actually want it.'

Maya's eyes widen as she scans my face. 'Why would you not want it?'

'Because it would mean so many things would change. I like the way things are now. I mean, I might have to move away or do a lot of travelling, and there's so many things to think about. There's Deen and Ma, and there's the Divas. And there's you.'

Maya sighs and steps forward, linking our fingers together. 'If you move, I'd come with you. If you travel, we would figure it out.'

'But you have a stable job at the school. One that you love. And you just started that mentorship programme for women of colour in football. You're so passionate about that,' I say.

'Yeah but . . .' Maya shrugs. 'I love you more than either of those things. Obviously.'

I smile, but I also know that I would never ask Maya to give up what she has. And I'm not sure if I'm ready to give up what I have either.

'It's not just about that. I mean, when Jen told me, for a moment, it felt like I was stepping into some kind of dream. But when I thought about it, I wondered if my dreams have changed,' I say. 'I love coaching the Divas, and I love the life we have here. I don't think I want another life.'

Maya studies me. 'Are you sure about that? Because this is a really great opportunity, and I don't want you to give up on that for any reason, if it's what you want.'

'It's not what I want,' I say, and this time I say it confidently. This time, I know that I mean it. There's a past version of me that would have leapt at an opportunity like this, who would do anything to be in that world. But I'm not that person anymore. 'I wouldn't mind a few changes in my life, though.'

Maya gives me a confused smile. 'OK . . . what kind of changes?'

'Well, I would like the Divas to finally beat your team in a game, for one,' I reply.

Maya rolls her eyes. 'Never going to happen.'

I break out into a grin. 'Also, I would quite like to leave my apartment behind.'

'You like that apartment,' Maya says.

'Yeah but . . . I could like another one. One where you and I live.'

Maya's smile widens. 'Yeah, I think I'd like that change too.' She leans forward and presses her lips to mine, before looping her hands through mine. We walk like that, hand in hand back to my apartment, and towards the rest of our lives.

Acknowledgements

A big thank you to everyone who has made this book possible. Thank you to my agent, Uwe Stender, for always being my number-one advocate. Thank you to my editor, Sanah Ahmed, for all your brilliant editorial insight, which has helped shape this book into what it is now. Thank you to the entire team at Orion for your hard work.

Thank you to all my friends and family who have always shown up for me. You know who you are by now.

Finally, thank you to my readers. I wouldn't be here, sharing my stories, if I didn't have your support throughout the years.

Credits

Adiba Jaigirdar and Orion Fiction would like to thank everyone at Orion who worked on the publication of *The Perfect Match*.

Editor
Sanah Ahmed

Copy-editor
Jade Craddock

Proofreader
Holly Kyte

Editorial Management
Anshuman Yadav
Jane Hughes
Charlie Panayiotou
Lucy Bilton
Patrice Nelson

Audio
Paul Stark
Louise Richardson
Georgina Cutler-Ross

Contracts
Rachel Monte
Ellie Bowker
Tabitha Gresty

Design
Charlotte Abrams-Simpson
Nick Shah
Deborah Francois
Helen Ewing

Photo Shoots & Image Research
Natalie Dawkins

Finance
Nick Gibson
Jasdip Nandra
Sue Baker
Tom Costello

Inventory
Jo Jacobs
Dan Stevens

Production
Ruth Sharvell
Katie Horrocks

Marketing
Isla Newton

Publicity
Sian Baldwin

Sales
Dave Murphy
Victoria Laws
Esther Waters
Group Sales teams across Digital, Field, International and Non-Trade

Operations
Group Sales Operations team

Rights
Rebecca Folland
Tara Hiatt
Ben Fowler
Maddie Stephens
Ruth Blakemore
Marie Henckel

RAISING READERS
Books Build Bright Futures

Dear Reader,

We'd love your attention for one more page to tell you about the crisis in children's reading, and what we can all do.

Studies have shown that reading for fun is the **single biggest predictor of a child's future life chances** – more than family circumstance, parents' educational background or income. It improves academic results, mental health, wealth, communication skills, ambition and happiness.[1]

The number of children reading for fun is in rapid decline. Young people have a lot of competition for their time. In 2024, 1 in 10 children and young people in the UK aged 5 to 18 did not own a single book at home.[2]

Hachette works extensively with schools, libraries and literacy charities, but here are some ways we can all raise more readers:

- Reading to children for just 10 minutes a day makes a difference
- Don't give up if children aren't regular readers – there will be books for them!
- Visit bookshops and libraries to get recommendations
- Encourage them to listen to audiobooks
- Support school libraries
- Give books as gifts

There's a lot more information about how to encourage children to read on our website: **www.RaisingReaders.co.uk**

Thank you for reading.

---

[1] OECD, '21st-Century Readers: Developing Literacy Skills in a Digital World', 2021, https://www.oecd.org/en/publications/21st-century-readers_a83d84cb-en.html

[2] National Literacy Trust, 'Book Ownership in 2024', November 2024, https://literacytrust.org.uk/research-services/research-reports/book-ownership-in-2024